I0817796

SHADOW
OF THE
LOST

Other Books by

RYAN D GEBHART

THE JEWEL OF LIFE

SPLENDOR OF DAWN

HIDDEN WITHIN

FADING LIGHTS

SHADOW
OF THE
LOST

A Novel

IN

THE JEWEL OF LIFE

RYAN D GEBHART

Hardcover ISBN 978-1-7326355-7-9

Paperback ISBN 978-1-7326355-8-6

Distributed by Ingram Publisher Services

Printed in the United States of America

Cover design by Fiona Jayde Media

This one is for Nick

Acknowledgements

Shadow of the Lost came about because I wanted to tell Jaerol's story, a story that is unlike Devlyn's in the main series. While the pages are filled with vulnerability, hope, and optimism, they are read through the lens of someone who is grieving and unwilling to let go of his pain, or even acknowledge it.

Although this novel takes place between the events of *Splendor of Dawn* and *Hidden Within*, I was unable to write it until this past year. To put it simply, I was not ready to explore these characters and themes. I'm incredibly lucky to have people in my life who have expressed their love and support as I very slowly came out of the closet. From that first time I told my parents, and my mother said that she didn't understand how 'it' worked to my sister's quick-witted response of 'google' it, I am so grateful for your encouragement and the laughs that came along the way. But for the person who showed me how to love all of myself, I am so happy you are in my life. I could not have written this novel without you, Nick.

I also want to thank C. H. Williams. There is so much about our broader LGBTQ community that I have not experienced. I am so grateful that you were willing to share your own experience with me and correct my blindness toward the trans community. Thank you for your patience and for opening my eyes so that I could better represent a trans character. I am so grateful for your honesty and friendship.

The list of affirming people that I would like to thank is endless; truly, I am the person I am today because of you all. As always, thank you, Micheline Brodeur. I could not have asked for a better editor. I can't thank you enough for everything you've taught me over the past years and always challenging me to be a better storyteller.

Ryan D Gebhart

21 June 2021

Sirein Sea
Wooded Hills of Thellion
PARENDIOR
PERRIEN
Gneal
Selma
Undal
Reryl
Lake Saeryndol
Mount Verinien
Arenthyl
Septyl
Winshyl
Ozhyl
Delming Wood
Audun
Cyrillean Pass
Cyril
Everin
Belin's Watch
Derin
The Kryslen Mountains
Stellantis
The Eldin Wood
Overen
EVELLION
KRYSEN
Verenthyl
Brunst
Hamil
Plains of Mindale
Werly
Binton
Farenton
MINDALE
The Purged Desert of Dwonia
Joph
Ashton Wood
Freiton
New Castle
Dwora's Gap
Haulk Wood
YANIL
Nyner
Nuqtol
The Shadow Mountains
Mount Cyngol
Lankor
Dornal Marsh
Havirly
Zorik
Kinzdol Islands
Tempestien Sea

The Unarian Sea
River Bethyl
The Loudien Mountains
The Illumined Wood
Coureny
Erithel
Lucilla
Mount Saecrien
Kweil Aitch
Roselan
SORENTHIL
Myrium
Peran
Daerinth
Ruins of Quellion
Plains of Orithil
GISTORIA
N
W
E
S
Hendil
Dead Wood
Brie
TIEL
Harding's Crossing
Eddle Port
Nairin
Joque
Ja'mare
Jahro Islands
Erynien Bay
Dagger Point
Suderrif
Jadien
Map of the Continent
EKLEAN
Inscribed in Ink
by the Hand of
RDG

Part One

Denial

Chapter One

Meridephaen – 9056.3E

Day broke, and my knees quivered. Today was the final day of the Grand Tourney, and Kiron and I walked beside each other, holding hands while alone. We had both advanced through the ranks of the tournament exceptionally well. Neither of us had the highest scores, but we were still competitive compared to our strongest classmates, even Razcul who topped every bracket. It didn't matter what event he participated in, he obliterated his opponents.

In the early rounds of the tournament, nearly a month ago now, I had been part of a group challenge against Razcul's team. He hadn't needed the team—the rest of them didn't have to lift a finger, and for the most part, they hadn't. Watching Razcul race toward you was a terrifying spectacle. In fact, I had almost darted in the opposite direction to get out of his way. Everyone knew he would be named the champion after the final match at the end of today.

Today, the high feast day of Meridephaen, represented

the most important day of the year for the Cyndinari. We marked that day with the final rounds of the Grand Tourney, bringing an end to the month-long tournament. Today celebrated not only our graduation from the Imperium, but for half of us, it was also a day of sacrifice for the greater good of the Erynien Empire. Those who lost today would forfeit their souls to the student who beat them, transforming the victor into a shadow elf for the Erynien Empire. The victors would never know death due to sickness or old age. They would live on, consuming countless more souls to elongate their lives.

Kiron and I had planned and schemed for this day. We would not become shadow elves. We had seen how it changed our kin. Elves who took the souls of others to elongate their own lives changed afterward, and not in a good way. Over time, their skin would scar and blister, decaying to a grey ashen color, as if their bodies had forsaken them, preferring death over their corrupted state. Neither of us wanted that to happen, especially to each other. I'd rather gouge out my eyes than see Kiron's bronzed flesh decay before me.

I brushed my hand through his cinnamon hair, pulling him closer.

"Sentimental, are we?" He smiled. I couldn't see it, but I could hear it on his voice.

"Only when I'm around you."

"You sure it doesn't have anything to do with last night?"

"Oh, it certainly does." I laughed. "I love you, Kiron."

"Well, obviously. You made that quite clear last night. I'm pretty sure our entire wing of the Imperium knows how much you love me."

"We weren't that loud. Were we?" I blushed, the embarrassed warmth flushing up my face and to the tips of my ears.

Kiron only smirked in response. I wanted to drag him back to our apartment at that very moment and I would have, if the Grand Tourney wasn't today. Missing it would not only have led to expulsion on our graduation day, but we would both likely be fed to our classmates. Probably to the Grand Tourney winner as an additional prize. The thought of letting another elf consume either of our souls was appalling. Being trapped in a corrupted husk of what had once been a Cyndinari seemed worse than coming face to face with Ramiel—especially if that corrupted husk was Razcul.

"Do you feel confident?"

"Oddly, yes. I might feel differently if either of us are paired with Razcul today though."

"I don't think either of us are high enough in the bracket to be paired with him."

I squeezed him closer to me.

We walked toward the Coliseum through the winding alleys of Broid, the imperial capital of the Erynien Empire. Although the great stadium wasn't only used for the Grand Tourney, the tourney was the most anticipated event every year. The stands were filled with spectators every day of the Grand Tourney, but the day of the final round was the only day that Erynor himself came to view the matches. As emperor, he led the Cyndinari and it being the high feast day of Meridephaen, he also guided the devotion and thanksgiving to Meridiel, the anadel who guided the Cyndinari.

The alley opened onto one of the many plazas surrounding the Coliseum. Given its elliptical structure, broad boulevards radiated from the impressive structure at different points and darted through the city to major urban nodes. The grandest boulevard linked the Coliseum to the imperial palace, the second grandest linked it to our school. The other three major boulevards led to the only city gate, the cathedral, and the docks along the harbor.

Kiron and I didn't walk along that major avenue from the Imperium though. It was too public and we preferred the shadows of the quieter, less traveled streets, where we could hold each other's hand. We were missing out on the colorful banners and flags, and assorted festivities that took place along the main parade route, and I briefly regretted avoiding it. Our classmates would be enjoying those cheers and festivities.

As we crossed onto the packed eliptical plaza surrounding the Coliseum, the colorful flags and banners fluttered in the parade, and matching flags danced on poles atop the arena's highest walls. We no longer held each other's hands—it wasn't safe here. And neither of us needed a classmate to call us flamers just now. Not today. Not before our separate matches. Our minds had to be clear today. We couldn't let ourselves become angry or distracted due to unwelcomed taunts. We had a plan and we had to stay focused. If we failed—if someone discovered our intended ruse—we would end up dead, our souls fodder for shadow elves.

The cheers of the gathered crowd encouraged us on, and I looked over at Kiron to see my own wide smile at the excitement mirrored on his face. Despite the violent competitions ahead of us, it was an exciting day for Broid, for the entire island of Cynethol, and for the Erynien Empire. Celebrations and feasts would last throughout the day and stretch into the night. Many of our classmates wouldn't sleep tonight as they celebrated their achievement in the finals. We wove our way through the festive crowd and toward the competitors' entrance, one of the four impressive arched portals into the Coliseum. Colorful ribbons and papier-mâché sculptures of dragons lined the portal. On the opposite side of the arena was the imperial portal, where the empire's elites entered, but only when Erynor was in attendance. The other two portals were the entrances for nobles and anyone wealthy enough to purchase seasonal seating. The general admission didn't have to purchase tickets, they simply entered through any of the arcades between the four main portals. The earlier someone arrived, the better the seats they would get.

We passed through the competitor's portal and into a torchlit antechamber. Only a dozen of our classmates waited inside, most still outside enjoying the festivities. Part of me hoped some would enjoy themselves too much and make an easy opponent.

"Hi there, Jaerol; hi, Kiron."

"Hi, Olivia, how are you?" I asked.

"I'm all right, although I was pretty nervous this morning. I'm up against Darol today, and he drank more than he should've last night. I'm not looking forward to having his soul inside me for the rest of my life though. He'll probably keep belching for all I know."

"You already know who you've been paired up with?" Kiron asked.

"Oh, yeah, the list is in the main hall. Sorry, I was so nervous when I looked at it that I didn't see anyone's grouping but my own."

Kiron and I didn't bother saying goodbye. We rushed

out of the antechamber and into the main hall, and my anxiety rose when I saw the list engraved on the stone plaque that hung on the far wall of the hall. All of our names were carved into it, and after today's finals, that same plaque would join the others lining the Imperium's great hall. Students would look on our names in admiration and as a reminder that half of their class would die, losing their souls to the victors who would be starting their new lives as shadow elves.

Kiron found his name before I could find either of ours; he moaned and stepped away letting out another moan, both hands covering his mouth, tears falling from his anguished eyes as he took in gasping breaths. Was he against someone much stronger? Did he have to fight Razcul? Neither of us could outmatch Razcul.

"Who are you up against?" I asked, trying to sound cheerful, still unable to locate either of our names, and worried about his reaction.

He shook his head, his gasping breathing now on the verge of a panic attack. Kiron never had panic attacks. He'd been the one who had shown me what to do to get through one, but right now, he seemed to have forgotten everything he had told me to do. I rubbed his back, trying to settle him down, not caring what any of our classmates would say. They already knew about us. But still, I didn't feel like dealing with the jeers. I had to focus on my own upcoming match, as did Kiron. I had to help get his nerves under control because I couldn't lose him. We had planned it all out, planned on winning our respective matches. Then we would pretend to be shadow elves for a while before disappearing. The Erynien Empire would never find us and we'd be together. We wouldn't be immortal but our lives would be our own. We would age naturally, grow old together, and eventually depart Teraeniel.

I scanned the inscribed list. I finally found Kiron's name. It was in the left column, and I had to know whose name had terrified him so much. Who was he so afraid of?

Then I saw. *We'd been paired—we had to fight each other!*

My heart stopped in my chest and I bit back a scream when I read my name next to Kiron's. Before I could react further, our classmates crowded around us, laughing, taunting. Someone said we should've known better. Our relationship was forbidden. We both deserved to die. I couldn't see properly. Everything was in a haze. I tried to take a deep breath and hold it in to steady my nerves, but I couldn't do it. It was just too appalling.

Kiron, always the stronger one, eventually came to himself. He grabbed my hand and pulled me into a corridor away from our classmates. I couldn't focus, and barely registered the closet he pulled me into, shutting the narrow door behind us. He squeezed me in a warm hug, and the shock faded enough that I blinked, slowly coming to myself.

One of us would have to kill the other.

"We can run. Please, let's run, let's get as far away as possible," I pleaded. "It's already part of our plan, just sooner than we intended." I heard the hysteria in my voice, half cry, half terror.

"We can't." His voice was steady, firm.

I trembled in his arms. He was so strong. Why was he so strong for me? How was he so perfect? He surely was the pure image of what the Cyndinari were meant to be. How had our people gone so far astray? Why did we have to kill each other?

Why did we have to become shadow elves? Why couldn't I be me? Why couldn't we be together—forever and always?

There was no way that we could sneak off now—everyone else knew we were to fight each other, and they would be watching, aware of our contest on some level, even as they fought their own battles. I was barely aware of time passing, but knew we had to be present for the opening ceremony. Emperor Erynor Meridien would lead the chant commemorating Meridiel, sanctifying the final round of the Grand Tourney.

We never should have left our apartment this morning. We never should have returned to the capital after we had snuck away to the beach the previous week. We should have swum across the sound to the other Kinzdol Islands, beseeched the goblins for refuge. They would have declined and probably reported us, but we should have tried something.

"I want you to do it, Jaerol. I want you to live."

"No, please, don't ask that of me. I can't. I won't recover, I could never recover from that."

We argued. I couldn't kill Kiron, I was too weak. He was the strong one—always the strong one. I would never be able to live with myself after that. I don't know what I said, but finally, Kiron gave in to my pleading that he be the one who lived.

"All right," Kiron paused. "I'll do it."

"Thank you, Kiron, thank you. I love you. I will always love you." I kissed him as we both cried and held each other tight.

Chapter Two

Ten years later – 9066.3E

The Temple of Ceur was just an echo of the frenzied panic it had been only an hour ago. Although the corridors were far from empty outside the Chamber of Light and the ei'ceuril and temple knights still ran about like chickens with their heads chopped off, the impending sense of doom was gone.

Liam and I had waited outside the Ceurtriarch's apartment for Devlyn for quite some time before deciding that it was time to head back to our respective quarters. The boy was no longer in the temple.

The storm that had served as a trumpet for the shadow elves and Erynor, announcing their attack against Ceurenyl, continued to rage outside. There was nothing natural about that storm. Its intensity had diminished as dawn came and the sun started to rise, but rain still pelted the city and the distant rumble and flash of lightning kept everyone on alert. With Erynor heading back to Broid, the storm would dissipate. I didn't know if it had come through wielding or something more sinister, but it *was* linked to Erynor.

The storm reflected my tempestuous mood far too well. Ridiculous as it seemed, and for a number of years now, there had seemed to be some kind of link between my disposition and the weather.

Far more accustomed to the tropical climate of my childhood on the sunny island of Cynethol, once a place of delight, thoughts of that now-wretched island had turned to the taste of ash in my mouth. I couldn't think of it in the same way. Not anymore. So much of my youth had been spent there, in bliss with Kiron. I had linked those perfect sunny days in Broid and the surrounding countryside with my emotions.

But when I had moved to Gneal after the Grand Tourney and the loss of my best friend, my lover Kiron, not even the sunniest day during the height of summer could melt the ice that had encased my heart that day. It wasn't hard for the frigid kingdom to reflect my icy temperament, and I realized that I took some comfort in it. Gneal had nothing to do with how I felt or what had happened to me—what I had done. But blaming Perrien's climate for affecting my moods required less self-awareness, and I did not want to remember that day. Reliving the Grand Tourney, even in a memory, was the last thing I wanted. I had spent the last ten years strengthening those mental blocks and barriers.

Moving anywhere north of Lankor and Tiel would once have been unbearable. Not only was it frigid most of the year, but the only body of water was a mostly frozen sea. Kiron's plan had worked though—I should have known that he wouldn't go through with our hastily and desperately modified plan. Instead, I had lived and he had died and my superiors had sent me as far north as possible for my first assignment as an Erynien emissary, assuming that I too had become a shadow elf following my victory over Kiron. But not consuming his soul meant that I was unchanged and would age at a mortal's pace; my skin would eventually wrinkle and my hair thin, but neither would decay from the inside out. I would not become more of a monster than I already was. It didn't matter without Kiron though.

Life without Kiron wasn't life at all; not even Ceurendol reformed could breathe new life into me. Not after that day—not after what I'd done. Tossing me into the fires of Mount Cyngol would have better results. That certainly wouldn't breathe any air into my lungs, but it would melt my heart efficiently enough. Lost in my misery as always, I was surprised by a question from the lethien, the half-elf, half-human who walked at my side.

"What's wrong?" Liam asked. I stared back at him, not responding. "You didn't just say goodbye to your brother," he snapped. "You didn't just hear that beast of an emperor threaten your only surviving relative." Liam hated me.

I was as sure of that as I was of my blasted Cyndinari heritage. As if my cinnamon hair and bronze skin wasn't evidence enough, memories of Cynethol that trickled through my mental barriers ensured that. Shaking my head, I tried to walk away. I had spent more than enough time with Liam already as we had sat in Therril's office throughout the night, keeping an eye on Devlyn while the shadow elves destroyed Ceurenyl. I didn't understand why Therril had insisted that I wait in his office. I had assumed it was for my own safety. Ceurenyl was under attack by my people. If anyone had found me alone in a corridor, I would've been lucky to get away with a few bruises and a swollen eye.

I'd rather nurse a bruised eye for a week or two than spend hours alone with Liam again. But no, Therril had asked Liam and me to wait in his office, first for Devlyn to arrive, and then hours longer with him until they'd decided to send him away. I had no idea how Therril, who had spent the entire day in the temple, had known to expect Devlyn's arrival; he certainly never told Liam or me that Devlyn would stumble into the office through a window that was not a window. My curiosity didn't care to dwell on it for long. Devlyn was now flying away toward the Illumined Wood to begin his novitiate.

I honestly didn't think Erynor was going to let him escape. If I hadn't heard my former emperor speak himself, I wouldn't have believed it. There had to be a reason. He wouldn't have just left Devlyn unharmed. Devlyn was a Phaedryn—although an inexperienced one without anyone to train him, since he was the only Phaedryn alive now. It didn't make sense that Erynor would allow the boy to escape. Even if Erynor didn't see him as a threat, surely there wasn't any benefit to letting Devlyn learn how to bond with the phoenix.

That wasn't all though. Erynor knew Xanth and I were here, Xanth locked away for murdering the Chair of Arantiulyn, while I was free to roam the temple. How much did Erynor know about that night Xanth tried to smuggle me into Gwilnor, only to be subdued by Velaria and Devlyn? The only logical way for Erynor to know any of this was through his servants of Shadow. Like in every other city, I knew that they were littered throughout Ceurenyl, but for Erynor to also know about the dealings inside the temple meant that there were also servants of Shadow skulking around among the temple's residents. That was a harrowing thought.

Did Erynor know I wasn't a shadow elf? Erynor had been at the Grand Tourney that horrible day, watching from the imperial balcony, surrounded by advisors, shadow elves, and scantily dressed attendants. He hadn't called me out as an impostor or tried to stop me from leaving the arena with the other victors. If he didn't know that I wasn't a shadow elf, surely, he knew that I had no love for the empire. That was evident after he had called me a traitor and a coward last night during his booming ranting to the entire city.

A traitor, sure. But I'd rather be a traitor to the Erynien Empire than any other nation—although Tiel was a narrow exception. I was trying to figure out what my role would be now. No longer an Erynien emissary, but a known defector, cursed by the Erynien emperor himself. I would never be able to go back to Cynethol. Not even my uncle could protect me; hiding me as an apprentice vintner at the winery on his estate would be impossible. Someone would recognize me, would kill me on the spot. Neither could I ever visit Kiron's tomb in the catacombs of the Imperium. If I ever returned to Broid, I might as well wear a sign plastered on my back labeling me as a renegade and a Luminari sympathizer.

"I hope Yelaris is keeping Devlyn safe," Liam said, snapping me back to the present. Wrapped in my self-pity, I hadn't noticed that he still walked with me. I suppose we were both heading to the lower levels of the temple. Still, he could've followed at a different pace if he didn't want to be around me, or taken another route altogether.

"Do you think he made it to the Illumined Wood yet?"

"I doubt it," he said, as we walked through a mostly empty corridor. "Yelaris is a fast flier, but not that fast. She flew me from Gneal to here, remember?"

"Vividly. The Perrien soldiers I was with nearly all died of fright at the sight. Your uncle, General Lex, threatened to have them all flogged for cowardice and thrown in Gneal's dungeons afterward. I was more shocked to learn that there were still free dragons after Erynor sought to either make them his subjects or destroy them. I guess he wasn't as successful as my magisters at the Imperium stated. I was even more stunned to discover one had bound herself to Velaria. I never expected that a free dragon would trust a Cyndinari."

"Do you think there's more out there? Free dragons, that is."

"It's possible. Can't imagine where they're all hiding though. They're not exactly small creatures, are they?" I answered, continuing the conversation despite my desire to be away from him after all our recent togetherness.

"I suppose not."

We walked in silence, crossing various corridors and descending through the Temple of Ceur to find our respective rooms. If not for the rain lashing against the windows, the sun would have poured through here. I desperately missed the sun. It's not that I minded this storm, but I'd been cooped up in the temple long enough. I didn't know how much longer I was going to be able to make it without snapping at someone. The ei'ceuril and other temple residents already thought I was strange because I often sat in the southern window niches. It wasn't the same as walking outside in the sunlight and it certainly couldn't compare to sunbathing on one of Cynethol's beaches. But, since I couldn't leave the temple, my options were limited.

Ceurenyl reminded me of Gneal. The skies were often grey and overcast, and because this city was up in the Laudien Mountains, its climate was similar to the more northern city's. The snow took too long to melt in both cities and summer was all too brief. Not like in Broid, where the summer-like warmth started in spring and stretched well into the autumn months.

I brushed the thoughts of Broid and Cynethol aside. They weren't safe. Besides, I would never be allowed to leave Ceurenyl. I couldn't even step a single foot outside the temple. Not because I was a prisoner, but because I was a kien wielder. And that was reason enough. I was a danger to the realms, just like all kien wielders. The only way we weren't a danger to ourselves or others was to be locked away in the Temple of Ceur, where wielders couldn't interact with the erendinth. I was safe here though. If Erynor were to send shadow elves to deal with me in the temple, they would have to pass through the Chamber of Light, which would incapacitate anyone with ill intent, crushing them in its luminescence.

Still, I missed my freedom. The temple was large enough to get lost in, but it wasn't the same as getting lost in the wilderness or city streets. I wanted to lose track of time while sitting on the sandy beaches of Cynethol, the sun kissing my skin.

No, I wasn't going to think about Cynethol. I didn't need to go down that depressing path again.

"Who were the others?" Liam asked.

"I'm sorry?" What was he talking about? What others?

"The others. The other shadow elves who killed my

family—devouring their souls. I saw what happened in Gneal when I killed one. All the souls trapped inside were freed at once. I want to find the others. I want to free my family from those eternal prisons. You were there. You have to know who they are."

I had rarely visited Gneal's castle dungeons, but Liam remembered seeing me on the other side of the bars. He had been the only lethien among the prisoners—all the others were full elves.

I had arrived in Gneal shortly after Liam and his family had been imprisoned. One of the female prisoners had continued on with the entourage that had traveled with me to Gneal and who presumably took her on to Broid. I didn't learn until much later that she was Devlyn's mother and Liam's stepmother. Erynor had wanted her as his personal slave. She allegedly knew something that Erynor sought. Some secret knowledge or weapon that could turn the tide of his renewed conquest of Eklean and beyond in his favor was hidden in Cor'lera. Erynor had heard Lucillia's prophecy before he'd killed her—or rather, tried to kill her. As a child, I had learned that Erynor had succeeded in stabbing Lucillia, but I had learned here in the temple that Erynor had never stabbed the woman. He had been unable to and instead, had fled from the Illumined Wood with his army, all of them burned in the process. Erynor was so wounded that he had had to go into hiding after that, only revealing himself again in the past century.

"You know I had nothing to do with how your family was treated."

"You were there, Jaerol—you were there and did nothing."

"There's that anger and blame again." I was being unfair since this was the first time that Liam had actually voiced it. He didn't need to though. The way he looked at me had already made it clear how he felt about me. If he could, he would probably turn me over to Erynor himself. He wanted me dead. At least, that had been his intention since Velaria had rescued him.

He still blamed me for alerting Perrien's officials that he had been freed, even though I personally hadn't cared and hadn't told anyone that a prisoner had escaped. I hadn't known who Velaria was at the time. Clearly, she was an ei'ana, but her appearance had stunned me. She looked like a Cyndinari. How had a Cyndinari become an ei'ana? How many were like her? I had never dared to believe that there were Cyndinari free of the Erynien Empire. Why wasn't I born like her? Why weren't Kiron and I allowed to be free? I pushed those thoughts away.

"If you're as innocent as you claim to be, how could you just stand by and watch? Butchering my family would have been a kindness compared to what they did."

"I never watched—you know that." The accusation stung all the same. I was aware of what had become of the elves in Gneal's dungeons. Velaria might have freed Liam, but countless others had had their souls stolen and were still enslaved within one shadow elf or another, preventing them from transitioning to Lumaeniel. "I…I couldn't watch."

"You didn't stop it either."

A ping reverberated in my chest. What was that? A second ping followed the first crack on my frozen heart, followed by a wash of emotions. Had Liam's tone managed that? The accusations? Or was it a memory of Kiron? He had often spoken to me in a similar fashion. Those sad eyes sprung in my mind—Kiron wasn't supposed to be the one to die. I struggled to regain my icy composure—it was supposed to be the other way around. It was supposed to be me.

Chapter Three

As the week went on, details of Erynor's assault against Ceurenyl trickled into the Temple of Ceur. Everyone had heard that first explosion, and considering how loud it was, like many others, I too feared that the entire temple would collapse. Several days had passed before I overhead a group of temple knights mention that the blast had happened at the city gate. I had asked whether the gate still stood, but none of the knights would dignify me with an answer. Everyone knew what cinnamon hair, bronze skin, and pointed ears meant. They all expected me to do something horrendous inside the temple so I could return to the Cyndinari as a hero.

Since gaining a degree of freedom in the temple—something that Xanth would never know—I'd been allowed to walk the temple's corridors without too much attention, but everyone knew me by my hair and skin. Despite Mother Velaria Treyven sharing the same Cyndinari features, whatever prejudice was still directed at her due to her lineage paled in the shadow of her authority as Chair of Azurelle. As a nobody Cyndinari and prior Erynien emissary, I bore their full disdain. None of the temple knights would speak to me.

I had to wait for the rumors to spread through the lower levels among the lay votaries before learning that the city gate had been destroyed. The temple knights had taken large casualties at the gate and now blamed anyone with red hair for their comrades' deaths. While I knew precious little of the Erynien Empire's greater schemes, I had assumed that they would eventually siege Ceurenyl but had also assumed that Lucillia would have been Erynor's first target. Openly attacking Ceurenyl first made little sense, even if the Ei'ana of Septyl would be his greatest adversary in the battles to come.

When Xanth and I had first come to the city, the shadow elf had mentioned infiltrating Gwilnor Academy, but only in passing. I had assumed that Erynor wanted to dissolve the ei'ana from within their order, rendering them useless in the war to come. Even as Xanth briefed me on their intent, being in the company of a repugnant shadow elf meant that I had stopped listening to him as we passed through Ceurenyl's city gate. I had never seen a gate and wall crafted from stone not native to the Skylands built so well. I knew elves were responsible for Ceurenyl's founding and construction long before the Great Migration from the Skylands, but they had used the local stone for the city walls and gate. The old refurbished cities of Thellion could never compete with elven wielding. The invisible wields woven into the structure were impressive. I had been told that the wields had given the walls and gate their form.

Hearing that Ceurenyl's gate had been reduced to rubble was unimaginable. I refused to believe it without seeing it.

I had discovered early on that the closer I walked toward the Chamber of Light, the more likely I would cross paths with the upper echelon of the Ei'ceuril hierarchy, a group of individuals that I had no interest in interacting with. These poorly named wise ones and archstewards were a feeble reflection of their predecessors. Their ineptitude in wielding kien along with their inability to touch the erendinth here in the temple had poisoned the soul of the Ei'ceuril order. That same inability to press into the erendinth while inside the temple nagged at me.

I hungered to wield again. Even though I had never learned to wield with control—that balance had long been broken and forgotten—I had once wielded and interacted with the erendinth as often as I drew breath. At least, that's how I thought of the erendinth. They were just as essential as breathing. And severed from them in this temple, I was now suffocating.

Climbing the last elaborate stair to the main level, this one noticeably grander and more ornate than the ones in the lower, subterranean levels, I passed a group of huddled ei'ceuril. Wise ones most likely, clustered like nervous hens, looking at me as though I was a fox in their coop. I'd grown accustomed to these looks over the years, particularly when others had looked at Kiron and me disdainfully, whispering *flamer* behind our backs. Those whispers were always meant to be heard. For a time, their words had wounded me, but they had never seemed to bother Kiron. Another memory flashed. My hands could still feel Kiron's ears, my fingers caressing his hair, bringing tears and an ache in my heart. Fighting to regain my cool demeanor, I pushed past the ei'ceuril laughing among themselves, concealing my watery eyes as best I could. Did these old fools think they were the reason for my tears? They didn't know what pain was.

Finally reaching the doors to the Chamber of Light, I was appraised by the temple knights stationed there. I knew the appropriate words now, after I had embarrassed myself the first time I had tried to strut into the sacred space beyond. "I am not worthy to enter into such splendor, but by the will of Anaweh, the Creating Light."

The words stung. They spoke to a truth I never wanted to speak. I wasn't worthy—not just to enter into that illumined space, but to live. Kiron should be the one still alive, not me.

Overwhelmed, I passed through the doors and into the Chamber of Light. The transition was blinding. However the ancient ei'ceuril had managed to create that shaft of light, they could have at least toned it down a hair. Blinking, I waited for my eyes to adjust fully. The incredible space materialized—broad columns raced upward to carry sculpted arches, their corners rounded to pendentives as a wondrous dome sprung from them, seeming to disappear into the heavens.

"Remarkable, isn't she?"

I turned to find the ei'ceuril magister who taught theoreticals at Gwilnor Academy, Therril, standing beside me, gazing up in wonder. Undoubtedly, he'd seen it many times over his long life in this space.

"It hasn't grown familiar to you?" I asked.

"Not even after all my years in this temple could this space lose its splendor. Even on my deathbed, this will hold me in awe."

I started to walk away from Therril, who continued to

stare up and into the shaft of light. Sidestepping around the light toward the exit and into the city, I tried not to make my path overly obvious. I meandered slowly, seeming to take in the architecture, which admittedly, I was. That was one thing I did not have to pretend at. I had never been in a space more impressive. Even Broid's imperial palace paled in comparison to this, despite Erynor's allegations otherwise. The imperial palace might be grand, embedded with riches and luxury, but it was not the crown of Eklean, and certainly not the crown of all Teraeniel.

"Off somewhere?" Therril had followed me. A questioning eyebrow rose and his silver eyes glimmered in the light. Why didn't he have the green-to-silver eyes so common to the Luminari? "Hmmmm?"

"Nowhere in particular—trying not to gawk up at the dome." That was partly true.

"The dome is lovely, but not even it can compare to the chamber's centerpiece." Therril really was a good ei'ceuril. Not like many in the temple and the few I had known in Broid. "Are you aware that it's ill-advised to lie to an ei'ceuril? Here of all places, no less!"

"It's also ill-advised to keep a Cyndinari as a guest in the Temple of Ceur. At least, the looks I get from many of your brother ei'ceuril seem to suggest so."

"Ho-oh! They wouldn't recognize an advisable action if it came from Anaweh's own lips. Not that the Creating Light has lips; at least I don't think so."

I laughed. When was the last time that had happened?

"So, you do know how to smile. A bit out of practice by the looks of it, but no worse for wear. After all, you can't lose it by not doing it! Some of our younger members might have a different opinion—that's certainly what their actions suggest. And they think us old kooks don't know!"

"You're not referring to what I think you're referring to? Are you?" Was he really joking about sex?

"You're a smart young man, you figure it out." Therril turned and headed toward the exit that led back into the rest of the temple. "Well, what are you waiting for? Come on."

I started to protest, but the look Therril gave me forced me to reconsider. So instead, I followed the much older elf out of the Chamber of Light and into the corridor toward the cloistered portion of the temple.

The path Therril chose was easily recognizable—I had just walked it a week ago, but in the opposite direction with Devlyn and Liam. Why was Therril taking me to his office?

As we approached, I saw Liam waiting outside Therril's office. I groaned at the sight. I didn't have the energy to deal with Liam just now. He did not need to see my still tear-streaked face.

He turned when he heard us approach and saw me walking with Therril. Was that regret in his expression? "Oh, sorry, I'll come back later."

"What are you apologizing for? Now, come in, come in." Therril flourished a key then unlocked the office door, insisting that both Liam and I enter.

I stood uncomfortably close to Liam, my skin crawling at the proximity. "I should leave."

"Don't be a Cyndinari fool of an elf. Now, you two have been cooped up in this temple for far too long and I think it will do you both wonders if you got out for a walk and some fresh air."

"We're both kien wielders. Isn't it illegal for us to leave the temple?" Liam asked, crossing his arms and physically closing himself off to the possibility. Especially if I was involved. He wanted nothing to do with me. I felt a strong urge to punch him and tell him to shut his trap. He wasn't going to ruin my chance to get out of the temple for an afternoon.

"Hmm? What's that? My old eyes must have missed something. I could have sworn that all I saw were two responsible young knights leaving the castle for a breath of fresh air. Was I mistaken?"

I exchanged a pleading look with Liam, who only shrugged in return. He too wanted to get out of the temple, if only for a few hours. Did Therril say the castle? And there was nothing knightly about me.

"I thought that's what I saw. I also believe I saw a change of clothes just past that window." Therril turned and walked out of his office with a window that was not a window.

An awkward moment passed, even more awkward than when we had first been asked by Therril to wait in this same office a week ago. Granted, neither of us had known about the secret passage through that specific window at the time. Not until Devlyn stumbled through it in the middle of the night. Neither of us believed at the time that he had scaled the side of the temple.

I shrugged and took the first step toward the window. "You coming?"

Liam looked back toward the door. The questioning doubt lingering in his eyes was clear.

"That's why you were here in the first place, wasn't it?"

"He said he wanted to talk to me about something. I never thought he would secret me out of the temple. I also thought it would just be the two of us, him and me, I mean."

"Sorry to disappoint, but I don't want to miss this opportunity. I've had my fill of turned-up noses for one day, thank you. It'll be nice to be around normal people again." With that, I stepped onto the sill of the window displaying overcast skies and into a darkened tunnel with the next step.

Liam followed, but he had more sense and brought a lit torch with him, illuminating two sets of Septyl knight's uniforms. "Funny, I can't imagine Therril ever dressing up as a knight."

"I don't think he intended to. I can't imagine him dressing up like anything but an ei'ceuril. It's hard enough to imagine him wearing normal clothing, let alone a knight's tunic." I lifted one of the tunics off the hook up to eye level. "Do you think he planned this all along?"

"I would say he's smarter than he lets on, but I can't imagine anyone doubting his intellect. His sanity, perhaps. You don't become the theoreticals magister at the most distinguished school on the continent, if not the entire world, if you're a dolt."

I laughed, and Liam echoed it.

"I didn't think you knew how to laugh," Liam's words held a note of puzzled surprise.

"It's just as much of a shock to me," I replied honestly, still smiling, then realized that I was holding eye contact with Liam. Forcing a cough, I turned away. He didn't have any green in his eyes either. That was odd, even for a lethien. All the Luminari were supposed to have the emerald-to-silver eyes after Lucillia gave birth to the twins, Feolyn and Roendryn.

Liam walked past, deposited the torch into an empty bracket, and picked up the other uniform by the shoulders. "I can't believe I used to wear this on a daily basis. My training at Gwilnor to become a Septyl knight stopped once it was discovered that I would start wielding."

"I'm sure it didn't look that bad. Honestly, I find it hard to look away from some of the temple knights at times."

Liam turned his head to look at me. "Sorry, what was that?"

"I said, I would very much like to…"

"That's what I thought you said," Liam interrupted, coughing. He now looked at the uniform differently, as though questioning whether he wanted to change in front of me.

I brushed past him. I wasn't going to stand idly in a dimly lit tunnel the entire day while the opportunity to go outside awaited. My shirt was soon over my head and crumpled under my arm as I undid my belt next and slid my trousers off.

Liam's eyes widened. "Cyndinari don't wear small clothes?"

I smirked this time, noticing that Liam was trying not to stare between my legs. "You should read up on how the elves used to dress on the Skylands. Better yet, look at some of the artwork that survived."

"I have nothing against the elves, but I highly doubt they went without small clothes like the barbarian tribes in Dwonia."

I pulled up the new trousers. "You're mistaking the point. They were so comfortable in their skin back in those days that you'd just as likely come across one completely in the buff. Especially if they were out frolicking in the country."

"You're lying." Liam took his own shirt off now. His mixed elven and human lineage was incredibly alluring. I had never seen an elf with a chest so broad and biceps twice the girth of my own. "Besides, what's any of that matter? I'm not an elf."

"You realize that you're a lethien, right?"

"A what?"

"Half-elf, half-human."

"My da is from a human family and my mum was also a human."

"Those pointed ears speak to something other than 'just' human."

"Whatever." Liam exchanged his trousers and finished dressing. I'll never understand why anyone chooses to wear small clothes—they look incredibly constricting and uncomfortable. "Ready to find out where this tunnel goes?"

"Gwilnor, I imagine." I smirked again, looking at him from over my shoulder.

"Therril did mention us leaving from the castle."

Chapter Four

We passed through the only unbarred door out of the castle. The quad lay beyond it, and the largest arch I had ever seen. It spanned two levels of the castle and opened onto a bridge crossing a narrow stream. I sighed in relief once we crossed the last of Gwilnor's bridges and were past the last checkpoint of knights dressed just as we were. Fortunately, none of the ei'ana or students in the castle had recognized us. Not even the knights standing guard recognized Liam, even though he had trained with them for a time.

Heavy clouds hovered above, threatening another storm. After Erynor's successful assault on Ceurenyl a week ago, it was all too easy to associate storms with another attack. Just the other day, a small thunderclap had caused me to leap from my favorite window niche.

Despite not being able to feel the sun kiss my skin, my mood was greatly improved just by stepping outside for the first time in months and breathing in fresh air.

I set off at a quick pace, forcing Liam to call after me, "Wait, where are you off to?"

"To see if the rumors about the gate are true."

"Is it safe?"

"Is anywhere outside the temple safe?"

Liam didn't answer, but hurried after me anyway. Had Therril intended for this to happen as well? Did he hope Liam and I would become friends? It was a funny thought. Instead of dwelling on it, I continued to lead the way across the bridges, out of the castle grounds, and into the city proper. People filled the streets, cleaning up the debris following Erynor's attack the previous week. Some gathered rubble, others scrubbed burn marks off walls, while still more wandered about not knowing what to do, distraught by the continuing evidence of an epic battle.

Ceurenyl had been the only haven during the Ceurendol War—the only Krysenthien city that Erynor had failed to conquer fourteen hundred years ago. The people of Ceurenyl had lived freely and confidently with that knowledge. But now, that self-assurance had been shattered after Erynor soared into their city with a horde of shadow elves, blasting their gate to rubble for good measure.

I knew how they felt. Even with my frozen heart, I too knew what it was like to live in fear of the Erynien Empire. Every night throughout my life, I had fallen into a fitful sleep, terrified that my disloyalty would finally be uncovered. The first time I had slept through the entire night after the Grand Tourney was when the ei'ana and ei'ceuril had tossed me into a cell. I was a prisoner, but I was safe, locked away. I still couldn't believe that my duplicity had only been uncovered by the ei'ceuril in the Temple of Ceur. Their cells of justice could only hold the guilty, and the only thing that I was guilty of was being born a Cyndinari.

My innocence had been further proven when I had visited the Chamber of Light that first time and was supported every time after that. If I had pledged myself to Ramiel, I would have collapsed to the floor, unable to move. I had felt every pair of eyes that had stared at me when I had first entered the Chamber of Light. They had all expected—and still waited for—me to buckle under the weight of my own sin of treachery. Yet not even the perceived sin most accused me of had brought me to the floor.

Apparently, the Creating Light cared little for who I slept with. Given the whispers and the sneers I'd suffered all my life, I too had been surprised that my sexual orientation had not crushed me to the floor.

"What's wrong now?"

I had grown quiet again and didn't realize we had walked a good distance from the castle in silence. "It's nothing."

"How'd you manage to trick all those shadow elves so that they never knew you weren't one of them?"

"What do you mean?" I glared back, caught off guard by the question.

"You're an awful liar. Now, which question would you prefer to answer honestly?"

"Fine." For a moment, I considered telling Liam how I had fooled the Erynien Empire, but that required speaking about Kiron. I wasn't ready for that. I wasn't ready to say his name out loud. Not yet. "The ei'ceuril weren't the only ones surprised that I didn't collapse to the floor, that first time in the

Chamber of Light."

"I thought you said you were innocent." Liam halted, appraising me anew, as though confirming that he was right all along in his distrust toward me.

"I grew up thinking that Anaweh frowned on certain relationships."

"What type of relationship would Anaweh disapprove of? Well, aside from abusive ones that is."

"With other men."

"Oh. I see." Liam stopped looking at me and instead cast his eyes around to look at anything else. Suddenly, the cobbled streets were much more interesting than my potential affronts. "I didn't realize. Well, I didn't realize before your comment in the tunnel about how you felt about some of the knights."

"You'd be one of the first."

"Right." Liam cleared his throat and took a deep breath. "I kind of expected the same would happen to me when I first walked in. I was in bad shape at the time; a shadow covered my heart and I could barely stand on my own two legs. I have no idea how I managed to sit on Yelaris the entire way from Perrien to here. Flying on the back of a dragon isn't as easy as it looks."

"Neither is being carried unconscious in her claws. The bruises took less time to heal than I expected."

"Anyway, I assumed eleven years a prisoner in Gneal's dungeons were penance enough. That those past…um…actions were atoned for."

"Does anyone know?"

"I'm sure some suspect it, but other than some friends I grew up with, I haven't told anyone. Granted, I didn't exactly have to come right out and explain it to them either."

I laughed. The unexpected mirth came without warning.

"It's not that funny."

"Perhaps not to you," I said, still laughing. The imagery of Liam talking about those secrets while fondling a friend had me grasping my sides. How was this lethien—this half-elf, half-human making me smile again? The smile reached my eyes this time.

"Fine. Let's go see this ruined gate you so desperately want to gape at."

I knew the way better than Liam did, so I led him through the streets congested with confused and bewildered inhabitants. People repeatedly looked toward the temple, sitting on the mountainside above the city. They waited for some news of hope to come from there—any sort of reassurance that would bring a sense of stability to their lives. No one yet knew how many people had died from Erynor's attack. But by their grim expressions, everyone knew at least one family affected by a death or a missing person.

The number of people with those lost vacant expressions increased the closer we came to the gate, or rather what had been the gate. The city wall and its equally spaced guard towers rising over the buildings, had been visible over the past several blocks. Once we crossed another intersection, I could see that its straight horizontality dipped, its clean edges reduced to broken corners.

As Liam and I rounded the final building before reaching the plaza in front of the gate, my breath caught in my chest at the sight of the destruction. After a week, burnt buildings continued to smolder, the smoke refusing to disperse. There weren't any flames, but I knew from experience that the guts of those buildings still harbored charcoal, fueling the endless smoke. Only the stone exteriors remained, stained black by the once engulfing fires. None of the buildings' shells were salvageable. The entire plaza would have to be cleared before reconstruction could begin.

Among the many citizens were both Septyl and temple knights. Some of them continued to patrol, while most were helping to clear the debris that was cool enough to touch.

Walking past dazed citizens, I stood at the feet of what had been the gate. Liam stood beside me, gaping at the ruined structure.

"I never imagined destruction on this scale was possible."

"Your experience with the Erynien Empire was largely from inside a prison cell. Erynor brought Krysenthiel to her knees. A ruined gate is the least of his capabilities."

"What do you think will happen next?" he asked.

"As long as there are ei'ana in this city, he will never leave it in peace. But his plots reach every corner of Eklean. Ceurenyl is not the only prize he seeks. If he is not stopped, Lucillia will burn. As will any other city that spurns him."

Too stunned to remove our gazes from the ruined gate, it was only when someone shrieked that we turned away. A man was screaming as he ran from a smoldering house, his clothes singed and his face covered in soot.

He stopped in front of a pair of temple knights, frantically pointing toward the house he had come from. "Please, she's still in there—my daughter. We have to save her," cried the man.

"Where is she? Is she trapped?" one of the knights asked.

"Yes, it's a beam—she's under a beam. Please, hurry."

Five of the knights rushed into the house.

"Fools," sneered the man, no longer a fear-stricken father crying in a panic over his trapped daughter, but a deceiver, weaving his arms and squealing in glee.

Before he could finish his wield, I saw his wielded disguise fade. Ashen, scabbed skin not charred by smoke but by corruption eating from the inside out, had changed the shadow elf's appearance. Once red, now lusterless hair poked through the ruse. I rushed at the cackling shadow elf, lowering my shoulder and prepared to tackle the deceiver. Before I got to him, Liam more sensibly launched a heavy stone at his head.

I barely saw it fly past but heard it crack satisfyingly against his skull.

Moments later, the five knights came out of the house confused, but fortunately unharmed. Thanks to Liam's skillful throw, the shadow elf had not completed his wield of tenebrys. The other knights who had been standing by now recognized the shadow elf for what he was.

"Should we take him to the temple?" one knight asked, reaching out with his sword as though to poke the creature.

"Did your superiors teach you how they become shadow elves?" I asked, scowling down at the writhing abomination.

"Only recently, but yes."

"Judging by this one's corruption, it's over three hundred years old and has consumed dozens of innocent people's souls to extend his own life. They're trapped in this husk of wasted flesh."

The surrounding knights now scowled at the repulsive thing at their feet, all of them with drawn swords. They knew that this shadow elf had likely devoured the souls of people in Ceurenyl during and since the attack. They had not only every right to kill this repugnance, they had a responsibility to.

As they dithered over their next actions, the shadow elf started to come to himself, his forearms flexing, tenebrys electrified at his fingertips. The knights stepped back as he cackled again, but one determined knight stood her ground.

A fluid stroke from her translucent sword separated the shadow elf's head from his shoulders, letting loose a burst of lighted spheres to escape the rotting corpse. The souls of the enslaved anacordel disappeared just as quickly as they had appeared, eager to return at last to Lumaeniel. Who knows how long some of them had been deprived of their rest? They had been cheated not only by an early death, but also from eternal splendor in Anaweh's Light.

The knight who had executed the shadow elf wiped her sword clean on the rags that clad the shadow elf. In the confusion caused by the shadow elf's trickery and subsequent death, none of the others noticed, as I did, that under the cloak she wore to conceal it, her uniform was different from the others. She had sheathed her sword before anyone could get a closer look, so that any who might have noticed it would likely think its transparency was a trick of the eye and nothing more—certainly nothing special or magical.

I knew what I had seen and I knew that sword was made of a substance forgotten by many. This was no ordinary knight, and by the way she carried herself, this knight knew she carried a verathn.

I wanted to question the mysterious knight, but too many things were happening at once now that the shadow elf lay dead.

Pushing past the spectators watching the shadow elf's body disintegrate to ash before their eyes, I searched for the knight but she had successfully slipped away.

I peered through the growing crowd, unable to locate her. Liam approached from behind. "We'd better return to the temple before this attracts anyone who might recognize us."

Chapter Five

I woke in my windowless bed chamber on a stiff mattress not fit for a common criminal, longing for the plush pillows and soft silk sheets that I had grown up with in Broid. The memory of those luxuries called me to return home. I never would have anticipated that I would one day be lodged in a windowless room, confined to the Temple of Ceur, living a life constrained to idleness due to my ability to wield.

Everyone knew the risks associated with kien wielders. Even after all the years I had spent wielding in the service of the Erynien Empire, not once had I grown any closer to mastering any sense of control. None of us did. I had figured out when to stop before I lost control of the erendinth, but that was discouraged by the Imperium's magisters who had taught me. Kien wielders were exhorted to embrace their strength at the sacrifice of control. The world belonged to the strong, not the careful and hesitant. If the Luminari had been strong, they would never have been enslaved, losing their kingdom in the process. My magisters believed, as did most Cyndinari, that history was on the cusp of repeating itself. The prudent Luminari would never achieve their potential strength, and would kneel as slaves to the Erynien Empire once again, as would all Eklean and beyond.

Naturally, my magisters were wrong.

Devlyn had proven that he could wield with control. While I didn't have any indication that that control was tied to bloodlines, it certainly made Liam more interesting. Over the past month alone, I had purposely sought the lethien out several times each week. He hadn't started to wield on his own yet—probably because he couldn't in the temple. But perhaps, like his brother, he held one of the secrets to wielding with control.

Rather than waste away in the lower levels with the lay votaries, Liam devoted most of his time to training with the temple knights. He did not give the impression that he enjoyed sitting back and doing nothing. Granted, that same itch to do something—anything—productive was stirring in me too. Each day resembled the last and I had yet to do anything meaningful or fulfilling. I could hear my uncle telling me that boredom leads to reckless actions.

Aware that I had woken up at an unnecessarily early hour, I rolled over, hoping to look out the window. Grumpy at the lack—a clear design flaw—I tried to press into the erendinth, again. Too many months had passed since I had last touched ignys, terys, aquaeys, and aerys. I even tried to embrace umbrys. I still couldn't believe I had managed it at the Grand Tourney. It was only my relationship with Kiron that had led me to unlock the secret.

Giving to receive; receiving to give.

The mantra intrinsically linked kien and kiara. The riddle wasn't determinative—kien wielders only press into the erendinth, while kiara wielders only embrace them. It was both. While probably not the way the ancient elves understood it, I only came to understand it because of Kiron—because of what we had done together and what we meant to each other.

His face lingered in my mind but was beginning to fade as I came more fully awake. I wanted to hold onto his image longer, refusing to allow my thoughts to shift to anything else, lest the memory disappear. Kiron's face surfaced so irregularly now that I treasured every moment I could hold onto it. I refused to acknowledge that the sound of his voice was slipping from my memory, and even as I pretended that wasn't happening, it made me hold on to his now-infrequent image as long as possible.

Finally, I allowed Kiron's face to vanish. Groggy and uncaring, I got out of bed and went to the lavatory. It was early enough that no one should be awake yet, so I risked walking the corridors wearing just a robe.

Luckily, my inner sense of time had remained intact since telling time by looking out a window was impossible here. As I had expected, the corridors were empty, and I began to empty my bladder as soon as I reached the lavatory. Then, someone spoke from behind me.

"You know, if you follow through with your intent to join the temple knights, you might want to reconsider your preference to go without small clothes."

How long had he been in here? "I don't like them."

"You realize all the temple knights share rooms, right?"

asked a fully dressed Liam, apparently ready to start the day.

"Well, I'd better make sure we're sharing a room—one less person to make uncomfortable."

"I never said I was comfortable."

I questioned whether to challenge the lethien again, then decided not to bother. I took his wandering gaze as both a compliment and confirmation of his ease around me. "Who should I speak to about joining the temple knights?"

"Bastien's in charge of recruitment. He's had that role for years."

"Sorenth?" The name certainly sounded Sorenth.

"Yeah, all the way from Daerinth, I believe."

"Is that still considered Sorenth?"

"Why wouldn't it be?"

"Its prince is rather sympathetic to Erynor—he's practically in Yanil's borders as it is."

"You don't think he'd start a civil war, do you?"

"A civil war is the least Erynor is after. It won't be long until he tries to lay claim to all Eklean—and don't think that he'll stop with just this continent either."

Liam frowned. I could see that he wanted to do his part to ensure the liberty of Eklean, but as long as we're both kien wielders, incapable of controlling our wielding, the most we could do was become ei'ceuril or temple knights and protect the Temple of Ceur. I chuckled to myself at the thought of the first option and turned to wash my hands.

"What's so funny? Did you only just now realize that your robe barely covers you?"

"It's the perfect length and fit, thank you. But no, I imagined myself joining the ei'ceuril and taking their vows."

We laughed together at that and left the lavatory. He kept walking with me. Odd. His room, along with the other temple knights' quarters were in the opposite direction and up several levels. Those levels certainly had their own lavatories as well. What *was* Liam doing here? Was he seeking me out now, just as I had been doing with him? Surely it was too early for him to come looking for me if that was the case.

"So, what's training with the knights like?" I asked, debating how to ask my more pressing question.

"It's fine for the most part. Practically no one is the same age. It seems the most common thread is how long it took the men to get bored with their lives as lay votaries."

"Wait, are all the recruits able to wield?"

"No, not all of us. The younger a recruit, the more likely they're not a wielder. They joined for the right reason and were likely born and raised in Ceurenyl. Apparently, it's easier to join the temple knights than it is to join the Septyl knights."

"I wonder why that is."

"I suppose it has something to do with the prestige connected to Gwilnor Academy. Every Septyl knight training there receives an education before being knighted. We're mostly just trained how to fight here."

"If we wanted, could we attend lessons with the ei'ceuril?" I asked. The thought of training without a formal education seemed like a waste of time. Granted, I had already received an education from the Imperium, but I knew that they had fed us a version of history that didn't necessarily match up with actual historic events. Then there was the whole issue of their ethics.

"You realize how young the ei'ceuril in studies are,

right?"

"It can't be that bad."

"Some of them are twelve years old, Jaerol. That's what? A decade younger than you?"

"Fourteen to be exact. At least I won't be distracted by any other students this time around."

"I'll be sure to flick crumpled pieces of paper at you then."

"You want to go back to school?" So much for not being distracted during a lecture.

"Those poor kids would be scared senseless if they had to attend lessons with a Cyndinari. They'll need a strong knight to keep them safe." He winked.

"Me? Frightening?"

"It's the red hair and pointed ears." Liam ruffled my hair playfully as he said it.

My stomach clenched at the touch and my heart fluttered. When was the last time someone had run his hands through my hair? I glanced at Liam who was quite unaware of what he had caused inside me. It was silly, really; all he did was mess up my hair. But still, I felt something. It reminded me of my old self. Before…

"You okay?" he asked, his hands now back at his side.

"Fine," I said.

"Liar."

We walked in silence after that. I was beating my feelings down and I knew it. Kiron's face tried to bloom in my mind again, but I just couldn't deal with it right now. Not in front of Liam—not anyone.

"When are you going to speak with Bastien?" he asked as

we reached my room.

Why had he followed me all this way? I certainly did not need an escort. Especially inside the Temple of Ceur. I'd be more likely to be assaulted by a feather than anything actually threatening.

"I suppose I should speak with him later today, right? Want to hold my hand as I ask him?" I didn't mean to lace venom in my response, but there it was.

"I wouldn't mind standing outside the door, especially if Bastien approves of you taking lessons with the ei'ceuril. I was sincere about wanting to join you. I can't say I received the best education at the abbey school in Cor'lera either. I think their curriculum was skewed a bit, but in Perrien's favor, not necessarily the Erynien Empire's."

"Well, I guess they're one and the same now, aren't they," I replied.

Liam didn't make any sign to move, so I opened the door and invited him in. A hint of unease lingered in his tense stance, either because he didn't fully trust me or because he knew and saw that I was very naked beneath my robe. Admittedly, my robe was meant to be provocative. "I won't bite," I said, waiting in the doorjamb.

Whatever had frozen him, he snapped back to himself and followed me in. His gaze darted across the room and his jaw dropped when he saw my belongings.

"Weren't you a prisoner before you moved into this room?" he asked, taking in the overflowing chest.

"The ei'ceuril were kind enough to have the knights retrieve my belongings from the inn I had stayed at. After my innocence was proven, of course. The innkeeper decided to double the rate she charged me when she found out I had ties to the Erynien Empire. Said she would burn my belongings if I didn't pay in full."

Aside from my personal belongings and the trunks where my clothing was stored, the room had little furniture to speak of. There was only an uncomfortable bed, a writing desk with a rickety chair, and a wash basin. Since I hadn't expected to run into anyone in the lavatory, certainly not Liam, I hadn't bothered splashing water on my face to wash the sleep away or brushing my teeth. I crossed the short distance to the wash basin to do both now.

"I can leave if you need to get ready," Liam said, scratching his back as though he was nervous about something.

"Don't bother. You followed me back from the lavatory knowing fully well that I had to get ready for the day."

"I didn't expect you to start with me here."

"Prefer my disheveled look while wearing an all too revealing robe, do you? Didn't you point out that it didn't cover much?" I bent over the wash basin and washed my face. I wish I had a mirror, not just so I could make sure that I was adequately put together, a small luxury that I sorely missed, but to see if Liam was sneaking a peak while my back was turned and I was bent over.

"Hardly," he said eventually.

I turned around to dry my face on a nearby towel, disappointed to find him looking away from me. Pity. "What are you looking at?" I asked as I hung up my robe. He might be modest and avert his eyes, but I wasn't changing my routine for his sake.

His cheeks flushed as he turned around. I smiled, pleased

to see that he wasn't as chaste as I feared.

"What is it with you and being naked all the time?" His eyes flicked back between a blank wall and different parts of my body, unable to stop looking at me.

"Calm down. I just took the robe off to get properly dressed."

Instead of arguing my intentions, Liam sat down on the closest thing he could find, which happened to be my bed. I debated for a moment whether to comment on why he had to sit down. He wouldn't be able to continue pretending that he didn't like seeing me naked when there was visible evidence. I pretended to be undecided as to what to wear for my meeting with Bastien.

"How many pants do you have to choose from?" he asked, somewhat irritated.

"I suppose these ones will do." I grabbed the pair I had intended to wear all along. "When should I go see Bastien?" As much as I enjoyed tormenting Liam, it had gone on long enough.

"He's typically in his office early. I'd probably wait an hour or so."

I pulled my pants up and found a clean linen shirt. Fully dressed, I sat beside Liam on my bed. I certainly wasn't going to sit in that rickety chair. What would he do if I leaned into him? I can't remember the last time I had sex with anyone, and an hour gave us more than enough time. No one in the temple had been comfortable with me being a Cyndinari, so getting close enough to anyone to even suggest a bit of fun was out of the question. Even though I was fully dressed and Liam was sitting more at ease, he was still noticeably tense. I could try gauging his reaction if I just brushed my hand against his thigh. That was innocent enough to pretend it was an accident, at least, that's what I told myself.

"So, you're really going to go through with it? Liam asked before I could make a move.

"Joining the temple knights?"

"What else are you debating about? Actually, I take that back, I don't want to know."

I laughed. I didn't think he was interested in hearing what I had just been thinking. I glanced at his thigh again, although this time, I had to restrain myself—Ramiel's hell, he's pretty. The temptation to grab his muscled thighs and the rest of him coursed through me, and now I was the one sitting, attempting to hide what was growing between my legs.

"Well?" he asked, a hint of impatience in his tone.

"Well, what?" I was too distracted and hoped he was asking if I was going to grab every inch of his body.

"Are you going to join the knights?"

"Oh, right. If Bastien lets me join, then yes."

Our conversation was strained after that with too many awkward silences. There was only one thing on my mind just now, and I doubted that would change so long as I was around Liam. Was it the same with him? Was he also having difficulty thinking of anything but me naked again, holding me in his lap?

We eventually left my room and made our way to Bastien's office. Breakfast was over an hour away, but Liam had assured me that Bastien would be in his office now.

Living among the lay votaries wasn't all that bad, but they all resented their lot more than I did. Fortunately, it was mostly directed at the ei'ana. Still, none of them went out of their way to chat with me or even be friendly for that matter. They instead saw my presence as akin to an unwanted pimple. Doing anything about it would just make it worse. Few of the men in the lower levels were gathered in the corridors as we made our way to Bastien's office. While none of them had taken the time to get to know me, it didn't take long for them to learn one thing about me. I didn't care that they knew that I was gay, but dealing with accusations was debilitating at times. They might as well tease me for having red hair, which I could change if I had enough dye.

Liam and I reached Bastien's office without incident and I gave Liam a nervous smile. I had no idea what I was walking into but it felt like an interview.

"Good luck," Liam offered. "I'll wait here—I want to know if he'll let us study with the ei'ceuril."

Was that the only reason? Instead of asking, I knocked on the door and someone called from inside to enter. "Bastien?" I inquired to the man hunched over a parchment at the only desk.

"Yes?" Bastien didn't look away from his parchment.

"I'm Jaerol Solaris," I started, but he cut me off before I could continue.

"I know who you are, Jaerol. Aside from Ceurtriarch Ealyndol, you're likely the most well-known person in the temple, right now. What can I do for you?"

I breathed in sharply, surprised at Bastien's directness. I couldn't let that stop me. I had come here with a purpose and I intended to see it through. So I told him. I didn't think there was any need to mention that I only wanted to become a temple knight because I was bored. Most knights had high ideals, and diminishing their vocation to an escape from too much leisure likely wouldn't end well.

After telling him everything I thought necessary, he sat silently. I fought against the urge to fidget. Did knights fidget?

"You understand my hesitancy, yes?" Bastien asked at last.

"Is it because I'm a ginger or something else?" If Bastien wanted to comment on my disposition toward liking other men, I wasn't going to stop him. I did let that detail slip moments ago. I have no idea why I felt compelled to mention it, but it was too late to rescind it now. I had walked as close to that shaft of light in the Chamber of Light as I dared. And despite all the expectant stares, I had yet to collapse. The Creating Light wasn't condemning me for my sexuality—and it clearly hadn't stopped Bastien from admitting other young men with that orientation into their ranks. I had noted more than a few wandering eyes among the temple knights.

"Not three months past, you were held in the cells of justice as a prisoner, a convicted shadow elf and emissary of the Erynien Empire." Bastien ignored the bait.

I frowned. I had so hoped to challenge Bastien about that detail. After sitting alone with Liam for over an hour, my sexual frustration was getting the better of me. "I was an emissary, but I was not, nor was I ever, a shadow elf. My position among those monsters was purely motivated by self-preservation. Also, becoming a shadow elf isn't reversible."

"That being the case, it does not change your past. Think about it for a moment." Bastien was clearly frustrated, pressing his thumb and forefinger to the bridge of his nose. "What do you imagine would happen if I allowed a Cyndinari into our ranks? How do you think the knights would react? Many of them have lost loved ones and brothers and sisters in arms to the enemies of the Lucillian Alliance. To say nothing of the recent loss of life only a month ago. A hundred knights were killed at the gate—murdered by Cyndinari sc…" he stopped.

"Scum. Cyndinari scum. That's what you were going to say." I held Bastien's gaze. Despite growing defensive, I largely felt the same toward my people. The conflict resounded inside me—not every Cyndinari was evil.

"Apologies. I'm still rather emotional about the attack. We lost many good knights. I was bunk mates with two of the lieutenants when we were recruits."

"I'm sorry to hear that." I paused, stopping the memory of Kiron from surfacing. "I trust you're familiar with Liam Telvin?"

"Newer recruit, half-brother to the kien wielder the ei'ceuril won't stop blabbing about?"

"That's him. Did he tell you of our past? How I was an emissary at Gneal? How I knew firsthand what the rotating shadow elves had done to his family?"

"I find it hard to believe he's forgiven you, if that's where you're leading me."

"You and me both. But he's come to accept my past. He knows that I wasn't involved in any of the treacheries committed against his family by those shadow elves. And he also knows that if I had had the ability to stop it, I would have. I was just as powerless as he was in those circumstances." That discussion had never occurred, but I tucked it in the back of my mind for later. That conversation would doubtless occur. "He's waiting outside your office to see if you'll admit me."

"Is he now? I suppose I could make you two bunk mates—there are four to a room. We try to fill them as recruits join. Recruitment has been low recently though. I've lost count how many rooms currently have only three recruits. Liam's room is one of them. Renaud and Stephen are the other two."

I tried to smile, pleased with the turn of events. I couldn't just sit around and do nothing all day with the other lay votaries. "There's one other thing I would ask."

"Haven't you asked for enough?" Bastien had lifted a parchment, assuming that our meeting was finished.

"Probably, but is it possible for Liam and me to attend some lessons with the ei'ceuril?"

Bastien looked up from the parchment. If my asking to join the temple knights was not ridiculous enough, this certainly was. "You want me to authorize you to sit in a classroom filled with children? Do you honestly think that they'll be able to focus on their studies with a Cyndinari in the same room?"

"Honestly, I just want to get an accurate version of history. I'm curious to find out how much of my education was a fabrication. Liam feels the same."

"Read a book then." He returned to examining the parchment as I remained seated. Noting that I wasn't standing to leave, he looked at me again. "If it's so important to the both of you, I could arrange a tutor. But I won't allow any of my recruits or knights in a classroom with children."

A tutor sounded ideal. After all, I wasn't all that eager to sit in a classroom again either. "Thank you, sir."

"You're welcome. Now please leave. I'll inquire about the availability of a tutor and any ei'ceuril who are willing to take on two students."

I stood, and paused, unsure about how the temple knights paid respects toward their superiors. Was I supposed to salute? Rather than make myself look like a fool in case I made the wrong gesture, I simply left the office to find Liam waiting in the corridor. Even though I had told Bastien that he was there, I had assumed that Liam would have left. Didn't he have better things to do to fill his day?

"How'd it go?" he asked.

"Well, to start, you'll have to get used to another roommate."

"Really? I honestly didn't know if he would let you join."

"From the way our conversation went, I wasn't certain either." I scratched my back while talking, relieved to be away from Bastien's scrutiny. He was only doing his job, but I could do without his penetrating gaze. Despite an itch that had been plaguing me almost since I first entered his office, I hadn't felt comfortable scratching myself in his presence.

"What about taking lessons?" Liam asked as we walked away from Bastien's office.

"We won't be in a classroom, which is fine by me, but he's going to try to arrange for us to have a tutor."

"That actually sounds preferable. Want to grab some breakfast? I'm starving."

"Same. Where should we eat? With the lay votaries or the temple knights?"

"Well, you were just admitted to the knights, so let's go to their mess hall. Might as well get you acquainted with your new surroundings."

We walked the rest of the way to the knight's mess hall in

silence; fortunately, it was the closer of the two options.

Chapter Six

Despite Liam's assumptions, Renaud and Stephen cared less about my preference in small clothes and more about my cinnamon hair and pointed ears. They were both human. Renaud and his crystal blue eyes screamed his Sorenth nationality. Stephen also had blue eyes and blond hair, a trait apparently connected to the long-fallen Kingdom of Thellion, however, he had been born in the Evellion city of Cyril. Fortunately, at present, Stephen's hatred for Perriens far surpassed his feelings toward Cyndinari.

We were getting ready for our morning drills, and Liam had already gone, leaving me with Renaud and Stephen.

"Funny, Bastien led us to believe that you two were friends," Renaud commented, pulling his tunic over his head, struggling to find the right arm hole.

"He suggested more than that."

"What exactly did he suggest, Stephen?" I didn't feel like dealing with this today. I had dreamt of Kiron again last night. The dreams came more often now and I spent more nights lying awake in bed than I dared to count. I knew that I hadn't dealt with Kiron's passing. I also refused to believe that he was gone. He couldn't be gone.

"Settle down, Jaerol. Stephen didn't mean anything by it—did you, Stephen?" Renaud glared at Stephen, daring him to say otherwise.

"Sorry, I've been a tad irritated recently." Stephen took a deep breath. "The attack last month and not hearing from any of my family in Cyril has had me on edge."

"Sure." I finished getting ready and left the room.

Drills this morning consisted of melee combat, and I was hard-pressed to force down memories of sparring with Kiron on finely grained sand of cyndaryl. The night after our first sparring match had led to many firsts. The Cyndinari still practiced the ancient elven customs, and despite one's gender, clothing was not permitted on the sacred cyndaryl.

The temple's training rooms were a far cry from the arenas in Broid. Sparring without the high noon sun beating against my exposed skin made the entire occasion much less pleasurable. Would Meridiel appear in the temple and spit on me for forsaking our people's customs? Elves were killed in public displays in Broid for committing less-offensive crimes.

Sir Daphnel oversaw the morning's training and paired me with Liam, presumably because Liam was the least likely to accidentally murder a Cyndinari. That was still debatable. Any sign of the ease between us brought about by our once intimate conversation about secret things had long disappeared.

Our chests and backs were already sweaty. None of the men training wore a shirt. New recruits learned that mistake the hard way. Interestingly, there weren't any women among the recruits. Was there a bias against female knights? Perhaps these people were less developed, just as my magisters at the Imperium had insisted. The training rooms were deep inside the temple, hidden away in the subterranean levels. And while those recesses were often cool, these rooms had no windows for ventilation. Despite how thin one's shirt was, it would quickly become a sweaty smelly tangle. It was also more difficult to grab and hold a slippery torso.

Liam lunged at me, and he and I grappled while I tried to keep his arms from wrapping around me. The lethien had an unfair advantage over me. Not only did Liam have the heightened agility and prowess common to elves, but he also had the added strength common to humans. Neither of his racial gifts were diminished by the other. Liam's broad frame could easily overpower me and as my mind strayed to thinking about his gifts, Liam took advantage and slammed me on my back, then pinned me to the floor. It happened almost too quickly for me to register, and I was embarrassed.

"You didn't have to be that rough." I heaved, gasping for the breath that had been knocked out of me.

"I don't think you understand how fast you are." Liam kept me pinned. I squirmed under the pressure, just as his arms tightened. "You're not getting out that easy."

Again, I writhed under him. I was no novice when it came to sparring. I tensed my legs and then with whatever strength I had left, somersaulted backward. Our positions reversed in a fluid arch. The sudden movement caught Liam by surprise, and now he gaped from underneath me, pinned to the ground. "And you don't understand how strong you are."

Liam grinned. "Oh, I'm aware of that." Still grinning, Liam arched his back and thrust his legs so that he stood, taking me with him since for some reason, I held on as he lifted me then slammed me again to the ground onto my back. "You could make this easier on yourself."

I couldn't move. Liam had entangled my legs with his own while still managing to exert the downward thrust that kept me pinned. The practice bell dinged and he released me.

"Good work, men. You'll be ready for practice swords before the month is over," said Daphnel.

I followed the line of recruits out of the training room and toward the baths. The temple had access to the mountain's many streams which led to the bath halls inside the temple. They were less common on the upper levels, as the individual residences of the ei'ceuril tended to have their own private lavatories and bathtubs. But on the lower levels of the temple, the residents lived more communally. While the baths could be used by anyone, they were primarily used by the knights and lay votaries.

As they streamed into the bath hall, the recruits discarded their sweaty pants and small clothes, as none had kept his tunic on for the morning drills, and shoes were a foolish endeavor when grappling. The baths in the temple, however, were not like the baths in Broid. I remembered those baths fondly. Who wouldn't enjoy the grand majestic structures filled with pools of steaming water fed by the island's rivers and then heated with the erendinth? Some of the pools were covered by vaulted ceilings, while others sat exposed to the sun in a colonnaded courtyard. Some baths were large pools, large enough to host several dozen people, while others were more private—more intimate.

I tested the water with a single toe, withdrawing it immediately. All the rivers around Ceurenyl were fueled by melted snow, and these baths were fed by those rivers, and because the baths were in the temple, the waters couldn't be warmed by wielding.

Goosebumps raced across my skin. Cyndinari were the elves of the high noon sun and summer. Our Skyland of Cyndinare had hovered over the warm southern seas. The Cyndinari wanted nothing to do with the cold. If it wasn't for the stench from sparring, I might have foregone the bath altogether, something I considered each day before taking a full step into the large pool, freezing with snowmelt. I lingered at the far edge of the pool, waiting for the goosebumps to recede.

Still roused by the grappling session with Liam and thoughts of what often went on in those more private baths in Broid, I watched the other recruits laugh as they jumped or dove into the water. Water splashed across the tiled floor, turning the carefully placed mosaics slick.

I didn't have the chance to ease myself in. Amid the raucous laughter, Renaud came from behind, grabbed me in a bear-hug and pulled us both into the water. It felt like my heart stopped beating the moment we hit the water, even before we submerged.

Swimming up from the depths, I turned on a laughing Renaud and lunged at him, pulling him back and under the water. I was furious. I still hadn't forgiven him or Stephen for their comments that morning. We grappled in the water, Renaud pushing hard for the surface to breathe, something I intentionally wanted to prevent. When we both came up for air, I heard the laughter filling the bath hall, some clearly directed at us.

Renaud was just as furious as I was now. "It was for your own good," he hissed. "You should be thanking me, not trying to drown me!"

I stared daggers at the Sorenth. "Who hit you on the head as a child? Have you lost all your senses?"

"Listen, mate. I don't know what you were thinking about or who, but not everyone in this pool will reply kindly to an uninvited surprise, if you get my meaning."

I did—crystal clear. And despite the freezing water, I felt the crimson blush on my face. I was sure that not even my hair was that red.

"Next time, try grappling with someone other than Liam."

It was only after I was fully dressed and alone that I allowed any introspection. Secluded in a small chapel, one not spacious enough for even a dozen people to sit comfortably in the pews, my mind wandered. I had been thinking of the baths in Broid. Modest behavior was not something the Cyndinari were accustomed to, especially those who called the imperial capital their home.

But no, that wasn't what had brought the arousal. It wasn't anything I was thinking of or even looking at, and there was plenty to look at. Instead, I had still been feeling Liam's arms around me, his body pinned against mine. The sensation had left me tingling. It was the first time since Kiron that someone had touched me and actually sparked something. Instead of shedding a tear at the decade-old loss, I fumed.

"How could you let that happen? How could you permit an entire people murder so much of its youth? Why would you bring me into a culture that does that? How could you let me…?" I couldn't finish. I raged at Anaweh. The chapel's door was closed, but even if it hadn't been, I didn't care. "Let them hear. Let them hear my sins and how you allowed them to happen. I didn't choose to be born a Cyndinari. I didn't choose to be a wielder. And I certainly didn't choose to be…"

"You didn't choose any of that." Ealyndol had somehow come into the chapel. "The choices you have made though… those are yours. They make you the fine young elf that you are."

The sudden, almost stealthy appearance, had me nearly leap off the pew, yet my anger kept me seated and had me pressing on. "How can you even suggest that? I'm looked at as though, at any moment, my head will spin in circles round my neck. As if being a Cyndinari wasn't sin enough." My blind rage had me forget who I was talking to. This wasn't a bartender who pretended to care about my problems; this was the Ceurtriarch, High Archsteward and Arbiter of the Light.

"Few in this temple have known hardship. Most of us were brought here as boys, our suffering largely limited to being torn away from our families at a tender age, only because we could wield. Do not mistake me, for it is a traumatic experience, and has led to lasting damage." Ealyndol sat beside me. "No one in this temple understands what you went through—the courage required to say no in the face of evil. How many of your kindred managed what you did?"

"If they did, they were probably killed on the spot."

"None of us choose the life we were born into. If I had not been a kien wielder, I would have become the Aryl of Lucillia. Instead, I had to abdicate all my rights and claims to the Lucillian throne. My sister did just fine and her daughter is doing just as well now."

"I didn't know you were the youngest of a past aryl. That must have been difficult." Thinking about someone else's life was easier—it was easier to show sympathy for someone else.

"I turned out all right." A gentle smile reached Ealyndol's eyes.

"Forgive me, but how is it that you're here?"

"There are some perks to being the Ceurtriarch. And besides, it's always so crowded in the Chamber of Light and its radiating chapels. Even my private chapel is seldom vacant. I don't know what brought you to this particular chapel, but before today, I have been its only visitor for quite some time."

"Sorry."

"Don't be silly." Ealyndol closed his eyes and hummed a soft tune. It might have been a prayer, but I couldn't identify it. Either way, the Ceurtriarch was done speaking. He had come here to pray after all, not soothe an angry Cyndinari.

I tried to stay in quiet prayer for a while longer but my riotous thoughts wouldn't calm enough to truly meditate. Ealyndol did not seem to have any issues with tapping into contemplative prayer. I stood and made my way quietly to the door.

"Take care that you do not close away the pain for much longer. Even my fading eyesight can see it eating away at you. It would be a shame to watch it corrode all the good and light inside you."

Ealyndol's kind words at my back as I left only made me angrier than when I first entered. I wanted to take the Ceurtriarch's words with an open mind, but he had no idea what I had gone through. What I had done.

My denial of the events at the Grand Tourney in Broid's Coliseum was all that had held me together over the past ten years. I had stayed whole by not letting myself acknowledge the loss—by not feeling it. I didn't know when that had worn down: surely only after I had left Gneal. Had it begun after I had been taken prisoner and locked in the cells of justice? Was it when I first walked into the Chamber of Light? Or was it when Liam had made me smile that first time?

Whenever it had happened, I wanted to reverse it. All I felt now was rage. I wanted to wield the erendinth more fiercely than I could ever remember and willingly lose control. I wanted to tear away every stone from the temple's foundations—wielding terys and ignys to bring this confining and maddening structure to the ground.

I had never felt so irrationally angry.

Part Two

Anger

Chapter Seven

14 years earlier - 9052.3E

My uncle Teran's manicured gardens welcomed me before any of his staff noticed that I had arrived. Teran maintained an orderly estate and owned one of the finest vineyards on Cynethol. Many had wrongly assumed that he had gained his wealth through those vines, but he had only purchased the failing vineyard and estate after he had gained a sizeable fortune. He had never married and had amassed his wealth through his contacts with the Goblin Guild. They seemed to prefer collaborating with a Cyndinari who had not become a shadow elf, at least whenever possible.

As a child, I had always enjoyed visiting Teran's estate. My father had even occasionally allowed Kiron to join us on our vacations. Today, my family had remained in Broid, unaware that I had left the city. As far as they knew, I hadn't left the Imperium's campus.

Teran's attendants knew me and they had skipped all the formalities reserved for my uncle's usual guests and had left me on one of the estate's terraces where I fidgeted alone.

Muffled voices came from behind me, somewhere inside the manor, but not from any of the rooms immediately adjacent to the terrace where I sat. Teran always had visitors. Every time my family had vacationed here, we had seen a stream of guests coming and going. Some stayed a few days or even weeks, while others hurried off before their horses were fully rested. That was part of the reason I had come without giving any notice. Teran was so used to uninvited guests that my showing up on his doorstep without warning shouldn't be an issue.

I clenched my thighs as the voices quieted and concentrated on keeping my hands from shaking. Despite myself, I looked over my shoulder to find my uncle walking through the opened door.

"Nephew," he called, cheerily.

"Uncle Teran." I stood, forcing a grin.

"To what do I owe the pleasure?" he asked, embracing me warmly. "Please, sit, sit," urging me back into my seat.

"I wanted to see you. I hope that was all right. I know I should've sent word ahead."

"Don't be foolish. You're always welcome here. Where is Kiron? Your mother seems to think you two are inseparable. She won't believe you showed up at my estate without him."

"He's still at school—at the Imperium."

"Shouldn't you be there as well? It was your choice to attend there, you know."

I broke eye contact. Teran had advised me against attending the Imperium. He had never said why I shouldn't, but he had promised I would have a much happier life without receiving that kind of education.

"You saw tenebrys wielded for the first time today." He wasn't asking a question.

I nodded, trying to hold back my tears. I had never seen anything so horrible. It had been a perfectly sunny day in Broid and then it was as though all the light disappeared. I could still see somehow, and I think the other students could as well, but it wasn't just my vision that had been affected by the wield. It was as though I had forgotten what the light looked like, as though it had never existed.

"Come, let's take a walk along the coast." Teran stood even before he finished speaking.

I followed and Teran led me through the orderly gardens, past the vineyards, and to the coast, not speaking. Once, when I started to talk about something at school, he just grunted, uninterested. His jovial demeanor had completely changed. I hazarded a glance over my shoulder.

"Is anyone following us?" he asked, ruefully.

"Should there be?"

"Well, my competitors have paid off my entire staff, so they report everything back to their benefactors. Fortunately, I too have paid them off. They can eavesdrop as much as their hearts desire on my estate, but if they want any golden crowns from me, their eyes and ears need to stay on the estate."

"Wouldn't it just be easier to hire new staff?"

"Perhaps I might if I had someone to share the burden of managing my estate. But even then, my competitors would only pay off the new staff. It would be a never-ending cycle. It's quite exhausting having to find out who paid off who. This way, I'm happy, my staff is happy, and so are my low-life adversaries."

"Is selling wine really that competitive?"

"More than you would think. There's a new ice wine on the market now. It's becoming quite popular. The grapes are restricted to some back-water village in Perrien. I'm sure the wine's been around for centuries, but its only just starting to be traded past Perrien's borders. Hopefully, it's just a phase. We don't have the right climate to make ice wine here on Cyneth-ol. And I have no desire to travel to Perrien to invest in another vineyard."

"I'd rather you not move that far north either."

"You and me both!" Teran chuckled as he slipped his sandals off to walk barefoot on the sand, inviting me to do the same. "Still, none of my competitors own a vineyard. At least, I don't think they do. And if they do, I'll have to find myself better spies."

I stared back. "You're paying off their staff too?"

"I have to. I can't let them catch me unaware."

"Is someone after you, uncle?"

"No, not after me. They know where to find me. More so, they want to keep tabs on me. Make sure I stay on Cynethol and find out who I'm in contact with."

"Why would you ever leave our island? Surely there's no-where else in Eklean that you'd rather live." Leaving Cynethol had never crossed my mind. Even so, after seeing tenebrys wielded…maybe I could leave this place with Kiron. We could be happy and free somewhere.

"The rest of the continent isn't all that bad. Don't listen to everything your magisters say about Eklean. Some king-doms could use a bit more sun though and their people show it too! I'd invite every Evellion to our beaches for a month, nobility included—especially the nobility. Light knows they could use a beach day. If only to let their hearts melt just a tad. They could also use a tint of sun on their pasty skin."

We laughed together, remembering our own vacations together at this very beach.

"If you don't mind my asking, uncle, what have you gotten yourself into?"

"It's not so much trouble than it's curiosity over my contacts in the Goblin Guild."

"Why would anyone care if you're speaking to goblins? They're part of the Erynien Empire."

"Not of their own volition. Believe me, if our ancestors hadn't landed here in the Kinzdol Islands, the goblins would have been more than happy to keep their distance from us. Especially after many of our people became shadow elves and worse. But no, they're concerned about my contacts on the mainland. Acquaintances I've made over the years while I apprenticed with the guild. I don't want to overly trouble you, Jaerol, but not many shadow elves look favorably toward me. A regular elf rising to my stature without joining their ranks is quite the scandal at court. It also doesn't help their propaganda machine. My life is a testament to the fact that you don't have to become a shadow elf to become a powerful and influential elf." Teran paused, looking past the coastline and over the Erynien Sea. On clear days, Yanil's coast was just visible.

"I never wanted you to attend the Imperium, Jaerol. Your parents heard from me regularly after you had passed your exams and decided to enroll. I would've given you everything if you hadn't chosen to attend. Still, you enrolling didn't stop me from naming you as my heir."

"Your heir?" I looked back over my shoulder at the peaked roofs of the estate rising just above the beach's sand dunes. I loved everything about this estate. Especially the wine produced here. My uncle knew that I had started sampling it well before I should have.

"I understand your decision. Propaganda about the Imperium is fed to you even before you can read. And it's not like you can read anything here on Cynethol that states otherwise."

"I don't understand." Teran was jumping from one topic to the next with every breath.

"There's a certain pride for a family when their child is accepted into the Imperium, especially among families who've never had the wealth or prestige to send their children. You're the first of your family to enroll in the Imperium, well, I should say the second."

"The second? Who else—did you attend?"

"Ramiel's hell, no! No, my sister."

"What? My mother never got in."

"You're right. She didn't. But Laela did. You'll find out soon enough if you don't know already."

I couldn't pull my eyes away from him if I tried. "Who's Laela?"

"Your aunt. She was the cleverest of the three of us and the oldest. Your mother looked up to her as though she were an anadel in the flesh. Your mother tried to imitate everything that Laela did. Especially attending the Imperium—even after Laela lost at the Grand Tourney."

I knew what the victors did to the losers at the Grand Tourney. I had attended my first Grand Tourney this past summer with the other rising third years, finally deemed mature enough to attend. Even so, I had known what happened before I had seen it for myself. The other students rarely talked of anything else but the Imperium's graduates.

"The entire family was invited. I was of an age and was attending a different institution that eventually led to my apprenticeship with the Goblin Guild. Even when I was younger, I wanted nothing to do with the Imperium and the goblins understood my desire to get away from Cynethol. However, your mother, not old enough to attend, was granted an exemption because our sister was a contestant."

"Uncle, why are you telling me all of this?"

"Because I love you, Jaerol, and every second you stay at the Imperium leaves me sick to my stomach." His eyes brimmed with tears and he cupped the side of my face.

The touch brought tears to my own eyes. After seeing tenebrys wielded in the classroom, I didn't know what to do with myself. Part of me wanted to run away forever. The furthest I had managed to get was Teran's estate. But even if I wanted to flee for good, I couldn't leave without Kiron. That was part of the reason why I had come here alone. I knew I would have to return to the Imperium at some point.

"What do you want, Jaerol?"

I collapsed into Teran, hiding my tears in his tunic, now sporting a damp splotch. He held me and rubbed my back, trying to soothe me. Even for an understanding uncle, this type of behavior was not acceptable for a Cyndinari. I imagined Kiron and me sailing away from here with Teran. Yanil or Tiel would be the obvious destinations. Both fell under the empire. I had no intention of going any further north—how anyone could live so far away from the sea was a mystery to me.

My lapse into fantasy didn't last long. The reality was that running away from the Imperium and trying to escape from Cynethol was all but impossible. We wouldn't be able to leave from any dock without our escape being discovered by a shadow elf. Teran squeezed my shoulders.

"Is it possible to get away? Can Kiron and I get away?" I spoke to his damp shoulder, too miserable to lift my head.

"It's risky. I doubt I could remain here if anyone caught hint of my involvement."

"So, you'll help us?"

"Bring Kiron back to the estate, and we can discuss this further. I don't think he would appreciate you deciding his future."

"Thank you," I said, hugging Teran tightly.

"Come, let's get you back to the manor. Mierella has been cooking all day. If I didn't know better, I would say she had more connections in Broid than I do and was informed of your departure well in advance." Teran smiled encouragingly as he ushered me back to the manor.

Chapter Eight

Dorien sat opposite Liam and me, a broad wooden desk separating us. After weeks of Bastien petitioning the ei'ceuril for a tutor, Dorien was the only one to reluctantly agree to it, which he was quick to remind us when we entered his spacious study. I was shocked to discover that Dorien was a wise one. Surely, he was too young for such a prestigious position. Most of the temple's wise ones that I had seen were wrinkly old men. Not a hint of grey touched Dorien's slick black hair, a clear indication that he was Tieli or Yanilean. However, his complexion was remarkably light for someone hailing from either of those kingdoms, a likely side effect of never leaving the temple.

A large tome lay open in front of Dorien, a small leather notebook beside it. I could just make out the tiny script meticulously scratched across the pages.

"As I understand it, you're both under the impression that your educational foundation was either misleading or flawed." Dorien didn't look up from his notebook, but turned the page, uninterestedly. His sleeves were rolled back twice, to make it easier. The quantity of billowy white fabric of his ei'ceuril robe appeared four times more ample than it needed to be, convincing me that the more senior an ei'ceuril was in their hierarchy, the more fabric they incorporated into their robes. The Ceurtriarch and archstewards likely had difficulties walking without tripping over their hems.

We both nodded. Did Dorien see our response? Did he care? He certainly didn't give any indication one way or the other.

"I can't say that I'm particularly knowledgeable about the Imperium's magisters and their teaching methods, nor what version of history they taught you in the Kinzdol Islands, but I cannot fathom why one of our own abbey schools would knowingly mislead its students. If your doubts are verified, Liam, we'll have to conduct a full investigation. Each school will be assessed, and past and current students will have to undergo testing. The piles of paperwork that would necessitate would keep the junior ei'ceuril here busy for a decade."

"Sounds daunting," Liam offered.

I couldn't help but imagine the bureaucratic backing necessary to carry out such a task.

"I certainly won't be the one leading such an inquiry. Some steward with hopes of being promoted to a wise one will surely want to prove himself. The poor chap will eagerly volunteer for the assignment. Sadly, it'll take him so long to conclude his findings that he'll have missed his opportunity to become a wise one. To say nothing of attracting ire from other wise ones and archstewards as he debases the abbey school they're associated with."

I had never visited any of the abbey schools while residing in Gneal, but I had heard enough talk about the schools from the various councilors and others coming and going from the castle. It seemed that the majority of the Perrien Council wanted to eliminate the abbey schools altogether, thereby also pushing out the largest contingent of ei'ceuril. But none of the councilors had devised any alternative to the educational system. Providing any resources or funding for a new school structure was openly mocked. The consensus seemed to agree that there wasn't any need to replace the schools. Perrien's wealthy citizens rarely sent their children to the abbey schools as it was, preferring to hire private tutors for their offspring. It was only the children from the working and impoverished classes that seemed to benefit from the abbey schools, a collection of people that the Perrien Council cared little for. In their minds, most of those people would enlist in the Council's expanding army. The councilors frequently commented that the only education their soldiers needed was knowing how to listen and follow orders. Not even the Erynien Empire had that dismissive an understanding of its soldiers.

As an Erynien emissary, I had had the unfortunate and difficult task of discouraging the councilors from closing the abbey schools. My superiors in Broid had relayed Erynor's intent to keep the abbey schools open. No one ever said why, but I gathered that Erynor desired to spread his own version of history and ethics across the continent. Implementing that into an already established network of schools would certainly be easier than starting from scratch.

"I can't say anything about the other abbey schools, but

Devlyn gave me the impression that the one in Cor'lera had gotten worse after I was taken prisoner. Entiel wasn't the abbot when I was a student there, but he did teach."

"I never had the pleasure of meeting Abbot Entiel," started Dorien, "but Steward Elias spoke quite highly of him the last time he visited the temple. Granted, that had to be over a decade ago. In fact, it was Elias who petitioned for Entiel to become the new abbot. He still sends the annual messenger bird to provide an update on the school and its needs. He and Entiel were quite beside themselves when Cor'lera started their little revolt against Perrien. I doubt it will lead to anything substantial, as it is only one small village, even if they do produce the finest wine I've had in years. Hopefully, their rebellion won't impede the production from their wineries." Dorien paused a moment, no longer interested in his notebook. He appeared to be thinking of something, perhaps pondering the quantity of his collection of Cor'leran Blue ice wine.

"Despite Entiel and Elias' troubles, I am envious of those two and others like them. In any other age, their miniscule ability to wield would have barred them from rising in our hierarchy, but because their wielding provides no threat, they're granted a dispensation to leave the temple and take on prestigious roles in the outside world."

"There are ei'ceuril kien wielders outside the temple?" I asked, my mouth agape.

"They can barely sense the erendinth, but to become a steward, a man must be able to wield. The rituals simply don't take hold over non-wielders," Dorien answered.

"Are there a lot of stewards outside the temple?" Liam asked.

"A small percentage compared to the population here in the temple. Still, they're weak men and would have been cast aside in a different age. Before the Balance was lost, they would have likely been rejected from joining the ei'ceuril. Our standards were once much higher—something painfully apparent to me when I'm with the novices. But, given this age, there's little we can do to correct it."

Liam glanced over at me, evident concern in his expression. I didn't see anything inherently wrong or troublesome with weak kien wielders outside of the temple, but Liam sure did. I'd have to ask him about it later. Whatever it was though, it looked like he wanted to leave Dorien's study. He took a deep breath instead, keeping his concerns to himself.

Dorien again began to thumb through his notebook, appearing to search for a particular page or passage. "I suppose we should discuss my role as your tutor. Firstly, understand that I don't have to do this. My time is extremely precious, so I will not tolerate tardiness. If either of you will be late, don't bother coming. I will not accept an apology. The arrangement will end. Understood?"

"Yes." Liam and I answered together. Dorien was probably only a decade our senior, but his presence commanded respect. However he had become a wise one at such a young age, he wore the mantle and large billowy robes well.

"Secondly, our purview of study will largely revolve around historical accounts. From my conversation with Bastien, I understand that is your primary weakness. I will not be instructing you in ethics or morality, nor will I spend any time on languages or arithmetic. And I certainly will not spend any time on theoreticals or any other forms of philosophy. If you want to broaden your understanding in those fields, I suggest you find another tutor or pick up a book. Will this be an issue?"

"No." Liam and I answered again.

"Good. Now, Jaerol, I assume you are mostly interested in learning about your people from a different historical perspective and their place in Eklean. Particularly, since your ancestors migrated to what is now Cynethol."

My immediate answer was a resounding yes, however, everything I knew of the world was through the lens of my people and how they saw the world. It was very possible that they didn't believe they were doing anything wrong. From a young age, I had been groomed and nurtured to look down on the other races—they would be so lucky to belong to the Erynien Empire and bear our fruit, according to our teachings. The various kingdoms of Eklean and across all Teraeniel should be groveling at Erynor's feet, kissing his toes and washing them with their tears of gratitude for his mercy.

As sons and daughters of Cyndinare, we were the elves of the high noon sun, our position and status in the world is dictated by the very stars. We were gods to the rest of the world, and even the other elven kin should prostrate themselves before us.

I thought of my upbringing—only my uncle and Kiron had believed differently. Despite wanting to know the truth of my people, I also wanted to learn more about the other kingdoms and races. Were they truly as lost and despicable as I had been taught? Did dwarves truly wander purposeless through their mountains without us? Were merpeople little better than mindless fish, swimming through the oceans without any form of civilization? Were they better off belonging to the Erynien

Empire with the Cyndinari as their lords? From what I'd learned, the giants had certainly benefitted from being part of the Erynien Empire. There were rumors that they had started building cities in the Frozen Mountains, linking northern Eklean and northern Qien along the Skrein Sea.

Questions that I had always wanted answered revolved in my head. Questions that I never allowed myself to dream of having answered when a student at the Imperium and certainly would never voice. Even so, one question burned brightest of them all.

"Is it true that my people were the reason the elves had to leave their Skylands?" I asked at last. I didn't know how much time had passed, but Dorien had to be curious about what was going through my head. Doubtless he could see the wheels turning behind my eyes. For the first time during this session, his notebook didn't hold his attention.

"Are you familiar with the Sha'ghol?" Dorien asked.

"The once-rulers of the Cyndinari?"

"Precisely. I've no idea how they managed to usurp the Cyndinari aryls, but they were undeniably in charge when your ancestors left Cyndinare and migrated to the Kinzdol Islands. It is theorized that they were the first to meddle in tenebrys. We have no way of knowing how they encountered that power, but it is also speculated that they communicated with Ramiel. That version of history seems less credible. I doubt it's anything more than a bedtime fairy tale for children. Now, whether the Sha'ghol ever contacted Ramiel and whether tenebrys is real, again, I'm highly doubtful."

"But what about the Skylands? Why would the ancient elves leave if not for the *Darkness*?" I asked.

"Another fairy tale most likely. Some cataclysmic event certainly happened on all the Skylands, but the Darkness? What, a large dark cloud? That hardly sounds threatening."

"Didn't Aren and the other Phaedryn who flew to Cyndinare find the Sha'ghol studying the Darkness? Weren't they experimenting with it?" Liam asked.

"Yes, I've heard that story too." Dorien returned to his notebook, bored. "Everyone needs a hero and a villain. I never bothered researching this Aren Lorenthien and by all accounts, the Aryl of Mar'anathyl failed to rescue the Aldinari from their Skyland. Hardly a hero if you ask me. The Luminari must have been fond of him for other reasons to have named their new capital city after him."

"What about tenebrys? I've seen shadow elves use it. I've seen them devour other people's souls," Liam protested.

"I'm sure you saw something." Dorien discarded the idea with a flick of his hand, his sleeve unrolling in the process. "But again, a story for children. There are only seven erendinth. Where would this other power have come from? The seven anadel who created Teraeniel brought the seven erendinth from Lumaeniel. They didn't create the erendinth; those powers are intrinsic to their nature. If the legends of Ramiel are true, and he is truly imprisoned somewhere beneath Teraeniel, he's just as likely to create a new erendinth as I am to prepare my own supper." Dorien neatly rolled back his sleeve as he spoke.

"Shadow elves attacked Ceurenyl, all of them wielding tenebrys. Countless people died—their souls fed on by those shadow elves," I said, my voice rising.

"Yes, we were attacked. But don't be naïve. Soul sucking

elves? I've read the reports about these so-called shadow elves. I'm not sure what they did to themselves, but the only result was just making themselves ugly. A nasty experiment gone horrendously wrong. A shame too, as I've heard nothing but positive remarks on your people's appearance. Quite the handsome and beautiful lot."

What happened next, I couldn't remember. My mind blanked and before I knew it, Liam and I were in the corridor and the door to Dorien's study closed behind us. My throat felt raw from yelling. Liam looked at me approvingly. Was he impressed by whatever I had just said? Flashes of my memory came back to me. "Did I really call Dorien a dimwitted fool, blindly following Ramiel's designs?"

"Yeah, and it was magical. I've never seen a hint of emotion from that guy. I honestly mistook his face as that of a statue, carved from limestone."

"I guess we won't be having a tutor after all," I said, walking away from Dorien's quarters.

"Good riddance. How in Ramiel's hell did that one become a steward? A wise one no less! Good thing we never asked his opinion on Anaweh."

"Seriously, probably another fairy tale."

Walking away from Dorien's quarters meant we also walked away from any hope of having a tutor. He was right about one thing though: much better to read a book. I still hadn't stumbled across the temple's library but knew that a visit was imminent. Surely a place like this would house an impressive collection.

Lost in my own thoughts, I was surprised when my body electrified as my hand grazed Liam's. I stopped walking and saw an embarrassed smile spring to his very apologetic expression. The connection had been brief, but it felt like a moment frozen in time, a moment that I did not want to end. I had to restrain myself from grabbing his hand, and strove to hide my elated expression. Embarrassment at the unexpected touch was the furthest thing from my mind. In fact, my mind immediately raced to not just holding his hand but pulling him close somewhere secluded and away from prying eyes.

"All right?" Liam asked.

Did he really not know? Was he numb to the touch?

"Yeah, I'm fine. Still thinking about Dorien." I lied.

"That's it?"

I smiled a stupid smile in response. Was he flirting with me now? He had to know what he was doing. We stood so close that I felt his triceps tense under his shirt sleeve, sending my heart racing yet again. My heartbeat hadn't settled from the hand grazing yet. Coming back to my senses, I took a deep breath to calm myself. I didn't need any more uninvited surprises.

I felt like a teenager again. I took that first difficult step away, breaking the magic thrumming through the static air. I pushed my fingers through my hair, partially just to ensure that it wasn't standing on end from the electricity I felt through my body.

Chapter Nine

Our training today was devoted entirely to swords and despite Renaud's recommendation, I faced Liam. We'd continued sparring with each other over the past few weeks and I had been much more careful in the bath hall.

Liam might have had the advantage when we grappled, but I had learned dueling from some of the best sword masters on Cynethol.

I tried not to let Liam's exposed and beautifully sculpted torso distract me. Instead, I smirked at his bearing. Not even the youngest students at the Imperium had held such an amateurish posture. Liam wasn't comfortable with the sword and held it like it was a broom handle or shovel instead of a sword. Finger placement mattered. It wasn't just how hard you could whack and slash—dueling required finesse. You had to be quick. I held my sword horizontally over my head, which admittedly was a bit showy, especially when surrounded by beginners. Grasping the wooden pommel felt right even though I preferred a real sword—I was a child the last time I had to use a wooden training sword.

The training bell dinged and I lunged at Liam, my practice sword whooshing as I rained blows on him. I missed hearing the metal sing through the air, and the glint of steel in the sun. I missed the sun on my exposed flesh, soaking in the salty sea air. But it felt so good to unleash the pent-up anger I was feeling.

The other recruits hadn't moved yet, but stood watching open-mouthed as my sword repeatedly whipped into Liam, who could barely raise his own sword fast enough to block half the blows.

I grinned, knowing the reddening welts would bruise. It was Liam's fault I was unraveling. It was Liam's fault that I couldn't stop myself from feeling again. I had managed just fine over the past decade.

My surroundings were a blur, all my focus on Liam. The old forms came back without thinking. Muscle memory took over and I fell into the comfortable maneuvers of *jienzu*. There was a feeling of wrongness about it here in the temple—jienzu was complimentary to wielding the erendinth. The only times I had ever felt remotely in control of the erendinth was when practicing the old sword forms in conjunction with them.

Knowing that I should also be interacting with the erendinth only heightened my fury. Liam continued to falter, but I was lost in the jienzu, slipping into one form after the other. Finally, someone pulled me back, wrestling the practice sword from my grip. I don't how he managed to get close enough, but he snuck through without getting whacked.

With the training sword taken from me, I slowly came

back to myself and gasped in horror at what I had done to Liam. He crouched before me, forearms shielding his face but I could see that blood flowed freely from his nose, both eyes were swollen, one more than the other, and he had more welts on his body than I could count. What had happened to his sword? I blinked in disbelief.

Whispers surrounded us, with the familiar taunt of 'freak' in a chorus. Renaud and Stephen, their eyes round in shock, still restrained me but it wasn't necessary anymore. I tried to shake them off, but they refused to loosen their hold.

Through a haze, I heard Daphnel call for a healer, then he spoke from beside me. "The four of you, to the baths. *Now*. The rest of you should be practicing."

I stalked away in a daze, avoiding the glares directed at me. Renaud and Stephen were just behind me, supporting Liam to a long bench in the bath hall.

Hunched over at the other end of the bench, I averted my eyes. I was appalled at what had happened. What had come over me? One moment I had been excited, looking forward to practicing with a sword again, to showing off my earlier training. But once I had fallen into the jienzu forms, I had simply lost track of my surroundings. I knew that my emotions were riotous, going from feeling unsettled to outright rage, but I had been managing to keep my emotions in check. Whatever had happened while performing the old forms, I had lost control, my inhibitions forgotten. No thinking had been involved. I had acted.

Most of the people I had practiced jienzu against were also well trained with a sword, performing the old forms with me as the air electrified with the erendinth. And I often practiced alone to perfect the forms, always with the erendinth. I tried to remember the last time I had executed the old forms and realized that it was likely while I had been in Gneal. Even before being captured by Velaria and sent to the temple as a supposed shadow elf, jienzu had been too risky in the city. While it didn't seem that any of the Luminari elves remembered the old forms, practicing them was not a subtle endeavor. Someone would have noticed a red-haired elf performing semi-acrobatic movements with a sword as the erendinth hummed around me. Liam had no way of defending himself against me. I kept telling myself that I didn't know what had come over me, but it was a lie and I knew it.

I knew I was angry, so incredibly angry and Liam happened to be on the receiving end. It also didn't help that Liam was the reason I was losing control over myself. He was barely recognizable after what I had done to him. In one breath I felt ashamed for it, but I quickly smothered the feeling. He deserved the blame for how I felt. If not wholly, then at least partially.

Renaud and Stephen risked quick glances in my direction. They looked at me as though I was a coiled snake, ready to lunge at any moment. They sat between Liam and me, at the farthest end of the bench possible, close to Liam, intent on protecting him in case I went into another frenzy. None of us spoke as we waited for the healer to arrive, which took longer than I would have expected.

Sister Lillianna was one of the few female ei'ceuril and had once been an ei'ana. Forsaking the Ei'ana Counsels was forbidden; the only exception allowed by the Seven Chairs was if a woman decided to join the Ei'ceuril and devote her life to the Creating Light. While Lillianna had not belonged to the Crimsyn School, she had been trained well enough as a healer among the Emradiels. The green sash at her midsection was all that alluded to her past life as an ei'ana.

"Oh, my," she gasped when she saw Liam. "I take it one of you is responsible for this?"

"Yes, sister." I answered, although the accusing glares from Renaud and Stephen were testament enough.

"Very well." Lillianna began applying a salve that smelled of lilacs and honey to the welts. "That will lessen the sting and clean the wounds, but it will do little to actually heal them."

"It smells nice," Renaud said. He couldn't stop staring at Lillianna.

"Why, thank you. It's quite different than what the Crimsyns would recommend, but I think the natural scents are just as beneficial. It's not only the physical wounds that need to be healed. And as I said, the ointment won't actually heal them." Lillianna applied the rest of her salve to the last of Liam's visible wounds. She couldn't see the welts on his thighs. But I somehow remembered where my wooden sword had landed. Despite having lost control of my emotions, I remembered everything I had done to Liam.

"How long will it take for the wounds to heal?" Stephen asked.

"If all I intended to do was apply this salve, then that would require quite a few weeks." Lillianna returned the jar to her bag. "But I've already received permission to take Liam outside the temple—beyond the temple's ward."

Despite the awfulness of the current situation, our eyes

lit up. Leaving the temple for anything was restricted for kien wielders. While my suspicions about Renaud or Stephen having the ability to wield were unconfirmed, few young men willingly left their home and family to serve as a temple knight. Most recruits had spent their adolescence in the lower levels of the temple and had only agreed to join the knight's ranks when they had grown bored with their purposeless life. Also, only kien wielders were not allowed to leave the temple, and I hadn't heard of either of them doing so.

"I thought that might interest you. And you're all in luck, as I'll need assistance. Liam isn't likely to walk all the way through the temple and up the stairs on his own. Do put your shirts on first, though. We can't have four shirtless men walking through the Chamber of Light."

Renaud and Stephen grinned, helping Liam first before getting dressed themselves. They resumed their positions on either side of Liam, his arms on their shoulders for support. They looked expectantly to Lillianna for direction.

"You know the way, dearies. We're right behind you."

They left the bath hall and Lillianna wordlessly signaled for me to accompany her, staying out of earshot from the three ahead. I expected that she would ask why I had done what I did. I waited for the accusations and the stern talking-to from this kind-hearted woman.

The silence pervaded. Lillianna showed no interest in asking any questions, and if she did want to, she was taking her time thinking them over.

I took mental notes of everything we walked by. We were indeed going toward the Chamber of Light. The temple only had one publicly known entrance, and to get to it, you had to pass through that hallowed space. The only other entrance that I knew of was that tunnel to Gwilnor in Therril's office. Were there more secret passages like that? Had the ei'ceuril documented them all or had they largely forgotten about the temple's secrets, just as they had forgotten how to wield with control?

Halfway there, the now jovial trio ahead were trading stories. Men always acted the same when someone was seriously wounded. There was concern at first, naturally, and they typically took the proper steps to see the injury tended to, but after that, they joked about it. They shared stories about their worst accidents and how long they had to stay in bed to wait for their wounds to heal.

I wished I could join them. Walking quietly beside Lillianna was painstakingly difficult, but I didn't think they would welcome me. I was the reason Liam was in that condition to begin with.

"I'm sorry," I said at last.

"You did no harm to me," she said at once. "You know who you have to apologize to."

"I can't believe I did that to him."

"Don't be mistaken. It's not just Liam that you owe an apology to. Those other two are your bunkmates, yes?"

I nodded.

"How well do you think they'll sleep after this?"

She was right. Lillianna's kind words seemed genuine and sincere. Perhaps that was why I didn't want to hear them. I deserved to be yelled at. Daphnel should have sent the meanest person at his disposal to discipline me, not this sweet ei'ceuril sister. I didn't deserve this.

As if hearing my thoughts, Lillianna said, "The pain we inflict on ourselves will always be worse than what anyone else could ever do to us."

No one stopped us from passing through the Chamber of Light and out into the entry hall. The doors to the chamber shut behind us, severing the light and casting the place into a dim glow. My skin crawled. This place, more than any other in the temple, always made me feel inadequate. My reflection looked back at me from the glossy stone, a stone that had an eerie depth, as though I could walk straight into it and never walk out.

Perhaps I deserved that. The cells of justice might not be able to hold me, but a cage of stone certainly could.

The introspection and self-condemnation ceased when the exterior doors opened. These doors were just as large as the ones that led to the Chamber of Light, but instead of flooding the darkened entry hall with a celestial light, this was the sunlight of high noon. Or, close enough to where the sun stood near its zenith.

Stepping outside to face the high southern sun, I couldn't help but smile as it warmed my skin, lifting my anxiety and dissipating my still-simmering anger. Liam wasn't the only reason that my mood had changed. Being locked in the temple was messing with my mind. Worse, it was poisoning it.

The sun's rays were better for me than the best of medicines and calming teas—not even the Crimsyns could have wielded a healing spell so effective.

Lillianna now took the lead and led us to the wholly underutilized temple gardens. Perhaps I could get permission to walk among the gardens on my own. I needed the sun—despite my hatred for what I was born as, I was still a Cyndinari. I wondered if Bastien or Daphnel could make an exception for me. Surely, they wanted to avoid another outburst just as much as I did.

Even as I thought it, I knew that would never happen. And not only because of the temple's stringent rules, but rather, the reason for those rules. Without trying, I sensed the erendinth. I felt them around me, begging me to interact with them.

Taking several steady breaths, I reminded myself what would happen if I gave in. I was standing on enough thin ice at the moment. I did know when to stop myself though. I could stop wielding if I lost control. At least that's what I kept telling myself, and most of the time I could.

We reached the gardens and Liam sat on a simple stone bench, still supported by our bunk mates. Lillianna drew close and placed both hands on Liam's head, her fingers tangled in his hair. I felt an unexpected twinge of jealousy. Startled and confused by my reaction, I looked away. Or rather, tried to.

I even tried turning my back to the others, pretending to take in the garden. It was certainly beautiful and breathtaking, but that wasn't why I was taking in the scenery. And I knew it. I wanted to deny my attraction to Liam, but as I looked at the breathtaking shrubs and flowers, I was only lying to myself.

I turned back around and my eyes locked with Liam's. My breath caught in my chest and my heart skipped a beat. I hated myself for it.

Liam had every right to hate me, and not only because I had just beaten him near-senseless. We had a past in the dungeons of Gneal. And while I had done nothing against Liam or his family, I hadn't done anything to stop it either. I had kept silent to preserve my own life, and Liam hated me for that. I was a coward. It would have been better for everyone if Kiron had been the one to survive the Grand Tourney. He would never have let the atrocities in Gneal's dungeons happen. He would have stuck to the original plan and escaped the Erynien Empire—not give up as I had.

However, at this moment, Liam wasn't looking at me as he had two months ago. I had noticed that he wasn't necessarily happy to see me every day, but the hostility had diminished some. His expression today was different. For the first time, the accusation and hatred did not linger behind Liam's gaze. To make it worse, his expression was soft and concerned.

Liam should hate me—he should be furious at me—he should want to return the beating and pound me to a pulp.

I wanted to turn away again; looking into Liam's eyes was too painful. I wanted—needed—to see the demand for revenge there. But this was entirely different. Only one other person had looked at me that way. Unable to bear the connection any longer, I pulled away. Why did that hurt even more? My chest ached with the broken connection. It felt much like when I had severed my bond with Kiron, just not as permanent.

In that momentary bond's absence, I felt a need rise within me, impossible to ignore. Did Liam feel the same? With Kiron, that feeling had sprung within us both at the same time, as though our feelings were shared and they did not solely belong to only one of us. A spark like that could not be lit by a single person.

That moment passed.

Before I could regret its loss, an enormous wave shot up from the nearby stream and over everyone, including Lillianna. There was nothing natural about that wave and its volume, which tossed all of us about, slamming us into the vegetation and garden benches and statuary before it receded. I ached horribly and felt the sting of many scrapes all over my body. Had I hit a tree?

From the moans and groans around me, the others were no better.

I pushed myself off the soaked grass, sopping wet and looked for Liam. Surprisingly, he still sat on the bench, but his eyes were hollow sockets of fear. He looked around, terrified, expecting accusation from the others.

He didn't need to explain. We all knew what had happened, even Renaud and Stephen. So, they *were* kien wielders.

Lillianna, the most experienced of all of us, approached Liam and placed a gentle hand on his shoulder. "You haven't done that before, have you?"

"What happened? What did I do?" Liam's voice cracked, and he shuddered.

"You just wielded aquaeys. The Eldinari are particularly gifted with that erendinth."

Chapter Ten

Bastien and Daphnel sat on either side of me at one of the taverns in the lower levels of the temple. The taverns weren't original to the temple, but when the Balance had been lost and kien wielders had been confined there, the taverns were the first additions to services available in the lower levels. Knights, lay votaries, and the occasional ei'ceuril frequented them often. While the upper levels of the temple felt more palatial, the lower levels were more like a town that never saw the sun, and to many of its residents, all that was missing were women. I didn't miss women for the same reason that many of the other knights and lay votaries did, but I certainly did find them more companionable than nearly every man in the temple.

I sipped my red wine, disappointed at the vintage, but I tried to hide that from my hosts. It didn't compare with the wine produced at my uncle's winery. They had both ordered a honey wine—mead was more common in these middle kingdoms and favored by the humans. By the looks of this tavern, the patrons enjoyed ale, wine, and any other type of spirits the tavern management could acquire. The place was crowded with other patrons, all too happy to ignore the Cyndinari sitting between two high ranking temple knights.

I took another sip, forcing a grateful smile and avoiding thinking about why Bastien and Daphnel had invited me to a tavern—alone. Like Lillianna, they too seemed content to simply sit in silence, although they did seem to also be enjoying their mead. I had no doubt as to why they had invited me here. They clearly wanted to talk about Liam. I really did not want to initiate that conversation—in fact, it was the last thing I wanted to discuss.

I had apologized to Liam. First in the temple gardens after he had calmed down from the shock of wielding for the first time, and later when we had returned to our shared room. On both occasions, Renaud and Stephen had been there and I had apologized to them as well. Then, I had apologized to Liam yet again when it was just the two of us leaving the dining hall after dinner together.

My wine glass was near half empty. I glanced sideways to see if Bastien and Daphnel were drinking at the same pace. I'd thought I was making my wine disappear quickly, but both of their glasses were empty and Bastien was eyeing down the bartender.

Once their glasses were full again, Bastien smiled. "Gets better with every one." He seemed relaxed, but I could practically feel the tenseness oozing from Daphnel's body. Granted, I might have been projecting my anxiety.

Daphnel took the lead. "So, do you care to tell us what is

going on between you and Liam?" he asked.

My throat suddenly felt dry. I moved to take another sip but restrained myself because I would have emptied the rest of my glass in a single swig. I gulped air instead, my face reddening as I asked myself that same question. I had lost count of how many times it had crossed my mind over the past week.

"It's complicated."

"So, finish your drink, order another, and uncomplicate it. You won't say anything that surprises us, boy," Bastien said, smirking at Daphnel instead of looking at me.

That was the first time I had ever seen Bastien smile. He looked genuinely at ease around Daphnel. I looked back at my other host, smiling back at Bastien, as though I wasn't sitting between them. And then it clicked. Of course.

I gave them each a more appraising look, my eyes widening in understanding.

"You were being sincere when I first came to you," I said at last to Bastien. I had wanted to pick a fight with him at that first meeting, assuming he had an issue with my sexual orientation.

"I had no reason not to be. I have no love for your brethren—they killed many fine temple knights when they attacked the city. But I have no problem with you being gay. How could I?" He locked eyes with Daphnel.

"I guess I will have another drink," I said as I emptied my glass. I felt my muscles relax now that I understood their relationship and immediately felt more comfortable around them.

"Do yourself a favor and get the mead instead. It's a good vintage and much better than the awful wine that makes it down here. The ei'ceuril keep the best for themselves. Getting anything past them is difficult, especially when wine is concerned."

As I waited for my next drink, I again looked between my hosts. "So, you two are…"

"Married," Daphnel finished for me.

"And for twenty-three years."

"Not always happily, mind you." Daphnel smirked into his cup.

A mead arrived for me and I took a relieved sip. It was indeed much better than the wine.

"Now, start talking. There's been enough angst due to suppressed feelings in this temple over the years," Daphnel said.

I took another long draught. Conflicted emotions flared inside of me as both Kiron and Liam's faces appeared suspended in front of me. Liam's face was clear. I saw him as perfectly as I had earlier today. Kiron, though, was fading. Indefinite features lined his bronze face framed by cinnamon hair. There was nothing especially Kiron about the features. Every Cyndinari stereotype looked like that. I ground my teeth at the reminder that I could barely remember what he looked like, although his eyes remained firmly in my mind. I could not let myself forget his silver eyes gazing back into my own, delving into my very soul. If he had asked and wanted to become a shadow elf, I would have willingly forfeited myself to him.

Bastien and Daphnel must have taken note of my silence, for Bastien asked, "That complicated, eh? It's not just about Liam, is it?"

I shook my head, reluctant to ask how Bastien knew.

Still, I couldn't speak of it. I held Kiron's name inside, willing myself to remember every freckle he swore he didn't have—he hadn't been able to see the freckles I had seen dotting his back.

"The young man would like an aged whiskey—from the barrel the ei'ceuril don't know about," Daphnel said to the bartender as he passed by, quiet enough to not draw everyone's attention.

"I've barely touched my mead," I protested, swishing its contents in Daphnel's direction.

"You're holding too much inside yourself as it is. In the meantime, I'll tell you part of my story to get you out of that pretty head of yours."

"Daphnel, you don't have to bring that up," Bastien said, his eyes imploring Daphnel to reconsider.

Curious, I looked at Daphnel. I highly doubted that he could tell me any story capable of distracting me from my own demons. What could he possibly tell me that would make me feel more comfortable here at the temple? I didn't belong here. I might have little choice about leaving because of my ability to wield, but this was not my home. I couldn't exactly return to Cynethol either. I'd be better off roaming the world—alone. At least that way I'd be able to feel the sun on my back again.

"I've already decided. You're a good lad, Jaerol, and you're clearly having a rough time adjusting to life in the temple. You should know, though, it wasn't easy for me to call this place home either."

The bartender returned with three new glasses, all filled with a golden liquid, reflecting the tavern's dim lighting. I took a hesitant sip and my nostrils flared at the smoky scent prickling back to my throat.

"Sure, not everyone here welcomed me with open arms, especially when I first joined. Some of my fellow recruits were just as bad as the ei'ceuril and their ideologies and pointedly rejected to even consider me as I am. But Bastien always accepted me for who I was and the others eventually came around and accepted me as their brother well before I went to see Mira in the Kedil Wood. I think some of the ei'ceuril used that time to write a treatise against visiting wielders like Mira. The Ceurtriarch hasn't read any of those pamphlets." Daphnel smirked at that. "Do you know of her?"

"Should I?" I racked my mind, trying to remember meeting anyone named Mira.

"I'll take that as a no. If you did, her name would likely be all the explanation needed."

I turned toward Bastien, who just shrugged his shoulders and took another swig of his drink.

"So, why is this Mira so important?" I asked.

"I wouldn't exactly say she's an important person since she does live in the middle of the woods, but she is important to anyone who has ever visited her."

"Why did you visit her?"

"After I was knighted, I heard a rumor about a wielder living in the Kedil Wood, just north of Trest. She had studied with the ei'ana at Gwilnor long enough to not be a harm to herself or others, but never took their counsels. From what I've learned of her, she spent a good deal of time with the Crimsyns, learning all she could about their healing practices. Anyway, she learned how to make someone's body reflect who they actually are."

"What, like reshaping a bulbous nose?"

"I'm sure she can and has." Daphnel chuckled. "That's not what I'm referring to though. I knew exactly who I was. I might have wrongly been called a girl as a child, but I never was and I was never a woman either. I was always who I am, and my fellow knights knew that well before I went to visit Mira."

I looked back to Daphnel, making sure I had heard and understood him correctly. Daphnel didn't have a single feminine quality to him, from his broad shoulders to his deep voice and scruffy beard. I had heard him correctly, but my mind could not connect what he had said to who I saw sitting in front of me.

"Ramiel's hell, I look more feminine than you do," I blurted out, immediately regretting it. I cursed my loose lips and the rest of myself for accepting that third drink.

"That's because you are," laughed Bastien, echoed by Daphnel. "And an idiot to boot if that's how you think."

I blushed, too embarrassed to apologize. "How? Can I ask that?"

"No, and even if I did understand how wielders do half of what they do, it's not a conversation I would gladly have." Daphnel took a swig from his drink, then cleared his throat. "Mira's not the only wielder to have offered such services over the years, but she was the closest to Ceurenyl."

"How many people have gone to this wielder?" I asked.

"Now, how am I supposed to know that? We're not part of some guild with member benefits. All I know is that enough people have gone to her that her abilities are no secret."

"Did it hurt?" I couldn't stop the onslaught of questions from pouring out, but even so I was only asking a portion of the ones coursing through my head.

"Look, I like you, Jaerol, and you've clearly been through a lot, but you're asking very personal questions. I know that you're not trying to be insensitive, most people aren't, and that you're just curious. I don't know what you experienced before coming to the temple, but the point of this is not to share my life story with you but rather to tell you that your journey will be easier when you let others into your life."

"It also helps if you don't beat those people already supporting you to a bloody mess with a practice sword," Bastien added.

"I did apologize to Liam—and to Renaud and Stephen."

"I would hope so," Bastien said. "Regardless of who you are or where you came from, good friends are hard to come by. Hold on to those people."

I couldn't say anything. I knew Bastien was trying to help, but I couldn't suppress the bubble of rage swelling inside me. I didn't need this—not now, not ever. My emotions had been unraveling for the better part of the past months and I could barely keep myself stitched together. It took every shred of my self-control to push my seat back and stand to leave.

"Are you sure you don't want to talk about it?" Daphnel asked, warmly.

"I'm certain." I turned away from them, my face warm.

"We're here to support you, Jaerol," said Bastien, grabbing my arm before I could stalk away. "We're not just your superiors. We don't have to be."

The last time I had trusted someone with authority over me had ended in Kiron's death. I jerked my arm away from Bastien. I didn't acknowledge either knight as I stalked away.

That small part inside of me, the part that kept pinging while around Liam, acknowledged that I was being an ungrateful ass. But right now, I was more comfortable with my long habit of hiding those feelings away. I didn't even have the decency to thank them for the three drinks.

I knew my anger had gotten the best of me and that I should turn around and apologize. All they had done was try to make me feel welcome, that I belonged here and could live happily in the temple. Despite what they had said and how they had said it, I didn't belong here. Their suggestion that it was otherwise had only made me angrier. I would not apologize and instead pushed my way through the exit.

Despite the late hour, the corridor outside the tavern was crowded with other men, knights and lay votaries intermingled, filling the air with a happy chatter. Any other time I would have taken this opportunity to find someone to share a bed with. Part of me still considered doing just that. Surely, someone here would sleep with a Cyndinari. I wanted—needed to stop thinking. Couldn't I get a single night without being reminded of Kiron? Of what I had done to him?

My heart raced. I barely noticed the attractive men in the corridor, dressed in loose fitting and revealing clothing. I pushed past them all, bumping into a few, which gained me a few unpleasant stares. I didn't make my way to my shared room. I couldn't be around anyone just now. Not yet.

Perhaps if I avoided Liam, I would stop thinking about Kiron. There was a definite connection linking them together, making thoughts of either one bring the other to mind. I continued to walk aimlessly with no idea where I wanted to go or even where I was going. I recognized a few landmarks, notable statues in wall niches, a stair hall that I descended instead of climbing as usual. Stair landings passed as I continued my descent. I was sure I hadn't ever gone this far below the temple. The cloudy white walls still emanated a soft light down here, just as they did in the rest of the temple. It wasn't enough to read by or keep you awake at night, but it did ensure that every crevice of the temple was searchable without a torch, although it was difficult to see clearly.

I hoped that the further I descended, the less likely it was that I would run into someone. I wanted to be alone—I deserved that. I didn't have a room I could go to for solitude, not anymore. I peered over the railing, trying to get a sense of how much further this stair went. I had already descended further than I initially anticipated, so I turned off the stair at the next landing into yet another dimly lit corridor. It was just as wide as the corridors occupied by the temple knights and the lay votaries. There was little ornamentation on the walls of the corridors above and this one had the same bare walls spaced with wide pilasters to thicken the structure. Considering the weight of all the stone of the temple above, I shuddered at the thought of the force pressing down on these deep subterranean levels. A second, longer look at the pilasters showed that they were wider than the ones above.

Unlike on the levels above, this corridor did not have any doors on either side wall, their smooth surface broken only by the equally spaced pilasters marching down its length. What was the point of having an endless corridor if it didn't lead anywhere? I now wanted to know what was at the end. Surely it had to lead to somewhere. Perhaps it was another tunnel out of the temple.

After walking for what felt like the entire length of the temple, I saw an archway at the end of the corridor. I passed through it and walked into an expansive chamber. Shallow vaults sprung from thick columns throughout the space. The same eerie light as in the corridor filled the chamber, except for one area where a warm light flickered from behind one of the columns.

Who would be hiding down here? And why? I couldn't imagine but I was sure that whoever it was, they did not want to be found. My emotions had finally settled down, diffused by the lengthy walk and my mind was now distracted by this discovery. For a moment, I considered quietly leaving.

Instead, a kernel of courage swelled in my chest. It resembled idiocy more than anything else but it pushed me forward and toward the firelight. My skin prickled and my heart raced as I neared the wide column outlined with a warm flickering light on the other side. Rounding the column, my heart pounded in my chest and I could feel sweat beading at my hairline and on my brow.

A bracketed torch came into view, lighting the accoutrements of a small camp. Bunched against the column was the most impressive armor I had ever seen. The firelight cast ripples on its golden hue and lit a number of metallic looking strips that had to be the closures. Then cold metal touched my throat, and I realized too late that the pile of armor did not include a sword.

I cursed to myself. Nobody knew I was down here. No one would even consider looking for me until tomorrow morning at the earliest, and only because it would be assumed that I had betrayed the temple.

"Who are you?" a woman asked.

"Jaerol Solaris." My voice was steadier than I believed possible and I thanked my years of training.

"What is a Cyndinari doing here?"

"I was hoping to find a quiet place away from everyone else above," I said honestly, my eyes catching the glint of the armor again. "You're the knight who killed that shadow elf a while ago by the ruined gate." I should have recognized the piled armor sooner. Granted, she had worn a cloak at the time, but the glint of her armor beneath that fabric had been unmistakable.

Her sword fell away from my neck and she walked around to face me. Golden brown hair hung over her shoulder, spilling down a simple white sleeveless shirt.

"You're not very good at sneaking around. I heard you while you were still in the stair hall."

"I wasn't sneaking around."

"Hard to believe that from a Cyndinari. You'll have to excuse my prejudice but the harm wrought by your ancestors was catastrophic. I'm Elayne Thenrel."

"You're a Guardian knight, aren't you? You don't look like the description my magisters provided."

"Were these magisters shadow elves teaching at the Imperium?"

"Um, yes."

"Dare I ask how they described my order?" Elayne sheathed her golden crystalline sword; apparently, I wasn't a threat.

"I'd rather not say—none of it was complimentary and clearly neither was it true."

"That's probably for the best. If their description didn't match, how'd you know I am a Guardian?"

"I served as an Erynien emissary for a time." I paused to raise my hands, expressing my harmlessness when Elayne unsheathed her sword in a flash, its point already at my chest. "It's complicated. If I were to be handed over to the empire now, a shadow elf would steal my soul before I could utter a prayer goodbye."

"Fine. You're not helping your case though." Elayne lowered her sword again, but notably didn't sheathe it.

"Yeah, not one of my strong suits. Anyway, because of that, I encountered every known knightly order in Eklean, and you definitely don't belong to any of them."

She responded with a derisive snort. "Children playing with swords, including the Luminari today. If only their forebears could see how far their orders have fallen. Tell me, Jaerol, has everything been forgotten? Do they even remember jienzu?"

"No one here, nor at Gwilnor that I know of. I recently lost control of myself while dueling against a friend. I hurt him pretty badly while practicing the old forms." I looked away, still ashamed of myself.

"Not particularly shocking. I doubt your instructors could teach proper control. They likely wouldn't recognize Balance if it punched them in the face."

"You talk of jienzu as though it were kien or kiara," I said.

"You're a wielder, I assume? Have you not noticed the similarities for yourself? The Arantiulyns liked to claim jienzu as their own. But it was Kyrendal who first developed the technique and it was widespread before we left our Skylands. He made it sound like he had learned it from someone else. It saddens me that so many have forgotten it."

"It doesn't have to be forgotten." I smirked.

"It would not serve my purpose well if others learned of my presence here."

"What if it was just a small number? Perhaps four people?" I proposed, immediately thinking of what better way to apologize to my bunk mates than getting them a proper jienzu instructor. Not only could they defend themselves better against me, but if what Elayne said was true, I'd also learn control—I wouldn't lose myself in the forms again.

"Fine. Bring your friends here on Gwynthaen at first light."

Chapter Eleven

I told Liam, Renaud, and Stephen everything about the night that started in the tavern with Bastien and Daphnel. None of them believed me. They couldn't imagine Bastien and Daphnel inviting me to spend time with them at a tavern and they certainly didn't believe that our superiors had bought me several drinks. They had assumed, as I did when Bastien and Daphnel asked to see me, that I would be expelled from the recruits and barred from training with the temple knights. I kept the rest of the conversation to myself though. Bastien and Daphnel had both revealed a lot about themselves, but that had been a private conversation and I knew they wouldn't appreciate it if I gossiped about it.

Still, even if I had forgotten about Daphnel's request to never mention what he had told me, I was too excited and wanted to move on and tell my bunkmates about Elayne. They had all grown up with stories about the fabled Guardian knights and had likely dreamt of a chivalrous career because of that order. Even Liam had heard stories of the knights who belonged to no kingdom—they served the Guardian Senate to keep the peace across the entire world. At the height of Krysenthiel, races of every kingdom and empire had once belonged to their order, before Erynor shattered the harmonious state of the world and the Guardian Senate had disbanded.

Once I finally convinced them that Elayne was real and that she was willing to train us in jienzu, they had all grown just as excited as I already was. I didn't think that learning better control of the old forms would better teach me control of kien, but I did hope. At the very least, I could learn enough control to not lose it while dueling a friend again.

By the time they accepted that Elayne was not only here but willing to train us, none of my bunkmates cared to remember what I had done to Liam. This had been the perfect peace offering.

I rolled over in my bed, trying to drift back to sleep. I didn't know if it was close to the first hour of the day, but I was done waiting. From the sounds in our room, I assumed that they had slept just as poorly as I had the previous night. No one was breathing the slow, heavy breaths of sleep.

I pushed myself into a sitting position and peered across the room. "Liam, are you awake?" I asked after not seeing any movement from Renaud or Stephen.

"We're all awake," came Stephen's voice from the adjacent top bunk.

"Is it dawn yet?" Liam asked.

"We'd be late if it was," said Renaud.

"Anyone else tired of waiting?" Stephen asked, his legs now dangling over the edge of the bunk.

Instead of answering, I hopped out of bed, feeling my way blindly to a lantern and lighting it. The small flame giving off just enough light so that I could see Liam's blush when I noticed he was staring at me. His blush wouldn't be noticeable in the dull glow from the stone—it certainly wasn't bright enough to keep anyone awake at night. Enjoying Liam's embarrassment, I splashed water on my face at the wash basin, ran damp hands through my hair to settle it, and got dressed. I still couldn't figure out if walking around naked made him uncomfortable or if he liked what he saw. His flushed cheeks certainly suggested the latter.

The other three followed suit, taking turns washing their faces and throwing on their clothes. The frigid wash water in the basin had scattered any remaining drowsiness.

We made a stop at the lavatory, and then I led them through the vacant corridors—due to the early hour—past the tavern Bastien and Daphnel had taken me to, and then down the stair hall nearest it. The temporary wakefulness from the frigid water in the wash basin had worn off. We were too tired to say anything and the only sound was our feet shuffling down the stairs. I counted off the landings until we reached the one I remembered from the other night and led them down the corridor.

It looked just as it had the other night, dim lighting and all. It didn't matter what time it was down here—the lack of windows in the lower levels of the temple ensured that. The four of us walking through this corridor was probably the most crowded it had been in centuries. Even though I had company, the walk felt just as daunting as it had the last time. I counted some of the pilasters we passed, growing disinterested after passing the tenth.

At last, we reached the archway at the end of the corridor and the chamber beyond. The lighting was just as dull as the last time, but I didn't see the additional glow of a torch, so I couldn't be entirely sure that we were in the right chamber. It looked the same and even smelled the same, but I started to second guess myself. The temple was immense and it was possible that there was nothing unique about this chamber. There could very well be identical ones branching off from each landing of the stair we had come from. There certainly wouldn't be anything unique about that musty scent at this depth in a mountain.

I looked around for Elayne, but she wasn't near the entrance, so we went deeper into the columned chamber to where I remembered Elayne's camp behind one of the wide columns. As I feared, there was nothing there. In fact, it didn't look like anyone had been here for years.

"Are you sure this is the right spot?" Renaud asked.

"Positive." I wasn't going to mention my theory about identical chambers on other levels.

"Lost, are we?" All four of us spun around at the voice.

Elayne was dressed similarly to the other night, only this time, her golden armor was hidden away somewhere, likely where she had set up her new camp. Her sword, the only identifiable feature connecting her to the Guardian knights, hung from her waist.

"Don't stare at me like that, it's making me uncomfortable." She crossed her arms and pivoted to the side.

"Sorry," I apologized for us collectively before making quick introductions, Renaud and Stephen looking stunned, as though they spoke to Anaweh in the flesh.

Elayne's gaze fell on Liam. "Quite the mystery to you." She approached him, cupped his chin, examining his bone structure. "I've only had the pleasure of meeting one lethien before. Elves and humans lived so near each other after we migrated from our Skylands, it was inevitable that some of our numbers would mate with each other. Once the Ceurendol War started though, the lethien villages were targeted by Erynor. To him, the mixture of elven blood with what he considered lesser races was an abomination. I didn't think a single lethien survived after he seized power. Truly, it is an honor to meet you, Liam."

"The honor is mine, Elayne."

"Sure, you believe her when she tells you that you're half-elf and half-human, but not me," I mocked.

"I can't help that she's more trustworthy than you." Liam smirked at me.

Elayne chuckled, apparently happy to be around people again. "Well, I know that you didn't wake up early on a Gwynthaen to simply meet me. Shall we get started?"

The four of us nodded, eager to start. I looked around to see if there were any practice swords we would be using. Not seeing any, I immediately regretted not stopping by the training rooms to secret some away. This session would be all but wasted if we couldn't actually practice.

"Now, I'm going to assume that none of you know how to properly meditate. So, take a seat, cross your legs, and close your eyes."

None of us were confident enough in our interior lives to argue the point, so we did as she instructed. We formed a slight semicircle facing Elayne, waiting for her to give more direction.

I had no idea what meditation had to do with jienzu and I struggled to not lose my patience at the delay either. My magisters at the Imperium had never even mentioned meditation in relation to jienzu. Meditation was something for the ei'ceuril, not for a student training to become a shadow elf. I kept my mouth shut. Comparing Elayne's teaching methods to that of my past magisters probably wasn't the best idea.

After some time passed where my thoughts wandered to the various jienzu positions, I started to wonder whether I should speak up. It seemed that Elayne had fallen asleep—her breath had become steady. Was she as tired as the four of us? In fact, I recognized Stephen's deep breathing. There was no doubt; he had fallen asleep. I peeked over just in time to see Renaud elbow him.

Was this how the Luminari practiced jienzu? Had I misunderstood Elayne the other night when she spoke of it? Perhaps the old forms meant two different things to the Cyndinari and the Luminari. That wouldn't be entirely surprising. It seemed that the only resemblance between the two elven kin these days were our pointed ears. Not even our eyes matched anymore but curiously, Elayne did not have the green-to-silver eyes like the rest of the Luminari. That didn't make any sense. She had the elven silver eyes, the kind the Luminari used to have.

"Only one of you knows how to breathe properly. Tell me, Liam, where did you learn?" Elayne asked. I opened my eyes again to see if she was doing anything different, but she continued to sit with her eyes closed.

"Learn how to breathe?" Liam asked.

"Breathing techniques are pivotal to meditation. While breathing properly isn't a guarantee that you'll have a good meditation, bad breathing can certainly be a detriment. Proper breathing helps ease your body to an appropriately relaxed state. The rest of you should listen to Liam's breath. Listen to how he holds his breath inside, cherishing it for a moment before releasing it."

I strained my ears to focus on Liam beside me. I couldn't tell how his pace was different than my own. As I considered yet again what I knew of jienzu, I almost asked how this was in any way related. Fortunately, Stephen spoke up first.

"What does meditation have to do with fighting with a sword?" he asked, speaking for all four of us.

Elayne grimaced, but she made no move to stand. "Tell me, Jaerol, what were you taught of jienzu?"

"It's a fighting technique used with a sword." I was never taught any of the theory behind the old forms, only how to use them while dueling. I wasn't even aware that there was any philosophy backing them up. Why did a fighting technique require a supporting theory?

"Using a sword well is one result of jienzu and Kyrendal did instruct his pupils while using a sword at times. But it's important to remember that a sword or any other weapon is just a tool. They have as much to do with jienzu as a hammer has to do with a house."

Elayne paused, as though she was frozen in place. I glanced to either side to make eye contact with the others and they all looked just as confused as I felt.

"We are anacordel," she started again. Clearly, she had been collecting her thoughts. "Ana is the breath of Anaweh's

Light within us—our spirit. Cor is that which we share with every physical creature on Teraeniel—our body. Del is the spark of life which animates us—our soul. As anacordel, we have the complicated task of balancing these three components of who we are. Bringing balance between our spirit and body and soul is uniquely our own experience. The animals and beasts, the cordel, have a soul and body, but no spirit. The anadel have a spirit and soul, but no body. Of all Anaweh's creatures, we are the most complicated.

"While it is possible to master balance in a lifetime, mortal or not, very few people achieve it. Jienzu is a technique that aids one to achieve balance. So yes, Stephen, meditation is intrinsic to jienzu," Elayne said, not as a reproach, but softly. "Its lack is the reason Jaerol lost control while dueling Liam. This world is out of balance—kien and kiara, the anacordel, Teraeniel, life and death—everything is out of balance. Ramiel has unhinged every facet of Teraeniel and I have no doubt that he is guiding Erynor to do the same."

She stood after that, offering me her crystalline sword. "You are unbalanced, Jaerol, as is every other Cyndinari. Take my verathn and try to strike me."

I looked at it hesitantly. I had seen my fair share of verathn before, but none were like Elayne's sword. Granted, the ones that I had seen were also corrupted verathn, manipulated by tenebrys, after they had been gathered from their fallen owners. Even here in the temple, I could feel the power coming off Elayne's weapon. "I've had some of the best sword masters in Eklean teach me to duel," I said, still taking in the sword's beauty.

Elayne smirked. "You think you can best a Guardian?"

She waggled her sword in front of me.

"But you'll be unarmed," came Renaud.

"You're right, how unfair." Elayne cocked her head, in mockery. "I know…" without finishing her thought, she tore off the lower portion of her shirt and then wrapped it around her head, covering her eyes. "That should even the odds some." She again extended her verathn at me.

I took it this time, balancing it in my grip with ease. I couldn't believe how perfect it felt in my hand. It seemed as though this sword was specifically crafted for me. Admiring the beauty of it again, I was caught off guard when Elayne landed a punch in my midsection.

"You didn't expect me to just dodge your swings once you were ready, did you? You're spending too much time ogling my verathn as it is."

Regaining my breath, I smiled back, easing myself into the old forms. Elayne might know more about jienzu than I did, but I'd never had a reason to doubt my own ability with a blade before. Holding this one made me even more confident than normal. I would have to be careful though since she was blindfolded.

Light on my feet, I leapt forward, swinging the sword upward. I didn't expect to land a hit. After all, I didn't really want to strike her. Granted, I wasn't expecting her to duck and kick the side of my leg either. How had she known exactly where my leg was and that all my weight was pressing down on that one leg at that moment? I stumbled backward, somehow managing to stay upright. I couldn't believe how quickly she had moved to attack me. It was as though she stopped time as her movements flashed in a blur. As I steadied myself to again press the offensive, she countered me with another blow, jabbing my side with a hard punch, and then with a final blow, she hit me square in the chest, knocking me flat on my back.

I blinked toward the ceiling, no longer holding the verathn. I had only attempted two strikes and neither came anywhere near hitting her.

"As I said, no balance." Elayne extended a hand to help me up.

Liam, Renaud, and Stephen gaped at Elayne, the question of 'how' forming on their lips. We spent the rest of the morning performing slow and excruciatingly painful poses. I quickly discovered that my body had muscles that I never knew existed. Many times, I nearly toppled over, unable to hold one position longer than for a single breath, let alone the thirty breaths Elayne had requested.

Eventually Elayne let us go, tired and sore. I didn't just feel physically drained, but emotionally exhausted as well. Every part of my being cried out, not necessarily in agony. It was something different, and it felt good. I didn't have the energy to continue or to put any thought into it, but there was something right about it. It felt as though my entire being was realigning. Not only was my physical posture misshapen, but so was my interior bearing. I could feel my inner being—my spirit and soul—stretching after long neglect.

Part Three

Bargaining

Chapter Twelve

13 years earlier - 9053.3E

Teran's estate was abuzz with staff making final preparations, even as the first guests arrived. The manor was large enough to accommodate twice the number of elves invited, but Teran always hosted his soirées on the terraces.

Kiron and I were chatting with one of our magisters, one of the few that did not make our skin crawl. Lys, like every other magister at the Imperium, was a shadow elf, but she had somehow managed to maintain a kind heart. We talked easily with her, neither of us feeling any pressure now that we were away from school for the weekend. And unlike most of tonight's guests, we didn't have to worry about traveling home when the festivities ended. Teran had shown us personally to our room when we had arrived late that morning. While Lys was a respected faculty member of the Imperium, even she had not been offered such generous accommodations.

The terrace filled as more guests arrived and the staff melted into the background, carrying trays laden with hors d'oeuvres and Teran's own wine in crystal glasses. The cheerful chatter that filled the area fell to a hush when a woman walked unaccompanied onto the terrace.

"She's beautiful," Kiron gasped, echoing the sentiment from the other party guests.

I couldn't argue with that. I had never seen anyone so beautiful before. Luscious cinnamon-colored hair fell over a single shoulder, giving a perfect asymmetry to her bronzed face, and complimenting her loose-fitting black gown. And no one could miss the onyx colored gem hanging from her neck, larger than many ripe strawberries.

Lys eyed us apprehensively. "Be careful around that one, boys. That is Yloran," she said, expecting us to know the name, and I did recognize it. There was only ever one Yloran throughout Cyndinari history: Yloran Eth Gnashar.

"Truly?" Kiron asked, also recognizing the name. "Isn't she a bit young to be a Sha'ghol?"

"If you had the power of the Sha'ghol, would you go around showing your age?" I returned, forgetting that Lys stood beside us. She smiled warmly and excused herself. She had spent decades educating Cyndinari teenagers and if there was one thing that we obsessed more over than living forever, it was our appearances.

"Way to be subtle," Kiron said, as soon as she was far enough away that he wouldn't be overheard.

Like every other shadow elf, Lys' bronze skin was decaying and scabbing to an ashen hue, and her hair had lost all of its sheen. Lys was one of the few shadow elves in attendance. Teran always appeared amicable around her, despite Lys being a teacher at the Imperium and a shadow elf. He had once mentioned that he was not well loved by their kind, but even so, some of the wealthiest and most well-connected Cyndinari had accepted Teran's invitation.

I glanced back at Yloran, and again compared her appearance to her supposed age. As a child, I had learned that the Sha'ghol had been around before we had to leave Cyndinare. If she was truly one of the Sha'ghol, that would make her…

Twelve thousand years old, a voice whispered in my head.

My heart skipped a beat, then pumped at an accelerated rate. Kiron and I had been making our way across the now-crowded terrace and when I froze in place, Kiron grabbed my hand and looked at me with concern.

"All right?" he asked, raising a questioning brow.

"Yeah. I'm fine."

"Liar." Kiron smirked, his smile bringing me back to my myself, making me aware of my surroundings again. No one seemed to have noticed my odd pause, and only Kiron brought any attention to it. I again glanced at the too-young looking woman. Twelve thousand years old?

Someone tapped me on the shoulder and it took all my formal training to not leap out of my skin. I turned to find a well-dressed young man, not ten years our senior. "Lady Yloran would speak with you."

Kiron gave me another questioning look before nodding and we followed him into the manor. Neither of us knew what we were getting ourselves into. Was questioning the age of a Sha'gol a crime? Especially if it was only in my mind? I hadn't even realized that there were any still alive. Did they hold any power or influence in the Erynien Empire? Erynor didn't seem the type to share his power with anyone, Sha'ghol or not.

A hundred similar questions spun through my mind as the handsome elf escorted us into the house. I caught a fleeting glimpse of my uncle before being ushered inside. To my surprise, he wore an approving, if not flat-out impressed expression. Had he planned this? Before the thought could fully form, Yloran strode into the salon where we had been taken.

"The answer is yes. Teran organized all this," she said.

My jaw dropped as I stared at the only woman I would ever consider leaving Kiron for. My heartbeat was unsteady and irregular. Kiron elbowed me and I hastily closed my mouth. For a moment, I couldn't tell whether I was more attracted to her or mesmerized by the onyx gem hanging from her neck. It looked even bigger up close.

Her fingers moved to the gem above her suggestively low neckline. Like every other Cyndinari, this woman cared little for modesty, as evidenced by the clothing of the guests on the terrace. Even my uncle wore an open silken tunic, his robe slit down both sides to reveal most of his thighs.

"Your uncle tells me you wish to get away from the Imperium—from the path that would turn you into a shadow elf, a mock imitation of immortality," she said.

I tried to answer but stuttered something unintelligible instead as my emotions raced. Had Teran betrayed Kiron and me? Why would he tell one of the Sha'ghol about our situation? Surely, she would deliver us to the authorities. The better question, barely able to materialize in my foggy mind, was how did my uncle come to know one of the Sha'ghol? I knew he was well connected, but this was on an entirely different level. This wasn't some wealthy goblin or a Lucillian sympathizer. I'd be less shocked to discover that Teran was a close friend with a Luminari aryl.

"I don't blame you, darling. If given the same opportunity, I too would prefer a mortal life." Yloran moved to the plush couch, crossing her legs as she sat. "These shadow elves claim they can still feel things, but I'm doubtful." She smiled at the handsome elf who had escorted us, clearly hinting at something more provocative.

"Are you really able to get us away?" Kiron asked, taking a seat on the couch opposite her, a small ornately carved table separating them. He leaned forward, hopeful. "Neither of us understood what we were agreeing to when we enrolled—what we would actually become."

"I doubt anyone is fully aware of what their transformation will entail, until it's too late." She settled herself more deeply into the couch, one arm now draped over the back of it, as comfortable as if she were in her own home. "Anything is possible, darlings. But do understand that you will become fugitives of the empire."

"What will happen to our families?" I asked. I had taken a seat beside Kiron, our legs brushing. The touch always gave me an added level of confidence.

"You'll likely never speak to them again," Yloran said without hesitation.

My parents weren't awful people, but they were loyal subjects of the empire. Would they turn me in as Yloran seemed to suggest? I was more concerned for my uncle though. My parents would immediately link him to my disappearance, blaming him for implanting rebellious thoughts into my head. They had even accused him of causing my tender feelings for Kiron. I had no idea what my uncle had to do with me falling in love with Kiron. How could he possibly influence that—even if he wanted to? All he had done was support and encourage us after we had chosen each other.

"When can you get us away?" I asked at last, weighing the various consequences. Regardless of the risks involved and the sacrifices we would have to make, it would be worth it. This was the right choice. Kiron and I would be together and free of the Erynien Empire.

"Even for someone who holds as much power as I do, getting you away from the Imperium while you are still students would be too difficult and it would be dangerous to attempt to smuggle you off the island as runaways. You should know that the Imperium guards its students fiercely. That friendly magister you spoke with earlier—do you sincerely believe she is here by accident? Her presence here is just as accidental as my own."

I tried to keep the disappointment from showing. How was this going to work if we waited until graduation? Only half the class would graduate at the Grand Tourney, and those same graduates left the Coliseum as shadow elves. It would be too late.

Yloran smirked. There was an unshakable confidence to her smile, a self-assurance that I immediately envied. I could never imagine this woman as the awkward teenager that I was.

Kiron interpreted her smile differently. "How can we trust you?"

Her smile narrowed but remained just as severe. "You cannot. All that you can trust is that I have little love for our dear emperor and his shadow elves. I am one of the Sha'ghol, one of the fifteen who first wielded tenebrys after Ramiel's imprisonment. I listened to his whispers and foolishly believed them to be truth. Our promised power from the Citadel is all but meaningless after the Cyndinari left Cyndinare." Yloran spoke as though she had just come from the Citadel—like she had never left it to fall into ruins on Cyndinare. "At first, we didn't know where the whispers came from. But we became the chosen fifteen—the Sha'ghol—and we were promised power unlike this world has ever seen." Yloran touched her necklace, the heavy gem now appearing to be an infinite void.

Kiron squirmed uncomfortably next to me. We knew the stories about the Sha'ghol of course. We knew how they had agreed to serve Ramiel in exchange for unimaginable power. But, neither of us believed those stories were true.

"You are still unsure about whether you can trust me?" She smiled. "It's true, I am bound to Ramiel. My power comes directly from him. All you can trust is my resentment toward the foolish pup. Draelyn or not, he does not sit above the rest of the Sha'ghol. He belongs among our number only because he inherited it from his mother as she died giving birth to him. Whatever the fool of a woman was thinking, she should have known that she could not survive giving birth to a draelyn."

"A draelyn?" I had never heard of such a thing.

"Perhaps another time darling. If you want to know more of them, read about Tenethyl."

"All right," I said warily. "Why would you help us? What do you expect in return?"

"There is no mistaking your relation to Teran." Yloran smiled, seemingly pleased "By agreeing to help, I'm fulfilling my own debt to your uncle. Don't bother asking for the details."

How had a Sha'ghol become indebted to Teran? I tried recalling everything that I knew of my uncle—all our private conversations and the various guests I knew had been invited to his estate over the years. I knew he wasn't just a vintner, because a Sha'ghol would never have become indebted to a simple vineyard owner. Did Teran's past apprenticeship with the Goblin Guild have anything to do with it?

"If it's not possible to get us away now, how do you plan on helping us?" Kiron asked, unable to hear the symphony of questions spinning around in my head. But somehow Yloran could. She stared at me. It didn't look like she had any inclination to answer my inner ponderings, but she did know them.

"I cannot physically save you, if that is what you are hoping for," she mocked. "Naturally, I could swoop into the Imperium, demand your release into my care, and carry you away to the Citadel. But powers being what they are now, that would lead to many annoying questions. Questions that I simply don't want to answer. I don't need doubt and speculation to follow my every step. I cannot allow my intentions to be revealed, not yet."

With every statement this Sha'ghol made, the more questions sprung into my head. Was she trying to sidetrack us, speaking of things that should not be possible?

"Then how do you intend to help us?" Again, Kiron kept his inquiry focused on the matter at hand, doubtlessly restraining his other questions to research later. If I had been alone with Yloran, our meeting would have ended with me not having a plan for escaping our current fate.

Yloran smiled again. "It would be criminal for two handsome Cyndinari such as yourselves to decay as shadow elves. I must do what I've been forbidden to do. The only way that you will escape your current path is to fool every person attending the Grand Tourney. You must learn to wield umbrys and make them all think that you are wielding tenebrys and stealing your competitor's soul. You will be granting them an early death in exchange for capturing their soul for an indefinite number of years."

Kiron's eyes lit up and I knew mine had as well. I didn't allow myself to think of the potential repercussions. So many things could go wrong. It would only take one person to see through our ruse for that plan to fail miserably. We also had to win our matches at the Grand Tourney.

"Assuming that works," Kiron scaled back his enthusiasm, "how would we get away from the Erynien Empire after that?"

"Smuggling away two alleged shadow elves is a much easier task than smuggling away students of the Imperium. Shadow elves aren't exactly the most reputable bunch of elves out there. No one would question the disappearance of two of them. You'll be assumed to be dead, of course."

Chapter Thirteen

Liam and I walked through the lower levels of the temple on our first patrol together, a patrol that had been pushed back an entire month. Bastien had insisted on a probationary month for both of us, although Liam had assured Bastien that he had forgiven me, and I had reassured him that my outburst would not happen again. The extra month came at the right moment too, since it meant that we'd been able to devote our free time to learning jienzu with Elayne. Despite building muscle mass in unexpected parts of my body over that month, I still had not grown accustomed to Elayne's understanding of jienzu. I had only held a sword that first time, the other three had not touched a sword, and she had yet to have us grapple with each other. Instead, hours upon hours had been spent in that forgotten chamber stretching our bodies into painful postures and learning how to breathe properly.

As much as I hated to admit it, I was starting to think that Elayne was right. After only a month, I felt more in control of my body. I couldn't say if my body, soul, and spirit were finally in sync after twenty-six years, but I had yet to lose control of myself since first meeting Elayne. And while I had never considered myself to be in poor physical shape, this training, these postures Elayne demanded of us in addition to our customary training under Daphnel's tutelage, was showing physical benefits for all four of us. I made it a point to avoid staring at Liam while in public, especially while in the bath hall. He was even stirring things inside of me when he was fully dressed; his clothes were getting tighter on him, his muscles all but visible beneath the fabric.

After passing so often through this area of the temple to reach Elayne even further below, I'd grown quite familiar with it.

The subterranean space had a stout character. Robust columns carried shallow vaults along the corridors. There was none of the rich ornamentation of the main level here in the lower levels where the lay votaries lived. None of the kien wielders who were kept here had chosen to become a lay votary, nor could they refuse to. It was either that or choose to become a temple knight or an ei'ceuril. I didn't know which ceurtriarch had mandated it but living in the temple without any pious position in service to Anaweh had been deemed unacceptable. I also wasn't entirely sure how these men served the Creating Light. All I had ever seen them do was waste away their days by meandering into taverns when they assumed evening had fallen outside. The lack of natural lighting down here disoriented everyone, and I often saw a handful of men in the tavern, regardless of the time of day. I didn't blame them, nor could I. I had done the same before enlisting with the temple knights.

"Could you imagine having to call yourself a lay votary?" I asked, positive we were out of earshot of the four we had just passed.

"Technically, you were one. Before you decided to stop sitting around doing nothing all day."

"They must have lowered their standards."

"I don't recall them ever being particularly high."

As we passed another intersection, we came across a larger group of men, all talking at once. Each seemed to speak louder than the last. They noticed us, and all but one hushed. I couldn't immediately place where he was from, since he didn't have the customary blond hair and blue eyes of most humans whose ancestors had belonged to Thellion. No, his eyes were brown, and his skin was likely only pale because he couldn't leave the temple.

"Heavy on the patrols recently," he said, shouldering through the other men. "Is it true what they're saying?"

"Depends. What are they saying? The ei'ceuril have been preaching the same dogma since Theseryn built this temple," I quipped.

"You think you're funny, don't you? I can be funny too, you know."

Liam, more imposing than either me or the man, stepped between us. "What are you asking, Dunstin?" He held his gaze as Dunstin took a step back. I couldn't believe it—Liam didn't even have to reach for his sword.

"About the witches at that school teaching a kien wielder—one of us."

"First off, they're not witches and I'd hardly say he's one

of you," I said, taking an aggressive step forward.

"Stop it," Liam threatened, standing between Dunstin and me. "He studied there for a couple of months, but he's with the ei'ceuril now."

"So, he's in the temple now?"

"Not at present. He's a novice and is spending the year in the Illumined Wood, just the same as every other ei'ceuril novice must do. Their wielding can't do any harm in that forest."

"But those greedy witches taught him. While they stole us from our families and tossed us in here to rot, they taught him. When are we getting out of this light-forsaken dungeon?"

"This is hardly a dungeon and mind your language when referring to the ei'ana." Liam's expression hardened. "Sorenth refugees are filling the city, constantly wondering when they'll get their next meal, let alone whether they'll have a roof over their head. Our every need is met here. Don't expect such hospitality from a real dungeon."

"A dungeon and our tomb," Dunstin challenged. "And my every need is not met. Perhaps some of those ei'ana can start by making reparations." The other men chuckled behind him.

"If you want to know what a dungeon is really like, keep doing what you're doing. I'm quite familiar with living in a dungeon and right now, I'd happily escort you to one. Be sure to enjoy your three meals a day, bath hall, and feathered mattresses and pillows while you can." Liam must be quite angry to even refer to that time, and not even that anger stopped him from flinching at the mention. I remembered what Liam had looked like at the time, his ribs protruding and so frail that a child could have easily snapped his arms and legs. It was a wonder he had recovered as well as he had.

"We have to reach our next check point," I said, pulling Liam away from the group.

The noise of the gathered men picked up again, and as we moved away, I heard Dunstin calling us faggots and suggesting that we enjoyed servicing ei'ceuril, only his words were much cruder and I could hear Liam grinding his teeth.

"Don't pay them any mind," I said, refusing to look back over my shoulder. A picture of Kiron immediately flashed through my mind. He'd used that same calming phrase, word for word, countless times at the Imperium. "Honestly, I would have said the same thing if I was in their shoes. And truly, some of those ei'ceuril…" I whistled suggestively.

Liam snapped a sideways look.

"Oh, don't look at me like that. Save your condemnation for Dunstin back there. Not all the ei'ceuril are holy men. Wealthy families across all Eklean want the notoriety that only the ei'ceuril can hold. It's a position of notable political authority, and a number of them are here for that and nothing else. Well, perhaps one other thing…" I smirked.

"You're incorrigible."

"Slander! I simply know more of the world than you."

"That's highly unlikely. What does a Cyndinari from Broid know of the world?"

I felt the mirth drain from my body. "You don't know what growing up in Broid was like. What they had put us through—especially those of us foolish enough to enroll at the Imperium." My skin crawled as the memories boiled inside. "You couldn't know."

"Then tell me." Liam must have read my emotions, for

his concern was clear. And for the first time since leaving the Imperium, I wanted to tell someone about my experience. I didn't immediately begin to speak, but as we continued our patrol I realized that even a month ago, I wouldn't have considered breathing a word of my childhood to someone else. My time at the Imperium and much of my childhood was tied to Kiron. Then the words began to tumble out.

"Every Cyndinari child is encouraged to take a preliminary exam when they are ten years old. One hundred of the ones who excel are selected to attend to the Imperium. For the most part, we had normal childhoods, but after the selection, we left our families to start our studies at the Imperium, and our childhood ended.

"Our magisters shaped us over the next six years to become the next batch of shadow elves. We were fed an imperial-approved history and philosophy. Anaweh was never mentioned by name, and Ramiel was understood as the Creating Light's equal—where there is creation, there was once the void. They are opposing forces that balance the realms. Other sects also thrive on Cynethol and the most widespread believe in an ever-expanding pantheon, claiming that all the anadel are gods and that godhood is achievable. They believe that Anaweh and Ramiel are the oldest and strongest of the gods. Even the holy tome of Theseryn mentions Ramiel's primacy in the creation of Teraeniel.

"In addition to our studies, we learned from some of the shrewdest and most skilled sword masters on the continent—again, I apologize for what I did last month."

"I already told you that I forgave you. Just don't do it again." Liam smiled back.

How could he smile like that? Had he truly forgiven me? "I won't. I promise." I tried to return an encouraging grin.

"Good. I might not be so kind to you the next time, and by the time Elayne finishes with us, you'll be easy prey."

"Just be happy that I'm learning to control myself. And don't think that I'll go easy on you either," I laughed back and we casually shoved each other as we walked on. "As you're also aware, our magisters taught us how to wield. Not like the magisters at Gwilnor Academy, though. All that they care for at the Imperium is power—raw, unsaturated power. Students are pushed to their limits daily. Every Cyndinari child dreamt of attending the Imperium. We had all looked forward to taking the exams, hoping to gain admittance. We had grown up with propaganda practically shoved down our throats. If we wanted to be our best selves, we had to make it into the Imperium and become shadow elves. Only then would we live forever and bring eternal glory to the empire and our emperor.

"The delusion wore off the first time we saw tenebrys wielded in front of us, during our third year. By that point, most students covet that power. Power is all we're taught to want. Kiron and I were among the few who never fit the Imperium's mold." I paused when his name came out. It was the first time I had spoken it since…

"Was Kiron special to you?" Liam asked.

"He died at the Grand Tourney with the other half of my graduating class." I stopped again. I felt my heart quicken and I expected his face to flash in my mind again but it didn't. I would give or do anything to see him again, even if it was just to hear his voice one more time. I didn't have it in me to tell Liam everything—I couldn't tell him that I was the reason

Kiron was dead. Even after all these years since that awful day, I could not admit that I was the one who had killed him.

"Oh, I'm sorry to hear that. Did I hear you correctly just then, half of your class was killed? How? And why?" Did Liam shift the conversation away from Kiron intentionally? Or was he simply shocked to learn that half of the Imperium's graduates were killed? It didn't matter and I was grateful for the transition.

"It's part of the curriculum. The surviving graduates take the souls of the defeated. All the surviving graduates became shadow elves, except me."

"That's barbaric." Liam paused and looked at me differently, as though only starting to realize the awfulness of the Erynien Empire. "You enrolled knowing that the person sitting next to you likely wouldn't survive graduation? Sorry, not just you, but your entire class." He pushed his hands through his hair, dumbfounded by the reality of the Imperium's cruelty.

"Except for Kiron, my classmates deserved to die. They would have done the same if they had been the ones to defeat their opponents. They were trained to be shadow elves after all. Not the most pleasant company."

"I guess that's fair."

Liam rubbed my back as we walked through the empty corridor, and it took some time before I realized that my face was wet from tears. I stopped and turned my head to wipe my eyes dry on my sleeve. "Sorry."

Liam had stopped when I did, and with a final pat on my back, he politely kept his eyes on the hall ahead of us. His hand had felt nice. "It's fine. I didn't think I had any more tears left after Velaria rescued me from Gneal's dungeon. I was wrong of course, and each nightmare brought with it a new stream of tears." Liam turned to smile reassuringly at me.

The last sounds from anyone but us were four intersecting corridors away. We were alone. Liam must have noted it too, for he started walking again.

As he did, I grabbed his hand. Lightning shot up my arm and laced through the rest of my body as his fingers tightened around my own.

I could no longer think. Rationality seemed like a luxury I had long ago forfeited. I pulled Liam closer and his lips touched my own. He didn't flinch—he didn't back away. He just stayed there, his soft lips against mine, his arm wrapping around my lower back.

I blinked as he pulled away, surprised at the length of the kiss. We had kissed longer than I had expected he would allow. Was he really that comfortable with kissing me?

Chapter Fourteen

After that unexpected kiss during our first patrol, the tension between us had become unbearable. I always felt guilty for kissing someone other than Kiron. This time was different though—I had enjoyed it. It was the first time that I had felt an inner spark of intimacy. I had presumed that all of those sentiments had shriveled up and died. Liam had taken it differently though; he didn't seem to know how to internalize it. We had both admitted our attraction to men months ago, but Liam seemed to have difficulty moving past not only finding men attractive, but acting on his attraction.

We hadn't really talked about our unplanned kiss. I had asked him how what we had done was any different from what he had done when he was younger. Liam had been quick to answer—it wasn't the same. He hadn't felt any meaningful connections just from touching when he was younger. They certainly had never kissed. And then he'd refused to discuss it further. But Liam's statement puzzled me. What had he felt when we kissed? Was it a confession of his feelings for me or was it something worse? Was it confirmation that he didn't want anything to do with me?

And with the amount of time that we had to spend training with Renaud and Stephen, as well as being bunk mates and even eating together, they had to have noticed how awkward we were around each other. Neither of them mentioned the strained atmosphere between the two of us, and probably assumed we'd had a lover's quarrel. Stephen had more than insinuated that he had already assumed that we were more than friends when I had first moved into the shared room. I still didn't understand how he had made that leap in judgement. What exactly had Bastien told them before I moved in?

To ease the strained atmosphere, I began a conversation about morning drills over our lunch in the mess hall when really, I wanted to pull Liam aside and rip answers from him. We ate our steamed vegetables and grains in an odd silence, interspersed with infrequent conversation, while the rest of the mess hall echoed with the voices of rambunctious young men, energized from the morning drills and refreshed from their baths. After my stunt with the sword, the other recruits kept me at an even greater distance than they previously had. I wasn't just a Cyndinari, I was also a freak because of my outburst. To them, it was worse than seeing a kien wielder lose control of the erendinth. There was no magical ward that could stop me from using a sword in the temple. For all they knew, the same thing could happen again, and instead of Liam, they could be the ones on the receiving end of a crazed Cyndinari's wooden practice sword.

My plate had been empty for some time when a teenager

approached our table from behind Liam. I didn't recognize the newcomer, but like many of the human men in the temple, he had the blond hair and blue eyes of Thellish ancestry. Those features were now largely confined to northern Eklean, and I had seen nothing but while living in Gneal.

"So, this is where you've been hiding all this time."

Liam turned with a broad grin, standing to enthusiastically hug the newcomer. "What in the Light's name are you doing here?"

I shared a questioning look with Renaud and Stephen.

"Last I checked, we were still cousins, despite what our uncles say."

Noticing the now-curious expressions at the table, Liam said, "This is my cousin, Alex Vaerin. And this is Renaud, Stephen, and Jaerol, my um, bunkmates."

Alex must have caught the hesitancy in his voice as he identified us, for he raised a questioning brow, but clearly didn't want to ask for more details. "Right, nice to meet you," he said and squeezed himself next to Liam on the bench. "Now, when were you going to mention you were restricted to the temple? I swear, no one tells me anything. Oh, it's just Alex—don't bother telling him that his one cousin left in Ceurenyl is now restricted to the temple, while the other is off in the Illumined Wood, just a little elf-boy, skipping through the forest."

I joined the others in bursting into laughter, and then was shocked to realize that my laughter was unforced, and had come readily. There was something curious about Alex—he easily sliced through the tension so efficiently that I could barely recall that I was still upset with Liam's behavior toward me.

"Did you know that it took me a month before I was able

to track down Velaria and get her to spill the beans? I get that she's this all-important Chair now, but the least she could have done was send a page to tell me."

"Sorry, I didn't think of sending a note either. Life has been hectic recently."

"You knew?"

"Yeah, Jaerol and I were with Devlyn when he made his decision to become an ei'ceuril. Never imagined that the Ceurtriarch would have a dragon waiting by to take him away from the city while it was under attack," Liam confessed.

"Yeah, I saw that other one from my dormitory window. It was massive and looked like it could swallow Yelaris whole."

"Ythinor," I supplied. Memories rippled at saying the name. "That monster would darken the brightest days in Broid and blot out the sun whenever he needed to stretch his wings. Erynor is rather fond of that beast and has referred to it as his brother. Rumor has it that it's the dragon that consumed all the Phaedryn—the phoenix in a constant state of death and rebirth in the dragon's belly."

"Must be some painful indigestion," said Alex, practically dismissing the veracity of it.

"Can't imagine it'd be worse than the heartburn I get after Jaerol adds his secret stash of spices to our meals," said Stephen, who had declined my spice pouch today.

"It's not my fault that the dishes in Cyril didn't prepare you to actually taste your food."

"I couldn't taste my next two meals after adding that one spice to my stew."

Admittedly, I had mixed up my herbs that night. Stephen's taste buds wouldn't have been the only thing on fire.

Alex looked at the four of us in turn and then asked, "So, any news of Devlyn and when he'll be back? The clearest answer I've gotten out of Therril was 'no less than a year and a day,'" he tried to mimic the older elf's voice but wasn't entirely successful.

"I've been told the same, also by Therril," Liam said.

"I found out that Devlyn's little girlfriend has also gone off to start her novitiate with the ei'ana. Apparently, the ei'ana and ei'ceuril novitiates are essentially the same," Alex said.

"The Lucillian princess?" Liam asked.

"Ellendren of the Royal House Roendryn, crowned princess and heir to the Lucillian throne," Alex mocked. "Nobility all act the same, don't they? Glad I don't have to interact with them more regularly."

"We're not all that bad, Alex *Vaerin*," Renaud said, with a stress on Alex's family name. Whatever the intent, Alex didn't even notice it, more intent on eyeing the food on the table. "Granted, whatever claim I had to the Sorenth throne is superseded by my ability to wield, making me unfit to rule, let alone leave the temple."

"Where were you in line for the throne?" I asked, disconcerted by this information.

"Honestly, pretty close. My father, Duke Marcel of House Lariviere, was the late King Dorian's youngest brother. Other than my father, few of the royal siblings had had many children, putting me at sixth in line for the throne."

"Hold on, you're a prince? And you never mentioned it?" Stephen asked.

"Titles don't really get you anything here in the temple," Renaud answered.

"The same is supposed to be true at Gwilnor, but I'd rather bargain on the existence of giants wanting to sit down for a cup of tea. They all get preferential treatment there," Alex said. "So, back up, this year long novitiate thing..."

"Year and a day," Liam interrupted.

"Right...and a day. They're completely alone during the entire time? So even if they wanted to meet up, Devlyn and Ellendren that is, and you know...get to know each other better, they can't?" Alex's eyes went round.

"I can't speak for Devlyn but Princess Ellendren never gave me the impression that she was interested in moving quickly in any sort of intimate relationship," Renaud said, understanding Alex's meaning.

"Princess aside, Devlyn's with the ei'ceuril now, he can't be doing what you're suggesting. Besides aren't they both rather young for that?" Liam clearly didn't enjoy others talking about whether or not his younger brother was sexually active.

"Pretty sure they are both in working order," Alex quipped then rolled his eyes. "And I get that Dev went off and joined this pompously pious group of old crusty men but you don't honestly think that he'll last long, do you? Anyone who sees the way he looks at Ellendren knows there's only one thing on his mind. And it doesn't involve getting old and wrinkly, surrounded by a bunch of other old and wrinkly men."

"Even if they wanted to find each other, I doubt they'd be able to. That forest's size isn't the only thing that makes it daunting," I said.

"Never found size to be daunting before," Alex chided, getting a quick laugh from Renaud and Stephen.

"I'm sure," I ignored the reference even though I likely

would have found it funny if Liam wasn't currently acting like a prude. "There's something magical about that place. My people are terrified of it. Granted, that's because it almost burned Erynor to a crisp and brought an end to his previous imperial reign."

"A shame it couldn't have done the job more permanently," Liam said.

"If it's so scary, why do they send a bunch of teenagers there? By themselves? Can't imagine what wandering alone in some ancient forest would accomplish." Alex seemed to have something else on his mind, his head turning frequently, sizing up the other recruits in the mess hall.

"I believe it has a lot to do with being isolated with yourself," said Renaud, careful to avoid saying anything too specific that would only have come from their training with Elayne over the past month. Temple knights weren't known for understanding the interior life. "Myranda told me of her time there."

"Sounds idyllic." Alex rolled his eyes. I had only just met him, but the thought of him strolling in solitude for a year through a forest was quite funny.

"I've never been an outdoors type, but I'd take it if it meant I could walk outside on a regular basis," Stephen said, looking longingly toward the wall where there should be a window.

"Makes becoming an ei'ceuril almost appealing," Liam said, giving me a funny look as he said it.

"But how do they reconcile sending kien wielders to the forest? Ei'ceuril or not, aren't they just as dangerous there as they are anywhere else outside the temple?" Stephen said.

"Who knows?" Alex was still scanning the mess hall, clearly growing bored with talk of wielders. "They probably don't care. Even if they do lose control of their wielding, what harm could they possibly do to a bunch of trees? Nothing but birds and squirrels in those branches."

"We'll have to ask Devlyn when he gets back." Liam shrugged.

"A shame he won't be moving back into the castle. Even if he did manage to avoid nearly every training session with the knights, it was nice having him around," Alex said.

"How is everything at Gwilnor? Intriguing rumors have been reaching the temple about them starting to let kien wielders study there again," Liam said.

"It's all anyone in the castle is talking about now. I think Velaria is leading that discussion, but there's more discord about it than common ground."

"How so?" I asked, curious whether the ei'ana had finally learned how to teach kien wielders control. A fleeting hope for learning how to control my wielding and live outside of the temple overcame me. From the way that Elayne spoke, Balance was far from returning. And from the little information that Yloran had offered me years ago, the only way for it to return was if both kien and kiara wielders reached their potential. And the only way for that to happen was if one wielder who had reached his or her potential taught the other. Conveniently, that wasn't likely to happen anytime soon. Erynor encouraged the imbalance, and Yloran implied that any Cyndinari who had reached his or her potential would have to answer to Erynor, ending any discussion of her training Kiron and me in anything but umbrys.

"Well, to be blunt, the Arantiulyns haven't forgotten that those two shadow elves killed their Chair."

Liam, Renaud, and Stephen all turned on me. "What? It's not like I could have done anything to stop Xanth. I'm still surprised that Velaria and Devlyn were strong enough to stop him."

"You're the other shadow elf?" Alex practically fell backward over the bench.

"I was never…" I started.

"…a shadow elf," mocked my three bunk mates together. "But I was an Erynien emissary. I'm innocent. I just wanted to stay alive and fooled them all into thinking that I was a shadow elf."

Fury shot down my spine. It must have shown, for Liam offered an apologetic look while Renaud and Stephen laughed.

"And you're all okay with this?" Alex asked, repositioning himself on the bench and keeping his eyes locked on me as though I would turn into a monster if he turned away.

"Well, it's not like the cells of justice were capable of holding him. Apparently, he has nothing to be guilty about. Otherwise, he wouldn't have been able to walk straight through the barrier," Liam said.

Alex glared at me. "Iron bars aren't good enough for the ei'ceuril, I take it?"

"Proving my innocence on facts alone would have been rather difficult."

"I can't say that I trust some magical jail cell to be a good replacement for a judge. Don't expect me to turn my back to you."

"That's fine. Now back to Gwilnor. Have the ei'ana

made any progress in instructing kien wielders? Have any of the kiara wielders actually reached their potential?" I asked, uninterested in proving my innocence to yet another person.

"I have no idea what you're talking about. The only gossip that reaches the male dormitories and the Septyl knights is about the arguments between ei'ana, the different Schools, and student wielders all seeming to know better than the other. Now that Devlyn's gone, none of us in the male dormitories are kien wielders, so we rarely pass on anything that a kien wielder would care about. It doesn't affect us, so none of us care. And even when he did live with us, few of us welcomed his, um…condition. I get that he's not going to destroy the city, but it's not something I'm exactly comfortable with either, and we're cousins. Imagine how the rest of the boys' dormitory talks. I guess the castle would get more crowded if kien wielders started to show up. They'd probably have to open up that unused southern wing of the castle again."

I frowned at the news. I had had a brief glimpse into the inner workings of the Ei'ana of Septyl when I had been cross examined by the Seven Chairs and wise ones. Their intent, other than the Arantiulyn wise ones, wasn't to determine my guilt, but to learn as much about the Erynien Empire's plans as they could. I had been little help. Some of the ei'ana accepted that a young emissary would not be privy to Erynor's plots. However, the others wasted just as much time arguing with the other ei'ana as questioning me. I couldn't believe that the ei'ana leadership was so dysfunctional. If left to their own devices, the only kien wielders who would walk Gwilnor's halls would be shadow elves after they returned to take the city, and seized the castle from the Ei'ana of Septyl.

Chapter Fifteen

The summons had come early, well before morning drills. I had no idea whether I was being summoned as a temple knight—only a recruit really—or as a Cyndinari and former Erynien emissary. The young boy who had brought the summons couldn't clarify why I was being summoned or who was summoning me. All that I knew was that it was a wise one. As I tried to decide what I should wear, I thought back on the past week, searching for something to explain why an ei'ceuril wise one would want to speak with me. Other than properly learning jienzu from Elayne, I couldn't think of anything else. And if the ei'ceuril had discovered that a Guardian knight was living in their cellars, I had no idea why they would want to speak to me about it. The existence and survival of one of the Guardians was sure to be a reason for celebration. If one survived, could there be more?

I abandoned the thought and decided on a silken green shirt, loosely tied at the chest. I might as well be comfortable if some ei'ceuril wise one wanted answers from me. Besides, I was tired of wearing the knights' standard issue tunic. Not only did the fabric not breathe well, but it was a hideous garment.

The boy who had come to my room had also brought me here, after waiting patiently for me to decide what to wear. As we approached the wise one's office, I could hear an argument of some sort spilling through the closed door.

The boy looked uncomfortably toward the door, then threw me an apologetic glance. Waiting for a pause in the argument, he rapped so lightly on the door that I was sure no one inside would hear that nearly inaudible knock.

The confrontation did not resume, and I started when the door opened, revealing two ei'ceuril. I recognized Dorien immediately, oozing privilege and self-worth as always, but not the other who was likely also a wise one given his equal discharge of entitled condescension. I noticed the grand chairs they occupied on either side of a small table and briefly wondered which of the two outranked the other. The ei'ceuril seemed to worship their imposed hierarchy and status more than they did Anaweh. At times, it was difficult to distinguish between them and servants of Shadow.

"You may leave us, Donald, and thank you for retrieving him for us," said the younger of the two ei'ceuril. "Please, come in Jaerol. I'm Steward Josthiel, and I understand that you've already met Dorien."

I entered the impressive office. It made Bastien's look like a broom closet.

"Pleased to meet you." I tried not to scowl at Dorien as I sat on a hard chair set across from them. I still couldn't believe that an ei'ceuril wouldn't believe that shadow elves were a threat. His willful ignorance had left me wanting to scream at him the last time I saw him, ruining any chances of Liam and me having a tutor.

"Oh, we've already met. Well, you were unconscious at the time—when that blue dragon of Mother Velaria's brought you and that other shadow elf here to the temple," Josthiel said.

"I was never a shadow elf." Even as I said it, I could hear my bunk mates mocking my automatic reply.

"Of course," Dorien supplied, shooting an irritated glance at his brother ei'ceuril. "I hope our summons came at a good time. Bastien says that your training with the knights is going well, although there was also mention of some uncontrolled rage. Is that true?"

"It is. And I've been meditating more often to control my anger better." It didn't seem that they knew about Elayne, and I had no intention of telling them. Especially given Dorien's belief that shadow elves did not steal the souls of their victims. I knew these men had been cooped up in the temple almost their entire lives, but that sort of ignorance was hard to forgive.

"Hmm, that's good," said Josthiel, uninterestedly. "Now tell me, why would you join the temple knights? Neither Dorien or I can seem to riddle it out. You were an Erynien emissary and studied at the Imperium. Surely, the life of a simple knight is beneath you."

"I wasn't exactly given many options here, was I? I had grown incredibly bored and the temple's library is rather chaotic and unhelpful."

"I'm afraid it's always been that way and no one has ever had the drive to organize the various rooms. To say nothing of the retribution we would receive from notable families across the continent whose ancestors donated the funds for those individual rooms." Dorien seemed bored himself, indifferent about the state of the library.

"We care less about the library and your boredom," Josthiel said, gaining another irritated glance from Dorien. Clearly, Dorien outranked the younger ei'ceuril, but that didn't stop Josthiel from speaking his mind. "Do tell us, why would you join the temple knights?"

"I just told you, I was bored."

"I'm sure you'd make a very capable knight, but *you* are a wielder," Dorien said, as though that obvious fact should influence my decisions.

"What difference does that make? It's not like we can wield here in the temple."

"Certainly not, but times are changing. I happened to be one of Devlyn's tutors during his short stint at Gwilnor. Naturally, as an untrained kien wielder, I was never permitted to leave the temple so he had to come to me for our private lessons. I was never able to see with my own eyes what that boy was capable of, but he seemed qualified enough." Dorien turned toward the window. "But I digress. Josthiel and I invited you here because we believe you are making a mistake in becoming a temple knight."

"You think I should become an ei'ceuril?" My effort to hold in my derisive snort was heroic. I had been assuming that I would be reprimanded for my actions against Liam. He had healed quite well thanks to Lillianna, but still, I had been expecting someone to discipline me for it. But being encouraged by two wise ones to join the ei'ceuril was the last thing I would have anticipated. In fact, it hadn't ever crossed my mind.

"Surely you can understand and respect the benefits of doing so. The temple knights serve their purpose well, but their renown caps at a certain position. If you desire to have any power in the temple, you've chosen the wrong path. And don't pretend that that doesn't interest you, Jaerol. Josthiel and I are quite capable of recognizing those with ambitions similar to ours."

"With us as allies, you'll easily rise through the ei'ceuril hierarchy." Josthiel extended his hand as an invitation to form an alliance.

I looked between the two wise ones skeptically. I didn't know anything about Josthiel, but Dorien had no reason to like me. In fact, he had every reason to despise me. While I had never called him an idiot in public, I did still call him that in private, and that opinion had not changed.

"Why the sudden interest in having me become an ei'ceuril?"

"Times are changing. The ei'ana are actively seeking means in which they can safely train kien wielders. If we can safely learn how to wield while outside of the temple, we'll be able to return to our cathedrals. They won't stand empty much longer, attended by low-ranking stewards with no pretensions to greater service. You are one of the few kien wielders in the temple who has intentionally wielded," Dorien had perked up from his previous boredom and now was leaning on the edge of his seat.

"What does that matter? If the ei'ana manage to successfully bring Balance back, I won't be the only kien wielder who wields outside of the temple. But even though I have wielded,

I'm just as likely to lose control of the erendinth as the next kien wielder is now."

"That might be so, but your past training has undoubtedly given you the upper hand. If you join the ei'ceuril, you will be one of the first to return to the world. You'll have your pick of any metropolis in Eklean. You'll be among the most senior members of the order, mingling with the aristocracy of wherever you choose to go to."

"Honestly, it also helps that you already have experience as an emissary," Josthiel said, looking less than enthusiastic about the talk of wielding. "You're the perfect candidate."

"I'd hardly consider my time as an Erynien emissary as beneficial."

"I disagree in that matter." Josthiel shifted, appearing sure of himself again. "Your familiarity with the Erynien Empire will be invaluable. As ei'ceuril, we must knit the nations back together to live in peace. Despite Erynor's flaws, he commands a strong presence in Eklean. His leadership can shape the world for the better."

I couldn't believe what I was hearing. This supposed wise one was encouraging cooperation with Erynor, and worse, it sounded like he expected the other kingdoms to willfully submit to the Erynien Empire.

"Strong leadership is the only thing that will bring peace back to Eklean and the larger world." Dorien smiled at me.

"Do you even know who he is? What he's capable of?"

"Difficult choices must be made by every leader," Dorien returned.

"He murdered nearly every female steward when he last reigned! He wanted to use their abbey schools to shape the next generation, brainwashing every child across Eklean. He orchestrated the Ceurendol War, brought about the Shroud severing the Luminari from their immortality, and every other anacordel who was to benefit from the Jewel of Life." I started to shake, enraged at these two ei'ceuril for their infuriating ignorance. I couldn't even mention that anyone loyal to the Erynien Empire was more likely to immediately kill me rather than engage in diplomacy.

"Yes, I've heard those stories as well. None of which are verified historical accounts. The best record we have of that elven war is from the diaries of one of our own. Oh, what's his name, Josthiel?"

"Benedetto?" he laughed in response. "Hardly a credible source. He didn't write a single authoritative text, only his private musings in his journals."

I put the name to memory, repeating it in my head, knowing I would have to look into these musings. These journals already seemed more credible than these buffoons. These two were pushing me past my limit. Granted, that limit had already been breached, and if it hadn't been for my time spent with Elayne, I likely would have snapped. I simply could not believe that there were ei'ceuril who believed that Erynor was a reasonable leader. I shuddered at the thought of him reclaiming his vast empire. I knew he had his sights on all Eklean and looked beyond this continent to the rest of Teraeniel. He likely already had members of his court in the other continents, either sowing unrest or already in positions of authority.

"And what about the war brewing across Eklean? What's to become of the people and kingdoms who oppose Erynor?" I asked.

"The stubborn northern monarchs, all descended from Thellion, will keep us in the dark ages, stagnant in their squabbles as they romanticize about a past that can never be reclaimed. Their refusal to corporate will only prolong this war," Josthiel said. "History only remembers the Kingdom of Thellion because it conquered the entire continent east of Dwota's Gap. And as for the Lucillian Alliance—it won't last the year at its current trajectory. I still can't believe that they closed themselves off in their city like cowards. Those elves have made their choice. They won't have a single ally left when they come out of their city again."

"History and politics aside, what is your decision on our proposal? With us as allies, you'll advance quickly through the order's hierarchy," Dorien said.

I paused, considering how to respond and thought of how Elayne would handle this situation. My pre-Elayne self wanted to let my temper fly, but the other more rational self didn't want to make enemies inside the temple. Especially since Josthiel and Dorien could make my life here extremely difficult.

"When you asked me to join the ei'ceuril," I said at last, "I found the idea laughable. No one has ever considered me a pious individual. But after talking with you two, serving Anaweh clearly isn't a priority to the ei'ceuril. You'll hand the faithful over to Ramiel in a handbasket to better serve yourselves."

"You fool," Josthiel shrieked. "This needless war will kill tens of thousands, perhaps hundreds of thousands. Who do you think is the true servant of Anaweh? The one trying to maintain peace, or the one rushing into a battle like a child? Eklean will burn under our current leadership. Ealyndol and the other like-minded Luminari will divide our continent down the middle, as the war between Luminari and Cyndinari is resumed. Enough humans have died at the hands of your elven wars." He was ranting now, and I stood to leave.

"You are both slaves to Ramiel. Goodbye." I turned away as Josthiel continued his rant, now spouting racial and homophobic slurs as I closed the door behind me. I could still hear him yelling on the opposite side of the door, and Dorien's voice as he attempted to quiet Josthiel but the calmer atmosphere in the corridor was welcoming.

I made my way back to the lower levels. I had had enough dealings with ei'ceuril and wise ones for one day. I could probably go another year without speaking to another one and be fine with that. There *were* decent ei'ceuril. I knew that, but after Dorien and Josthiel, I couldn't stand to make eye contact with one more just now.

Chapter Sixteen

I had all but isolated myself in the temple's library, which considering the temple's enormity, was shockingly modest. I had heard that Gwilnor's library was an incredible space, with all the books housed together, row after row of rare tomes lining the grand space, each shelf belonging to a distinct category in the broader library. The thought of perusing those books was overwhelmingly appealing.

Unfortunately, I was stuck in the temple and its library had a series of unconnected rooms, organized in such a manner that only the librarians understood it, and only after decades of attending to them. Each room offered only one desk, although some of the larger rooms had two or three, but none of the rooms seemed connected to a unified system. The segmented collections appeared to be individual private libraries donated by various patrons, and which the librarians had then shelved in their own areas as the books had come to the temple, rather than add the newly donated books to the current library according to subject matter. Each room offered a plethora of subjects that overlapped with subjects found in other rooms.

What I really wanted was a concise and accurate history. The Imperium had taught a skewed version of historical events, especially over the past fifteen hundred years. I had only just learned that the Ceurendol War had not started because a Luminari aryl had spat on Emperor Erynor, insisting all the while that the Cyndinari must submit to their authority. Further, the Lorenthien aryl might have become High King and High Queen of Eklean, but that suzerainty had been in name only. They had apparently only exercised their full authority once, and that was to abolish slavery, free the minums, and reallocate land to them for self-governance.

This was all news to me as I poured through the pages of a diary from a long-dead human ei'ceuril. Brother Benedetto had been born in Lankor, a country that was now a stark supporter of the Erynien Empire. He wrote adoringly of the Lorenthiens in Arenthyl, a city he dubbed as the heart of the world. The Imperium-approved version of history as taught to me was that the Yanileans had always deplored their Luminari dictators and after Nauto's Wrath had destroyed Lankor, they had earnestly entrusted their nation to the Erynien Empire.

Benedetto had been living here at the Temple of Ceur during Nauto's Wrath and wrote harshly of how his compatriots and the Yanilean, that country's leader, had responded. He had written, several times, *where are the Judges?* I had no idea how or why he thought that a judicial system could sway the Yanileans away from the Erynien Empire. If they were anything like those on Cynethol, they'd just as likely whip someone for saying anything favorable about a Luminari elf. Benedetto also claimed that Ramiel, the Evil One, had seduced his country from the Light, and those responsible had brought damnation on them all. While no one would ever confuse me for the religious type, it was refreshing to see someone write piously, especially after the meeting I'd had with Dorien and Josthiel.

I had not finished poring through a quarter of the diaries available in the room, but the prolific journalist had apparently filled hundreds of leather-bound notebooks and, according to one of the temple librarians, a fifth of the total number of diaries had been lost to the ages. Benedetto had lived long and had marveled at his increasing age at the beginning of every new diary. He wrote that if he had not become an ei'ceuril and had instead married and had had a family of his own, he would have so many greats in front of grandfather that he would have gotten winded by the time he finished listing them all. That was the benefit of Ceurendol, the Jewel of Life, the Life immortal of the elves shared with all. An unexpected side effect had been the change in his body, as if the hands of time had worked backward to bring his youth and vitality back at the age of fifty-three. Benedetto's parents had been dead twelve years by the time they'd reached that age, neither living past forty-one.

But after Krysenthiel had fallen and the Shroud poisoned the air, solidifying with every passing year, Benedetto had started to age. The latest diary I could find was dated in 7606.3E, forty-three years after the Fall of Krysenthiel. Ceurenyl was still secure, but Benedetto grumbled about not being able to wield in the city.

I pulled another diary from the shelf. In this one, Benedetto commented on his visit to Quellion, the crowned city of Gestoria. Thumbing through the pages, I soaked in the information. I had never heard of the Gestorians before. The Imperium's magisters didn't even bother to weave their own fabrication of the kingdom. Benedetto wrote of his awe of the Gestorian capital; limestone and marble spires pierced the clouds and gemstones glistened on every wall. The similarities between Quellion and the original city of Lankor, destroyed by Nauto's Wrath, were unmistakable and given that Quellion predated Thellion, it was clear that the city had served as a beacon for southern Eklean.

Turning the page, I read Benedetto's praise for the Great Library of Quellion. It wasn't like the elven library at Septyl, but according to his words, it was the height of human achievement at the time. He also wrote of the inadequacies of the temple's library. Just as I began to daydream of an organized collection again, the door opened. Ever on edge, especially with my back to the door, I looked over my shoulder and was shocked to find Liam entering. Was he now looking for me? I had thought he had been avoiding being alone with me.

"Not hungry for dinner tonight?" he asked.

"It's not time for dinner yet, is it?"

"Even in a room with a window, you've lost track of time." He smirked. Was that supposed to be a peace offering?

I looked to the meager window and saw that the sun had indeed set. The mess hall would have been swept clean by now, the leftovers taken to the homeless and the refugees waiting outside the temple doors. "I didn't even notice the time pass."

Liam took notice of the stack of books on the table, others sprawled open in front of me. "What's all this?"

"Benedetto's diaries."

"Who's Benedetto?"

"One of the few reliable sources I feel I can trust. An ei'ceuril from Lankor, writing during the Ceurendol War. To say that his version of history is different from what I had been taught is quite the understatement."

"Did you think Erynor was the good guy all this time?"

"Don't be ridiculous—that part was obvious. Anyone who teaches children how to wield tenebrys is a monster." I paused, my recent interaction with Dorien and Josthiel still fresh. I had told Liam and my other two bunk mates about it and none of them could believe it. Both ei'ceuril were clearly from southern Eklean, but they had never mentioned which country they had been born in. But for Renaud and Stephen, both from northern kingdoms that were currently under siege by the Erynien Empire, they found the two wise ones' position outright offensive. Liam was still puzzled by their thinking that shadow elves were not necessarily evil, just a failed experiment gone wrong, costing them their youth and beauty.

"Aside from how horrendous the Erynien Empire is, did you find anything else interesting?"

"Quite a bit actually. Have you ever heard of Gestoria?"

"The kingdom that the Erynien Empire wiped off the map? I hear there's nothing but ruins there now. Every city was said to have been razed and their fields salted."

"This is common knowledge here?"

"I would assume so. The Gestorians were part of Thellion, but their monarchy maintained their titles and rights, the only kingdom to do so at the time from what I remember. Legend also says they're the children of dragons."

"The children of dragons?"

"Most likely a fairy tale. Why the sudden interest in Gestoria?" Liam arched an eyebrow, now standing close to me.

"It's nothing, I'm just surprised that I've never heard of it before."

"Well, you did grow up in the Kinzdol Islands."

"Cynethol is very different from the other islands."

"Yeah, the goblins aren't the ones trying to kill us all." Liam leaned on the edge of the desk.

"That's because you aren't in debt to their guild." While I was genuinely interested in getting a better grasp on history, I had mainly come to the library as a distraction. My meeting with Dorien and Josthiel worsened my already awful mood, a disposition due entirely to Liam. I was beyond frustrated with him avoiding me because we had kissed. Last night, he again refused to admit that there was anything off between us. And as much as he tried to deny it to himself and to me, he had enjoyed that kiss as much as I had. After I had brought up him being distant last night, and getting wry looks from Renaud and Stephen, I had almost pushed the issue—audience or not. If they had not been in our shared room, I probably would have punched Liam square in his pretty face.

"Have you thought about what I said last night?" I asked, uneasy with Liam's relaxed demeanor. Perhaps he had come to find me to talk about it—about how he had been treating me since that first patrol.

"Depends. Have you?"

"The only thing I've been unsettled about is this distance that you're intent on keeping between us."

"Distance? We see each other all the time." Liam avoided looking at me, suddenly interested in one of Benedetto's diaries open on the desk.

"You know what I mean. Ever since that first patrol together—ever since we kissed—you've created this needless barrier between us." I unintentionally lowered my voice to a near whisper when I said kissed, as though it was something naughty that I didn't want overheard.

"I'm not trying to force a wall between us. I really did enjoy patrolling together. I can't pretend that I didn't, at least, not anymore. It's just hard to reconcile everything."

"What's so difficult about us kissing?" I asked, pressing the point. I heard the confidence rise in my own voice and I no longer tried to whisper.

"It's not just that—not that I appreciate the increased gossip behind my back. How do they all know anyway?" Liam grunted before spinning around and walking to the small window. "It's just, a year ago I was a prisoner at Gneal, and you—while I know you were just trying to stay alive—were an Erynien emissary. You were a guest of honor of the Perrien Council. I'm not trying to bring that up again, but it's hard to move past it, Jaerol. My da was killed by his own brother in cold blood and my stepmother's family in Cor'lera was rounded up and dragged to Gneal's prisons. With the exception of her two young children, all Evellyn's family was murdered, their souls fodder for the shadow elves that passed through trying to get information out of them. I'm the only one who survived that incarceration. Nightmares keep me awake at night. I can still hear them screaming. And I know you have them too. Jaerol, I hear you wake up, gasping as if you couldn't breathe a moment before—petrified."

I didn't know what to say. Liam wasn't accusing me, but he had experienced traumatic events. No one should have to go through what he had gone through. He didn't deserve that. If I could go back in time, I would liberate Liam and the rest of his family the moment I arrived in Gneal and learned of them in the dungeons.

My heart pinged, again.

Why was that increasingly happening around Liam? The more it happened, the more I felt a need to tell him about Kiron, and what we had been to each other. I took a deep breath.

"Kiron meant everything to me, and I to him." I couldn't find the words to transition to Kiron, but just started talking about him. I spoke of how we had met as children, studied together, passed the exams, lounged on Cynethol's beaches, swum with the dolphins in the Erynien Bay. How we had grown up on the same street and eventually attended the Imperium together. "I was only a child when others started to whisper behind my back. I was too young to understand what they were talking about, but I understood the laughter." I stopped then, not sure about what more I could say, especially as Liam was facing away, still looking out the window into the dark. Finally, he turned to face me.

"During our patrol, you said that he died at the Grand Tourney, right?"

"Yes." I felt another wash of tears brimming. I didn't want to think of Kiron anymore and I certainly didn't want to talk about him. It was torture enough that I couldn't remember the sound of his voice but now even his face eluded me. I knew that I shouldn't but I sealed myself off from my emotions.

It went against everything that Elayne was teaching us with jienzu but I couldn't deal with it right now. My tears would dry and my vulnerability would soon be hidden behind a wall of ice again.

"I am sorry about Kiron. He must have been a great person to have caught your eye. I'm sorry that he's not around anymore."

"You don't have anything to be sorry about. You weren't there. Besides, I'm sure it was more difficult growing up in a small village."

"It wasn't all that bad. Even if anyone assumed, they wouldn't say it aloud. Like you said, it's a small village, and villagers could be just as unforgiving toward the one who started the rumors." He paused, then added, "I'll be honest with you, Jaerol, if you are with me. Deal?"

"Deal."

There was another pause, and despite the apparent surge of courage that had arisen in Liam, he now faltered. And just as it looked like he was about to turn away again, he rushed on, "I've never felt this way before. I never had a Kiron in my life who meant the world to me. I never felt that burning desire in my chest to move mountains for the sake of another person." He paused, obviously uneasy about opening himself up to me as he rubbed his arm nervously. "You're right. I have been distant and yes, I've been doing everything I can to deny it. Because frankly, it's easier to deny my attraction to you than to deny what's going on inside me. It's much easier to pretend that it simply isn't there. And as much as I want to act on these emotions, this sort of thing isn't necessarily accepted here. Ei'ceuril constantly preach against two men or two women falling in love with each other. Not all of them, but enough to make me squirm under their judgemental gaze."

I stood to meet his eyes on the same level, and grabbed Liam's hand before he managed to turn away from me. The first hints of tears showed there. His vulnerability shook me to the core. The only person I had ever been that open with was Kiron.

"I'm really bad at making plans for the future. Whenever I do, they explode in my face." I squeezed his hand, attempting to convey some sense of reassurance. I knew that it was possible for us to potentially have a life together; Bastien and Daphnel were proof enough of that. "My emotions are equally knotted, possibly more. I don't know what I'm feeling for you, but you're doing things to me. It's as though you're taking a very physical chisel to the frozen pieces of my heart and chipping off the ice. For the first time in a long time, Liam, I'm starting to feel again. Light, it hurts!" Tears swelled in my eyes as Kiron's face formed in my mind. The image was clear and I could see him so well.

I wanted to push Liam away now; I wanted to turn away and hide my tears. I wanted to crawl inside myself and hold Kiron's face once more. Instead, Liam pulled me against him and wrapped his arms around me, hugging me tightly. I cried into his shoulder as he rubbed my back. Another ping sounded in my heart.

Chapter Seventeen

Meridenth was halfway over, and while I had long adjusted to not visiting a beach during the summer months, I could not reconcile being forced to stay indoors all the time. I missed the beaches on Cynethol where miles of crisp sand circled the entire island as rolling waves lapped against the shore.

My mind lingered on Cynethol's beaches and the times Kiron and I had snuck away from the Imperium on the weekends to relax by the water. The sun had warmed our bronze skin nearly every weekend when we were young. An even tan covered our entire bodies, gaining us questioning glares from our magisters. If our suspiciously darker skin didn't give us away, our sandy feet most certainly did. No matter how much we tried, there would always be grains of sand caught in some crevice. None of the magisters cared what we did with our weekends and time off, but the expectation was that we were locked away in our rooms or the library studying into the early hours of the morning. Only a small number of students did that, and, oddly, the magisters liked them the least.

Thinking of the beaches and my time with Kiron there, I hadn't noticed that there was a significant amount of swelling beneath my blanket. My eyes popped open as my hand grazed my groin, and I suddenly wished that my other bunk mates would make themselves disappear. All four of us were lying in our separate beds, exhausted from the morning's drills. I rolled onto my side, trying to make the tent in my blankets less noticeable in case anyone looked over. The room was bright enough that if anyone had looked, they would've easily seen the state I was in.

My mind continued to wander. Today was Meridephaen and now that I wasn't under constant watch from other Cyndinari, I considered allowing it to pass by without uttering a single prayer. My people's high feast day occurred on the summer solstice, celebrating Meridiel, our supposed guardian andel, the enthiel dedicated to the Cyndinari elves.

I knew all the chants and prayers by heart. Cyndinari children were indoctrinated at an early age and were expected to know how to properly praise Meridiel before they started school. Half the time, I didn't know whether we were supposed to praise Meridiel or Erynor. At one point as a child, I had believed that Meridiel and Erynor were the same person. My parents had laughed at that. I couldn't tell if they had found my thought funny or thought me foolish for believing in a spiritual entity. No one in Broid was a stout believer in Anaweh anymore, if ever. Instead, they seemed to place their trust in the emperor. My parents might not have been included among that number, but many others did believe in the anadel. Some called the anadel gods, and others claimed that godhood was achievable—Erynor and the other Sha'ghol were chief among that number.

I tried to not get upset about what my people believed in. Everything I had learned about the Cyndinari since coming to the Temple of Ceur was anything but flattering, especially in relation to Meridiel. It seemed that he was either blissfully ignorant of the atrocities committed by the Cyndinari or a willful participant in them and aligned to Ramiel. From what I had learned about the other enthiel, especially when the elves still dwelled on the Skylands, those anadel lived among the elves and frequently interacted with them. Doubting Meridiel's involvement in what had happened to the Cyndinari was becoming impossible. Celebrating his feast was going to be a challenge today.

What type of an enthiel allows his people to do what the Cyndinari had done? Did Meridiel even care? Did any of the anadel care?

Despite Meridiel's relation to Anaweh now, those probably weren't the safest thoughts to have in the Temple of Ceur. The last thing I needed was to be called a heathen, ejected from the temple knights, and forced to live among the lay votaries again. They had been all too happy to ignore me when I had lived with them at first. But now, ever since that first patrol with Liam, they had become all-out hostile toward me. For whatever reason, I was taking the brunt of their frustration.

I now hated patrolling the lower levels. The men down there were becoming more callous with every passing week. Taunts and insults about my sexual orientation followed me during patrols—no longer whispers, but brazenly vocalized for me to hear. The outbursts were mingled with their anger at still being confined as prisoners in the temple. Since the ei'ana were safely in their castle, I was taking the brunt of their disdain. It didn't matter that I was now confined to the temple as well, they resented that I had spent my entire life prior to coming to the temple as a kien wielder, free outside of the temple. The frustration had only increased once rumors about kien wielders learning to wield had spread like wildfire throughout the lower levels. As well, conspiracy theories ran rampant about how the ei'ana would only instruct the kien wielders that they liked. And given how most of the ei'ana were elves, the humans among the lay votaries had become divisive and hateful toward anyone with pointy ears.

Irritated and bored, I rolled over on my too narrow bed. My languid introspection had gone on long enough, and my earlier arousal had long been superseded by frustration. "Do you guys feel like doing something today? Anything?" I asked.

"Stephen and I have patrol duty all afternoon." Renaud didn't bother to roll over to face me. He too was on a lower bunk but was lying on his back looking up to the bottom of the bed over his own.

I shifted to look up and around the bed above me at Liam. I knew his schedule was open today. All our patrols were together. And now that we had made up after too long of a rift between us, I was eager to spend time with him instead of with Benedetto's diaries.

"Well?" I nagged.

"What sort of mischief do you intend to get us mixed in today?"

"Mischief? Me?"

"You know, you almost sound believable," Stephen said.

I rolled out of bed, and per usual, wasn't wearing anything.

"Put something on, won't you," Renaud hollered, chucking his pillow at my back, opening his eyes just in time to see my too pale backside. If it wasn't for my hair color, I could be mistaken for an Aldinari. My skin had never been this pale before, not even when living in Gneal. I had never considered walking outside in the Perrien climate to be a luxury while I had been an emissary.

"Still not comfortable with me, Renaud?"

"Not in the slightest! You're lucky I'm not as strait-laced as my father. His heart would give out if he ever discovered my bunk mate was a Cyndinari. No offence, mate. To say nothing of that same Cyndinari prancing around in the buff all the time."

"I could think of something to make his heart give out sooner." I winked, then shook my butt at Renaud.

"Don't be cruel," Liam said, his bare legs now dangling over the edge of the top bunk.

"Well, if you don't get out of that bed, I'm going to hop in just as I am. I'm bored."

Liam leapt from the top bunk at the mention but smirking as he did. He picked up my rolled-up trousers off the floor and tossed them at me before getting dressed himself.

"Pity." I pulled my trousers up, hoping all the while that I might be removing them again and soon. My plan had to work first.

"Well, if you two are off, give me my pillow back." Renaud held his head up in a half-crunch position. I tried not to look at his abs constricting in that position. "We still have an hour before our patrol and I don't intend to be awake for it."

I was soon in the corridor with Liam, and it was blissfully vacant. Before we even reached the first intersection, Liam turned to face me. "I wish you weren't so forward around them."

"You do realize that they know what's going on between us, don't you?"

"Considering how you were just staring at Renaud's abs and chest, I'm not sure if I know what's going on between us."

"Oh, right. I didn't mean to, but it was hard to look away," I admitted and wrapped my arm around Liam's waist. "I could remind you what's going on between us." I smirked.

Liam leapt back at the touch. "Not here." Liam had to reposition himself as he blushed. "Besides that, what did you have in mind for today? Don't pretend that you don't have Renaud and Stephen's schedules memorized. You knew they had patrol duty today. No playing coy either."

"Well, that didn't take long."

"What?"

"You were just angry at me for ogling Renaud. And now, you seem quite over it and curious as to what I have planned for us."

"Oh, well, your imagination wasn't the only one undressing the rest of him," laughed Liam, brushing a hand through his dark hair. "I never expected all four of us to have benefitted so much from training with Elayne. But seriously, don't be as forward about us around them. It makes me uncomfortable."

"You mean like this?" I grabbed both sides of his waist, twirled him, and brought him close. Our bodies pressed against each other, our faces nearly touching.

"I said, not here." Liam brushed my hands off but not before I felt what was between his legs stiffening against me.

I couldn't help but notice the meager effort to pull away. "Oh fine, and you were right. I did know about Renaud and Stephen's patrol today." I turned back down the empty corridor and jogged a few steps, hoping that Liam would chase after me. Looking over my shoulder, I saw that he kept pace just behind me.

Without looking, I nearly collided into Bastien. He must've just exited his office.

"And what, might I ask, are you two running toward?"

"Sorry, sir. I thought if we hurried, we could get some of the leftovers from breakfast for a snack," I lied, although I was hungry.

"You aren't a lay votary anymore, Jaerol. You know very well that your meals are regulated. And besides, all the leftovers were distributed to the homeless and refugees outside the temple."

"Oh, right. We'll be on our way then."

"Sorry to disrupt you, sir," Liam added.

Bastien watched us continue down the corridor at a much slower pace. I thought I saw a hint of a smile before I turned away from him. I partly expected him to call out our bluff.

"Is he still watching?" I asked.

"Does it matter? You're a terrible liar. You do know that, right? How did you manage to fool the whole Erynien Empire as long as you did?"

"You're seeing a side of me that they haven't seen since…" I froze.

"Since Kiron?"

"Since Kiron." My breath caught in my chest.

"I'm starting to understand what he meant to you. I never had someone like that growing up. And I certainly never anticipated to ever have someone in my life like that after I was taken to Gneal—not even before, to be honest. After Velaria rescued me, I never expected nor hoped for this to happen." Liam's fingers wrapped around mine. It was brief and no one was in the corridor to see. We had enough mocking disdain to deal with already. Fortunately, we weren't near the lay votaries yet.

I squeezed Liam's fingers before letting go.

"Come now, what's this plan you've been scheming?"

I looked over my shoulder again, just to make sure no one was near. "Follow me."

We turned onto the first stair hall and took two stairs at a time down. I stopped our descent after several landings, pulling Liam along before halting in front of Therril's office. I knocked lightly and looked about, nervous. The only way my plan would work was if Therril's office was empty. My heart pounded with each passing second. Despite having mixed feelings about Meridiel and my fellow Cyndinari, I wanted to make today special. I wanted this Meridephaen to stand apart from my past. Whether I wanted it or not, today was special to me. The summer solstice was engrained into my being as a Cyndinari. It was also the tenth anniversary of Kiron passing. I had to make today special for him. I knew I wasn't there yet, but the only way Kiron would rest in peace, was if I allowed myself to live in peace with myself.

Without an answer, I opened the blessedly unlocked door

and entered the empty office, pulling Liam in behind and closing the door. Unlike last time, there wasn't a lit torch waiting for us. Therril was not helping us sneak out of the temple this time.

"I hope those uniforms are still in the tunnel." Without waiting, I stepped through the window that wasn't a window and into the darkened tunnel.

"How are you going to change in the dark?"

"You're just upset that you can't see me naked again."

"I just saw you without any clothes on."

"What's your point?" I smirked, even though I knew he couldn't see it. I fumbled blindly for the hooks where the Septyl knights' uniforms had hung before.

"Find them?" Liam asked.

At last, despite thinking that I knew exactly where the hook was, I finally clutched a slip of fabric. "Here, hold these." I handed Liam both uniforms.

"How am I supposed to change if I'm holding both uniforms?"

"We have to change one at a time, that way we can hang our own uniforms on the hook without losing them in the dark. I can't do both at the same time. Especially since I can't see anything." I placed my discarded clothes on the hook and grabbed one of the uniforms from Liam.

Liam followed my lead, but before he could take the Septyl knight's uniform from me, he asked, "Where's the hook?"

"It's right in front of you."

"It clearly isn't. All that's in front of me is a rough stone wall."

I grabbed Liam by both shoulders, or at least I intended to. The other uniform was tucked under my arm and I grabbed his biceps instead. I had meant to position Liam in the direction of the hook, but I suddenly forgot what I was doing and dropped the other uniform.

Liam dropped his own clothes and turned around to face me. Our eyes had adjusted slightly, but we still could see precious little of the other person in front of us. This time, I felt Liam's hands venture to my waist, then slip under my tunic to touch my bare skin.

I froze.

I wanted this, and Liam stood a handspan away from me, wearing nothing but his small clothes. And this time, Liam's lips found mine as he pulled me closer to him.

Chapter Eighteen

My connection to the erendinth came in a rush, restored the moment I was on the other side of the temple's ward. Months had passed since I last felt them and I immediately pressed into them and wielded a globe of light. We had walked long enough in the dark tunnel.

"Don't do anything foolish," Liam said, still holding my hand.

"I won't. I'd rather not draw any attention to us. Therril will have to start locking his office door if we're caught outside the temple."

Natural light filtered into the secret passageway and I let my hold of the erendinth dissipate; the globe of light faded. We had reached the castle and the first staircase we came across led up. The stair hall grew brighter the further up we went and when we reached the main level of the castle, sunlight poured through the pointed arch windows. I felt a piece of me return as warm light washed across the little skin left exposed. I had not known whether it was going to be sunny today, but in the back of my mind I knew that it had to be. It was Meridephaen—all Teraeniel had to be sunny today.

Without thinking, I grabbed Liam by the hand and pulled him forward looking for an exit. Liam wiggled his fingers free, more cognizant of our surroundings. "Do you intend on having the entire city talking about us?"

I stopped and noticed that the corridor was far from empty. "Sorry, I got excited. Maybe they didn't notice. Besides, barely anyone knows us here and we'll have more to worry about if anyone does recognize us."

"Well, that doesn't mean we should draw unwanted attention."

"Fine, you're right. Now, come on, I want to get outside and really feel the sun on my skin."

"And how are you going to do that while wearing that uniform?"

"You really shouldn't ask something if you know you won't like the answer." I winked back. I had to remind myself to not grab Liam's hand again. I doubted anyone in the castle would recognize us, especially since we were disguised as Septyl knights. Still, the fewer people asking us questions, the better.

"Who said anything about me not liking it?"

We passed through the castle to the only unbarred exit without causing any disturbance. I gaped at the large arch on the opposite side of the quad. I was still in awe at its size. We walked across the castle grounds at a leisurely pace toward the city. I had to stop myself from sprinting across Gwilnor's bridges. Hopefully, the city would be in better condition since our last excursion. Thankfully, there wasn't any smoke rising in the distance today. Nine months had already passed since Erynor had sieged Ceurenyl. While the city seemed to have returned to normal, the overcrowded streets seemed odd. I had of course heard of Sorenth refugees flocking to Ceurenyl, but I never expected so many would have fled from their homes to a city that had just been attacked.

A cautious anxiety stirred in me. Any one of the newly arrived refugees could be a servant of Shadow, or worse, a shadow elf with a wielded disguise. I certainly didn't want to run into one of them again. I hadn't realized I had come to a near halt until Liam pressed his hand against my lower back to get me to start moving again.

"Is everything all right?"

"I'll tell you later." Too many ears surrounded us, seeking information. Even if none of them cared about the two elves dressed as Septyl knights, it wasn't worth the risk. I knew the Erynien Empire's tactics well enough to keep my guard up.

Following the gentle curve of one of Ceurenyl's main boulevards, I led Liam through the crowds and toward the city gate. A makeshift ramp that switched back and forth to avoid becoming too steep had been built over the rubble and a steady stream of new refugees entered the city.

Liam finally gleaned my intentions and grabbed my shoulder to spin me around. "Are you insane?"

I grinned without answering, pulling Liam along as the crowds separated for us. Reaching the ramp that spanned the rubble, I nodded to the knights standing guard. They all nodded back with no reason to be suspicious. We walked up the ramp and toward the peak of the ruined gate. Even as a pile of broken stone, we still had to climb a decent height to get over it. At the top, I nudged Liam to look behind us out at the city.

"Wow," he breathed in return.

The sun reflected off the slate roofs of Ceurenyl as the late morning sun wrapped around the southeast corner of the city. Beyond it, Gwilnor's grey towers sparkling in the light, the Temple of Ceur gleamed as a beacon. At this hour, it was hard to determine if the temple was illuminated by the sun or from its own inner light. The great dome looked like its own sun, poised on top of the rest of the impressive structure, with half and quarter domes radiating beneath it, either flowing from the central structure or buttressing it.

"What a view."

"Incredible, isn't it?" I replied. "But we didn't come here for the view."

Again, Liam stared at me.

"Don't be skeptical—you can trust me."

"About as much as I can lift this mountain."

"I never said I wasn't attracted to your muscles."

"You're ridiculous."

"And you're wasting daylight."

We walked down the ramp on the opposite side of the rubble to the bottom where we passed a long line of refugees trying to gain admittance into Ceurenyl. Another group of knights stood at the base of the ramp, questioning refugees before granting them entrance. Their questions were useless. Nothing these knights asked would reveal someone with ill intent toward the city. They might as well let everyone in and stop making them wait in line all day. Who knew how long these people had traveled and what hardships they had come across?

I nodded to this group of knights as well and they returned the same tired nod as the knights on the opposite side had done.

Instead of crossing the great bridge, which was miraculously still whole and unharmed, I led Liam down a path parallel to the city wall. The narrow path divided into a series of switch backs. From the adjacent riverbank, the paths looked like a large series of diamonds, crisscrossing the mountainside beneath the city walls. The river exiting the city on either side of the ruined gate fell in a rush. The waterfalls splayed rainbows in the sunlight just as we walked beneath one. Whoever had constructed these paths, had done so cleverly enough to ensure that they did not disrupt the waterfalls.

The river below flowed between the mountain Ceurenyl rested on and the surrounding mountains, but as we reached the bottommost path, the sound of the current was much clearer, the waterfall now well behind us. The river current and waterfall had washed away the noise from the refugees above.

I immediately tore off my shirt when we reached the pebbled riverbank. I longed for the sandy shores of Cynethol and the crystal-clear water of the Erynien Bay, but this was the closest I would get to that. The sun tingled my not-so-bronzed skin. If I didn't get any exposure to the sun soon, I would be as pale as an Aldinari! I kicked my boots off followed by my pants, Liam staring in disbelief.

"Are you going to swim in that uniform?" I asked.

"Swim?" Liam raised an eyebrow.

"Why do you think we're here? So I could sun bathe?" I walked into the river. My skin prickled—the water was freezing, but at least it wasn't frozen like the Skrein Sea. I had partly hoped that the river would have warmed up this late into the summer. My entire body clenched as the water climbed above my thighs.

"You look cold. Did you forget that this river is largely snow melt?" Liam laughed as he took his tunic off and neatly folded it on the ground beside the crumpled mess I had left. Liam was soon down to his small clothes and tested the water, dipping a single toe in.

"If you leave those on, they'll get soaked and you'll have to walk all the way back to the temple with a wet groin." I was fully submerged. I had made the mistake of easing myself into the river. It was best to plunge right in—the frigid shock would only last a moment. Instead, I was still shivering and my teeth clattered.

"I hate it when you're right."

I whistled as Liam removed his small clothes. I couldn't believe how attracted I was to this lethien. It was impossible to tell which elven kin he had come from, most likely a consequence of the human genes mixing with the elven ones. His skin was certainly darker than most elves, but not quite as dark as the Eldinari were fabled to be. And his mostly black hair had a tinge of red mixed in. I watched him walk slowly into the river, visibly freezing. I considered telling him to rush in, that it would be easier and less of a shock that way. My mind drifted and time seemed to freeze.

"Stop staring, you're making me nervous."

"The water's too cold for anything to pop up, don't worry."

"Is that supposed to make me feel comforted?"

"Certainly doesn't have that effect on me. Now, if we were at one of Cynethol's beaches, that would be a whole different outcome."

Without any warning, the water just above his knees, Liam lunged at me, tackling me under the water. We wrestled in the river, splashing, and laughing all the while. We fell into grappling positions, altering slightly to cope with the current.

I had been wrong about one thing though. The icy river wasn't enough to keep my arousal down, and neither was it cold enough for Liam.

We both froze where we floated, noticing each other at the same time. I could see all the way down to our toes in the clear water, but my eyes didn't make it that far. "I think that's the first time you've let your guard down around me."

"Yeah," Liam chuckled, blushing. "Whenever we spar together during drills, I have to think of my time in Gneal's dungeons to make sure I don't have any um…surprises."

"I'd rather you not think of that while we're touching." I looked away, ashamed that I had not been braver. Something should have been done to save Liam's relatives. Instead, I had done nothing as one shadow elf after another ventured down to the dungeons and returned with a triumphant sneer.

"Stop that." Liam grabbed the side of my face. "It's not your fault. And besides, just moments ago, you were laughing like I've never heard from you before."

Liam's touch made me forget about Gneal. Kiron used to touch my face like that. His hand would cup around the side, holding my jaw and cheek. I smiled and my heart pinged. What could I have done differently? Kiron should not have died.

I swam away from Liam and toward the riverbank. The current had carried us a good distance from where we had left our clothes. Water dripped off me as I walked back to them, Liam following behind. We sat on the narrow, pebbled beach, holding our knees to sit up.

"You're thinking of Kiron again."

"I miss him—today's the anniversary of his death. He shouldn't have had to die, especially not by my hand." I had never allowed those words to pass my lips before. I barely allowed them to surface in my mind.

Liam moved to place his hand on my thigh, but I shrugged it away and looked away from him. How did he not react to that news? I had just admitted to killing Kiron. He knew that Kiron had died during the Grand Tourney and that I had been the victor against my opponent without stealing my classmate's soul. Liam was smart enough but, surely, he hadn't already made that connection. "He was the only person I ever loved..." my voice caught in my throat; my eyes were wet.

"It's all right." Liam rubbed my back.

"No, it's not. I loved him and the world made me kill him. What if it happens again? I can't pretend that I don't have feelings for you. I shouldn't have feelings for you—I shouldn't have feelings for anyone. I can't let that happen again. I won't—I refuse to."

"Jaerol?"

I couldn't turn my head to look at Liam, my face was a blubbery mess. The memory of Kiron staring back at me as he died pierced my heart. Of all the times I could vividly see his face, it had to be now—and of that moment.

"Jaerol?" Liam pressed. I shifted my head around to look

into Liam's grey eyes. "I think I love you, Jaerol. And no one is going to make you hurt me."

Our bodies were still wet, and my salty tears only increased as Liam pulled me into a side hug. Our bare skin touching electrified my senses. Liam's hand moved between my legs, while his other hand guided my fingers between his own thighs. We looked into each other's eyes, asking each other if this is what we both wanted. Neither of us spoke a word and our lips met.

Part Four

Depression

Chapter Nineteen

12 years earlier - 9054.3E

The Imperium Gallery opened before me. Its grandeur always halted me in my steps, my breath caught somewhere between my lungs and throat. The gallery didn't have any doors, only two arched openings at either side of the elongated room. This space could have easily been another corridor, but the architects had chosen to design something grand instead. They had invited the finest Cyndinari artists to paint frescoes depicting Cyndinare.

Every plane of the gallery was frescoed with scenes of our ancient homeland, lost to the ages because of the Darkness. Even the barrel-vaulted ceiling was plastered with exquisite frescoes. A reddish gold tinged every image, as though the entire Skyland was enflamed. I had learned at a young age that the hue was a result of cyndaryl, the very substance that Cyndinare was made of.

Even after marking my fifth year at the Imperium, I could not understand how students and magisters alike could simply stride through this impressive space without pausing to appreciate the art and architecture. They didn't seem to take notice. Even when I was in a hurry, I couldn't help but slow my pace through the gallery. I probably could have saved myself a significant amount of time by choosing a different route through the Imperium, rather than pass through here.

Even though avoiding the gallery would alleviate my tardiness, I never once altered my path. Showing up late was always the preferable option.

I eventually reached the other side and passed through the arched portal. The rest of the Imperium was an impressive collection of buildings, connected with arcaded walkways. The complex was massive and dominated Broid's northeastern district. Only the palace on the opposite side of the city, separated by the Coliseum in the city center, commanded as strong a presence in the imperial capital, and that hadn't been constructed until well after the Imperium.

The palace had been built after Erynor had declared himself emperor. It was meant to exemplify that his reign would cast a shadow over the other Sha'ghol, who had held onto their power over the Cyndinari for several millennia. Not only was the palace complex larger, but it had also been constructed on the most desired hill of the city, requiring demolition of dozens of already palatial mansions, to clear the way for Erynor's palace. In addition to the sprawling complex, he'd also had his architects include a spire at its heart, stretching into the clouds and soaring over every other structure in Broid and the surrounding countryside. Even the harbor's lighthouses were now dwarfed by the palace's spire. The spire was the only one of its kind on Cynethol and had no precedent in Cyndinari architecture.

While the Imperium had always served as a school, it was originally built for the Sha'ghol as their residence and seat of power. They had envisioned it as their new Citadel and from it would sprout the Cyndinari culture and legacy, rivaling even Gwilnor Academy at its peak. Granted, that had been before shadow elves walked the Imperium's halls and when some of its residents had purer intentions. The Imperium's objectives were never completely guileless. After all, it had been commissioned by the Sha'ghol, alleged accomplices of Ramiel and the first elves to wield tenebrys.

In addition to our regular studies at the Imperium and learning to wield umbrys from Yloran, Kiron and I had devoted much of our free time to learning as much as we could about the Sha'ghol. Every bone in my body cautioned against trusting Yloran, but we had little choice in the matter. Uncle Teran trusted her; at least, he trusted her enough to assume she would keep Kiron and me safe.

I found my way to the library to meet Kiron where we now spent most of our free time. The brightly lit reading room spanned several levels, crowned with a glass dome, with balconies breaking the horizontality below it. While the reading room and adjacent rooms contained an impressive collection of tomes, the volumes that most interested Kiron and me were stored below in the archives.

The librarians and archivists were in a constant struggle against each other. Given Broid's humidity, both groups worried about their collections eroding. Wielders devoted a significant amount of time drawing moisture out of the library. However, the wielders would not have been necessary if the archivists had simply allotted a larger portion of their space for the library's more sensitive tomes.

The archivists consistently denied the librarians' request, stating that their books had multiple volumes and could easily be transcribed again if they were damaged. And if the librarians wanted to avoid that, they should simply hire more wielders to maintain an appropriate atmosphere in their allocated spaces. The librarians grumbled about the cost and their budget and that they could only hire kiara wielders. It was the only instance in Broid where the loss of Balance was acknowledged. A kien wielder was just as likely to lose control of aquaeys and inadvertently flood the library rather than remove the humidity.

I took the stair hall down to the archives, passing busy librarians and stressed students who had fallen behind on their coursework. The archives had a single point of entry, monitored by an apprentice archivist. While there were a few shadow elves among the librarians and archivists, the empire deemed them too valuable to be wasted sorting and categorizing dusty tomes. Those few shadow elves were only involved and oversaw the library and archives because of their positions among the Imperium's faculty. Rather, most of the librarians and archivists had attended an academy that did not meddle in tenebrys and began their apprenticeships at sixteen, the same age the Imperium's students would graduate and become shadow elves.

I scribbled my name on the archivist's ledger, earning a sneer from Ven, the apprentice archivist, as I moved on. "Your boyfriend's waiting for you," he said, hoping to frustrate me.

"Care to join us in the stacks one day? I'm sure you could

find another archivist to watch your ledger, for what, five minutes for you?" I smirked back. Ven was only a year or two older than us and had said something similar every time I passed without Kiron. It had bothered me at first, until Kiron pointed out that he was probably jealous of us and what we had together. There were so few openly gay couples in Broid that anyone who was too afraid to act on their true feelings tended to act out spitefully.

"Maybe I will," Ven replied as I walked through the opened door to the archives, freezing me in my place. "Don't expect it to be quick though."

I almost turned back, but instead walked on into the archives to find Kiron. Unlike the library's impressive reading room above, the archives featured no glamour or ornamentation. Low vaults spanned the chamber and every space felt like a catacomb. There was no central reading room down here, just a smattering of tiny rooms for private research. That was one of the reasons that Kiron and I had caught the attention of the archivists. We were always together researching in the same room.

I found Kiron reading in our usual room and closed the door behind me, exhaling as I entered.

"What has you all flustered?" Kiron asked, looking up from one of Broid's earliest records.

"I think you were right about Ven. I returned his jibe and he insinuated that he *would* join us behind the stacks one day."

"That's forward of him." Kiron returned to the tome in front of him. "Does that mean he knows what we're doing in the stacks?"

I laughed in response. Neither of us were brave or foolish

enough to try anything scandalous in a public setting, regardless of how abandoned the archive's stacks were on a sunny summer day. "Did you find anything new?" I asked, changing the topic.

"These early records don't make any sense." Kiron pushed his hands through his cinnamon hair. "How are we supposed to take these years as credible when they frequently comment on the Citadel after Cyndinare was lost to the Darkness?"

I grasped his shoulders and looked over his head to read the passage he was stuck on. I skimmed through it and reread the part that mentioned the Citadel. There was nothing exciting about these records—they read just as boringly as the archivists' ledger book. A name was provided, followed by a simple paragraph. This particular passage mentioned someone going to the Citadel as though they were walking across the city.

"How's that possible?" I asked.

"It shouldn't be, right?"

"Perhaps they called one of the buildings here in Broid the Citadel back then."

"Maybe. But aside from these early passages, we haven't found any evidence of a *new* Citadel. All the early records that we've come across include construction documentation and not a single report documents a replacement Citadel. The most likely candidate would be one of the buildings here at the Imperium but they're all accounted for. Do you think Yloran would give us an explanation?"

"Only with the caveat of killing us afterward. That would also let her know that we've been researching her and the other Sha'ghol. I doubt she would take that kindly."

"What if it's still possible though—could you imagine?" Kiron looked away from the heavy tome and up at me.

"What? The Sha'ghol going to the Citadel on Cyndinare?"

"Yeah. I mean think of it. There haven't been any official reports of any of the Sha'ghol in over a thousand years. I honestly assumed that they had all died before we met Yloran. What if they've spent all this time at the Citadel?"

"That's hard to say. And just because Yloran has little love for Erynor, that doesn't mean the others share her sentiment. They could have been hiding in plain sight all these years."

"I guess that's possible. But Yloran never gives the impression that she would allow herself to simply fade to the background. I doubt the other Sha'ghol are any different. Besides, it seemed that everyone at your uncle's soirée knew precisely who she was."

"She did make a comment about taking us to the Citadel. I don't think she intended for us to take it literally, but it hardly sounded like the Citadel was a thing of the past to her."

"She doesn't seem the sort to say anything that she doesn't mean."

"What if the Sha'ghol are immune to the Darkness?" I moved to take the vacant seat next to Kiron. "I mean think about it, if the stories are true and the Sha'ghol really did reach out to Ramiel, wouldn't an immunity make sense?"

"It's possible but I don't think the Darkness' origins were ever confirmed. I doubt any of the other anadel were involved in bringing it about but why would Ramiel send it to his supposed new allies? If it was really his doing, why not just cast it on the other three Skylands?"

I shrugged at the puzzle. It didn't make sense. Was it just a ploy to make the elves migrate back to the land below? "I'm suddenly not all that confident about asking Yloran any prying questions."

"I would've stopped you before you started," Kiron laughed and tousled my hair.

I glanced over at the door to make sure that it was in fact closed then turned on Kiron to kiss him. I'd only meant it to be a quick peck, but Kiron had other ideas and our lips didn't part. So entrenched, I barely registered him guiding me from my chair to sit on his lap, his arms wrapped around me, exploring my back before settling on my waist. Kiron's fingers dug under my waistband, crawling further down my backside.

Then the door opened with no warning knock and Kiron practically threw me off of his lap. My face turned scarlet when I saw a confident looking Ven smirking at us in the doorway. "Ramiel's hell, Ven, I wasn't serious."

Ven's shoulders slumped somewhat but not entirely as he came into the room to close the door behind him. I couldn't tell if I was more embarrassed or angry at the moment and while I had no interest in doing anything more with Kiron here and now, I certainly hadn't wanted it to be interrupted and stopped moments before either.

"So, I *was* right," Ven said.

"I never considered you stupid," Kiron said, the venom in his voice only a hint less than my own. "What do you want, Ven?"

He smiled hungrily at us both, his expression practically

screaming what he wanted.

"You're not getting *that*, not from us." I said. His shoulders slumped some more.

"How do you two manage it?" He pulled out the chair across the table from us and sat, looking defeated.

"Manage what?" I nearly made a crude joke about him bending over for whoever he fancied.

"Letting others know about you being together and then being seen in public as if it was completely normal and accepted. It's not!"

"Are you saying that no one knows about you?" Kiron asked, his voice now kind and concerned. Whatever venom he'd had due to the intrusion and having to stop himself was now gone. He didn't even seem to care what Ven seemed to think about it being unnatural.

"Not a soul."

"And you've never…" I left the question open.

"Ramiel's hell no! Once one person knows, even if they're a willful participant, the entire city would find out."

"Is that necessarily a bad thing?" Kiron asked. "You could let yourself be happy with another guy. What others think wouldn't matter as much if you're happy."

"You do hear what people say about you, don't you?" Ven grew defensive.

"It's hard not to hear it, but I'd rather them say and think whatever they want than be alone and without Kiron to love."

"And what they say and think doesn't bother you?"

"Of course, it does—it's infuriating—and the glares are even worse," Kiron said. He was the one who always calmed me down whenever anyone teased us. He had never mentioned that it had equally bothered him. I suddenly felt like a very selfish boyfriend.

Ven crossed his arms, closing himself off to us and visibly trying not to scowl. Whatever confidence he had mustered to follow me into this reading room had vanished.

"No one is going to force you to share your real self with the world—they don't need to know if you don't want them to. I can't speak for you but I'm much happier with others knowing that I'm gay; pretending otherwise is too draining," I said, offering a smile.

"Easy for you to say; you have each other."

"Are you honestly going to sit there pouting and claim no one has caught your eye? The Imperium is filled to the brim with handsome elves and I guarantee you that some of them are looking your way too," Kiron said.

Ven squirmed in his seat. "How will I know if they're also gay? I don't want to make a fool of myself or worse, get punched in the face because I winked at the wrong elf."

"It's a safe bet if he returns the same look you're giving him." I laughed, which actually made Ven smile.

"So, you two really aren't worried about someone hurting you because you're gay? Bliss and happiness aside, I'm terrified of what could happen if the wrong person knew and then did something to me or told others," Ven confided.

"We all have nightmares. They tend to fade the more comfortable you get with yourself. Those fears are only as strong as you give them merit." Kiron smiled reassuringly. He had said the same thing to me countless times before. I don't know if it had something to do with the reassurance not being aimed at me but at someone else, but this was the first time that

I actually believed Kiron. Sure, there were still bad people out there, people who wanted to make us disappear but whoever they were, they weren't here at the Imperium or on Cynethol.

"I should probably get back to that wretched ledger. I didn't expect this to last longer than five minutes." Ven winked as he stood to leave. "Thanks for this. I don't know if I'm ready for others to know yet, so please keep this to yourselves."

"Sure thing," Kiron replied.

"Oh, and if it's the Sha'ghol you're researching, those annals won't get you very far. Do you really think the Sha'ghol would let their personal dealings end up in a public record and accessible to students?"

For a split second I considered covering the tomes Kiron had splayed out. "Where should we be looking?" Kiron asked before I could deny anything and make a fool of myself.

"The restricted section, of course. You won't be able to get in though—I won't even be trusted enough for another decade or two before I can handle those scrolls. A good portion of them were brought from Cyndinare—the librarians keep insisting that they should be given access to them, but the higher ups have been rejecting their requests for centuries. That's the real reason the librarians want access to our space down here. Oh, that's another thing. Anything from before the elven migration to these lands below would never be written about in a book. That's a human thing that we later adopted. We only used scrolls back in those days"

I didn't care about the feud between the librarians and archivists. But it was clear that Kiron and I would likely never see the inside of the archive's restricted section. Documents regarding the Sha'ghol were one thing, but what else had been hidden away in there?

Chapter Twenty

I woke with Liam's arms wrapped around me and my back pressed against him. The sky had darkened long ago and the stars gleamed above, the full moon partially hidden behind a feathered cloud. We had spent the entire afternoon together by the river, the sun not setting until late in the evening. Liam had almost insisted we head back to the temple; we were both hungry and neither had eaten anything for lunch. I didn't want our time alone together to end and neither did he. Instead of returning to the temple, I risked wielding a fish out of the river. Liam was only angry for a moment. Neither of us had wanted to return to the temple—not yet.

Liam hadn't blinked an eye when I had wielded a small fire to cook the fish, a species he didn't immediately recognize. We had fallen asleep together after our late meal, our small fire flickering away in the night.

Liam squeezed me closer to him. "Can we stay like this forever?"

"Forever's a long time." I smiled.

"I hope it's longer than that."

The fire had gone out; not even the embers burned. The sounds of a small animal caught my attention. It crept somewhere behind us, oblivious to the two of us lying together. Other sounds followed the critter.

"Someone's coming," Liam whispered, before kissing my neck and moving into a crouch. I followed his lead. We had been using our clothes as pillows and pulled our trousers on. Despite the mysterious intruders, I noted that Liam didn't bother with his small clothes.

Still crouched low, we backed away from the remains of the fire pit, boots and tunics crunched against our bellies. As I slowly backed away, I started when a hand clamped over my mouth. My eyes shot open as someone muscled me away, keeping my mouth covered all the while. I assumed that Liam was suffering the same treatment, struggling next to me. I couldn't see him—I was too focused on trying to get away from whoever was holding me.

I thrashed in the much stronger man's grip, trying to elbow his gut. Unable to see the assailant, I gagged when an oily rag was shoved into my mouth then held in place with a leather strip tied around my head to hold it. Another set of rough hands bound my hands together behind my back. I pulled against the bindings without any luck, and then whoever had tied me kicked me from behind and I fell on my side. Liam dropped beside me, also gagged, tied up, and knocked to the ground by a different assailant. We faced each other, unable to scream the fear that radiated from our eyes.

Our faceless attackers dragged at the bindings on our

arms, forcing us onto our knees. From the corner of my eye, I saw a group of five approach us.

"When we were asked to stay behind following Erynor's attack, we never expected the river valleys to be so ripe for the picking. You see, we couldn't hide in the city. Unlike the shadow elves there, we're not able to disguise our appearance as they can. Instead, our band was ordered to wait here." The brawny man who seemed to be their leader now stood in front of Liam and me.

"Suin, our laws demand their execution. We watched them all day. Death would be a mercy for them—they deserve punishment for their deeds." This man was only a shade smaller than the first speaker.

"Our laws and customs only stand on our own land. You know this, Cairn. Need I remind you of the ones that you've broken?"

"Those were different. Not even the distance from Dwonia can forgive their offence."

"Even so, we have our orders." Suin leaned in close to our faces. "Drag them back to our tents. Strip them first. Tribe Laith will know of their crime. This custom we will uphold."

A knife roughly slashed through my trousers, then Liam's, as we still knelt, cutting my thighs in the process. The men who had bound us kicked us to stand. Suin had already started off back down the riverbank.

"If you think this is your punishment, don't get too comfortable, faggot." Cairn pushed me from behind to follow the others. "If we were back in Dwonia, you would not see the sun rise. From the moment you are discovered lying with another man, your guilt is known. If not for our orders, you would have been castrated when we discovered you. You would not sleep that entire night. Every man in our tents would beat you until near dawn. But we would not allow the sun to see you alive. The chief would end your disgusting lives and your mutilated bodies would be given over to the scavengers."

I shivered at Cairn's description. The Cyndinari were monsters, but they never mutilated bodies. The elven body was a beautiful piece of art—desecrating one was punishable by death on Cynethol. I couldn't see Liam in the dark but I was sure that he was as terrified as I was.

Cairn continued to describe what would have happened to us if we had been in Dwonia. I tripped several times, and each time, before I could steady myself, Cairn would shove me from behind, slamming me facedown to the ground. When I wasn't stumbling and falling, I felt the constant tip of a dagger poking my side. I was too sore to notice whether Cairn had drawn any blood and I didn't dare look down at the dagger.

"A strong leader would not care about the distance between here and Dwonia." Cairn came close to my ear to whisper, his dagger digging into my skin. "A strong chief would have honored our ancestors. If they saw Suin's handling of you two, they would spit on Tribe Laith and name him the son of none. Only with Suin's death and the next chief's repentance would the ancestors smile on us again."

I kept my mouth closed. Cairn didn't need any reason to dig his dagger deeper into my skin. Now, I could feel blood trickling down my side. The piercing pain was all the evidence I needed in the dark.

A large bonfire roared in the center of a semicircle of two dozen or so tents. Long shadows stretched from the tents in eerie forms, spidering away from the flames. Mud caked Liam and me, mud not formed from water, but urine and worse. Before entering the camp, we had been pushed face down into an area that seemed to serve as the camp's latrine, and were now covered in mud mixed with excrement. I felt sick from the stench. We were still bound, forced to kneel again with our backs to the fire. The mud on my back cracked. The fire had dried it out much faster than my front.

I couldn't look at Liam. I felt as though I had betrayed him, knowing that he was suffering because of me. With every step I had taken on the way to the tents with Cairn behind me, my depression had deepened. If we had stayed in the temple, none of this would have happened. We could have—should have—gone back there after our short swim. Staying outside the city walls had been foolish. I wanted to kick myself for being so stupid, yet again.

The crescent formation of tents fanned out behind us. I could barely see either end from my periphery. The largest tent was pitched at the center, between the others. It was directly behind us, on axis with the fire and the path they had created out of their camp.

I had yet to see any women in the camp. I wasn't familiar with Dwonian customs, but I thought that they were only upheld in what they called their exiled home. The men spat on us whenever they passed by. I felt defeated by it all. Memories resurfaced of nightmares suffered when I was young. While this wasn't an exact replica, it wasn't far from what I had feared would happen if someone had discovered my sexual orientation, although, those nightmares had Kiron suffering next to me. And now, someone else had to suffer because of what I had done. I hated myself. Kiron had known what terrified me. I had told him everything, even these parts of me that I was ashamed of. I had felt so childish to admit my fears to him. He never saw me differently because I was scared, in fact the fool seemed to love me more as I had shared more of my vulnerabilities with him.

The fire roared behind us, blistering hot. The Dwonians had tended to it all night, but now the campsite was quiet and all the Dwonians were in their tents, likely sleeping.

"Jaerol," Liam whispered. "Jaerol."

The sun started to rise in the east; in my misery, I hadn't noticed the stars fade, nor appreciated the beauty of the sky transitioning from black to purple, then to a burst of reds and oranges. Even in this state, I recognized it, but it couldn't touch that place inside me. That place that Kiron had shown me.

If Cairn had had his way, Liam and I would have been near unconscious from an even more torturous night, then beheaded by Suin. Even in my beaten and exhausted condition, my groin muscles tensed at the threat of being castrated. I barely noticed the burst of color in front of me, the clouds painted against the horizon. I'd probably notice them more if I had been born a Luminari. They sang with the rising sun, just as the Eldinari crooned with the stars, the Aldinari chanted with the setting sun, and my own kin praised the sun at its peak. I didn't think my spirit would be lifted with the high noon sun today though. Despite the lovely day I had had with Liam yesterday, it had also marked Kiron's death, and now, this next day, today, would likely mark Liam's death. I doubted I would survive the ordeal, and found it fitting that I should be killed a decade after I had killed Kiron. Meridiel himself was finally delivering my punishment for turning my back on my people and not uttering a single prayer in thanksgiving to the anadel yesterday.

My shoulders slumped. I had no idea how long we had been kneeling. The mud had long dried and my knees ached.

"Jaerol," Liam tried again, his voice pleading.

"I'm sorry." A weighted net fell over my already sluggish mind. I couldn't see past it and simply accepted it. It was better this way.

"You have to fight it, Jaerol. This isn't your fault. None of this is your fault and neither was Kiron's death."

Hearing Kiron's name resonated inside me, but even so, I could only feel the emptiness echo within my hollow shell. I started to shut down and closed myself off to my surroundings. Nothing mattered any more. We would be killed. The Dwonians would either do it here or they'd take us to a shadow elf who would consume our souls.

Liam was wrong though. This *was* my fault. It was always my fault. I'd been a fool to think I deserved to be happy. Gaiety wasn't meant for people like Liam and me. We deserved what would come to us.

Liam tried to get through to me, but hearing his voice made me feel worse. His entire family had been murdered, their souls devoured by shadow elves and I hadn't done a single thing to stop it. All I had ever cared about was myself. Kiron was dead because of my selfishness and Liam and I would soon follow him into death. Although, unlike Kiron, we wouldn't know the sweet embrace of Lumaeniel. No. Even if

Anaweh did permit my wretched soul into that blessed realm, Liam and I would more likely spend centuries inside the corrupted husk of a shadow elf.

Chapter Twenty-One

I didn't know when or how, or for how long, but I had fallen asleep, still kneeling, my chin nearly resting on my chest, my knees aflame. I opened my eyes to see Suin standing in front of us. The sun had set while I slept and only the fire lit Suin's face. I must have slept the day away.

"Tribe Laith demands your death."

Neither Liam nor I responded. We knew that. Even if Cairn hadn't gone into excruciating detail during our forced walk here, it didn't take much to understand how abundantly the Dwonians hated us for something we couldn't change about ourselves. I could more easily dye my hair blue than change my nature.

The Dwonians mostly spoke in the common tongue around us but had reserved some of their insults to their own language when striking us or spitting on us or worse. I knew that both my face and body were bruised beyond recognition. It didn't feel like any bones were broken, although I was too sore to be sure. I was positive that Liam was in no better shape.

"Our customs require that you should have died before the sun rose this morning. The sin I carry now from letting you live is heavy. Heavier still since you committed your grievance on the solstice in full view of the sun. Cairn is not wrong for wanting you dead. If he had been alone when we discovered you lying with each other during the day, he would have beheaded you. You would not have had time to blink."

I didn't think I could feel worse, but knowing that the first and likely only time that Liam and I made love together had not been a private affair made me ashamed for what we had done.

Suin turned away from us, his back to us and the fire, still ablaze. "I would say you're fortunate, but our orders are clear."

"Who's coming for us?" I asked. I couldn't believe how raspy my voice sounded. My throat felt like sand.

"You two will be together forever. Not bodily, of course. I hope your unnatural urges were worth it. I have half a mind to wipe that mud off you. That bright red hair and pointed ears might please Ianthol."

I had thought I was scared, that this couldn't possibly get worse. I had thought that we would die and that would be the end of it. Even knowing that our souls would likely be devoured by a shadow elf wasn't all that bad. But hearing that Ianthol was coming for us changed everything. He made other shadow elves look like pious ei'ceuril.

When he wasn't abroad on a military campaign, Ianthol lectured at the Imperium, and his appetites were no secret among students. Ianthol had his way with anyone he pleased, caring little for a person's gender, playing with his pets before devouring their souls. He especially enjoyed couples. He'd torture one at a time, having his fun and as if the assault wasn't enough, he would steal the one's soul after finishing, forcing the other to watch in horror the entire time. I was so horrified, I moaned.

"You've heard of him?" Suin looked over his shoulder, then left.

I sweated; moisture slickened the hardened mud as my heart raced. I still felt helpless, but I was determined that I would do whatever it took to prevent Ianthol from laying a finger on Liam.

The night dragged on until eventually I could only hear the fire crackling behind us. The Dwonians had finally settled down after a raucous night of feasting. My knees were no longer aflame, since I'd lost all feeling in my legs.

"Liam?" I whispered.

I still felt a heavy net weighing me down and all I wanted to do was curl up and hide. Something clicked inside of me though. Ianthol wouldn't just steal our souls. It would have been better if Cairn had killed us because at least then we'd have a chance of passing to Lumaeniel. But now, not only would we be at the mercy of Ianthol, but he would consume our souls only once he was finished having his fun with us.

"What?" he croaked back.

"We have to escape." For the first time since we had been captured, I contemplated wielding. I felt unhinged and unbalanced but we had to get away from here. Considering our current predicament, wielding seemed like the only option. I knew that I would likely lose control of the erendinth and the chances of escaping were slim, but we had to try something.

"Why now?"

"Ianthol."

"That bad?"

"Worse." I didn't know where to begin describing Ianthol. I didn't want to even think of him and the stories I had heard about him at the Imperium, let alone describe him.

Despite the fire roaring behind us, I felt chilled.

"No need to panic," hissed a voice in my ear. My blood froze in my veins, suddenly refusing to flow freely through my body—too terrified to move. I hadn't heard him approach. It was as though he had materialized behind us, waiting for the opportune moment to let me know that he was there and that he knew I was scared of him. "I can be quite kind to my pets. I can't remember the last time I was presented with two men at the same time. Are they also intimate with each other? Well done, Chief Suin. If I didn't know better, I'd presume that you wanted something from me. I was growing weary of your usual gifts. The Sorenth refugees are excruciatingly boring. They're all so predictable. Surely, you feel the same?"

"Our laws forbid it."

"Yes, so I've heard," Ianthol drawled. "But you're not on your land either, are you? Don't pretend that I don't know that you and your men have your own bit of fun before sending me my gifts."

"My lord…" Suin stammered.

"Now, now. I'm not known to be stingy. Quite the opposite." Ianthol breathed down my neck. "I would like them properly bathed and unbound the next time you find a pair such as these."

"But our customs demand…" Suin growled.

"I have already stated that you are not on your land. Please don't make me repeat it. I find it taxing."

"My lord."

"Now hurry up and douse them in water and clean your stench off them."

"The only water we have here is for drinking."

"Then you shouldn't have coated them with mud, spit, and piss. What did I say about repeating myself?"

Water soon splashed over our heads followed by three Dwonians for each of us to roughly wash the filth off with rags. I winced as the scab on my thigh opened, the sharp pain reminding me of the knife slicing through my trousers when we were captured.

"I am fond of lilacs," Ianthol purred as he watched the cleaning process. The flowery scent soon replaced the former stench.

Our skin had been scrubbed raw by the time Ianthol stepped in front of us to inspect his new prizes. "Ah, and who do we have here?" Ianthol crouched to get a better look at me.

I averted my eyes to avoid connecting with him. I didn't want him to remember me.

"I must admit, Jaerol Solaris, I had so hoped that you and Kiron would have joined me after my lecture that evening all those years ago. I was wounded when the two of you chose to leave the lecture hall before I could speak to you."

"You remember us? We were only two lowly students." I tried to play dumb.

"How many little queers do you imagine pass through the Imperium's halls? They can be such fun in their naivete." Ianthol scratched my chin. "It is a shame that Yloran got to you first. Her appetites are just as exotic as my own. Unfortunate that neither of us like to share."

"How'd you know we'd spoken with Yloran?"

"Come now boy, how ignorant do you think me? She was quite beside herself after the Grand Tourney. I don't recall any other two boys having such an effect on her. You must have known what she liked." Ianthol sneered hungrily at me.

"We never did anything like that with her." I shuddered.

"How curious." Ianthol stroked the side of my now clean face. "Take them to your tent Suin; I'll require privacy for the rest of the evening."

"The chief's tent is sacred," Suin protested.

"What have I said about repeating myself?" Tenebrys exploded from his palms and barreled into Suin's chest. It happened in a breath. The chief didn't even have a chance to look surprised or pained before he crumpled to the ground. "Cairn, you were his son and heir, yes?"

Cairn nodded, dazed at the sight of his dead father and chief.

"Your traditions hold that you succeed him following his death, yes?"

"There's the right to challenge, but yes, my lord."

"Will you take these two young men into your tent then and see that we are not disturbed?"

"My tent, or the chief's tent?" Cairn stammered.

"If you don't know which, then I'll be asking someone else the same question very soon."

"Yes, my lord."

We were pulled to our feet, and my knees screamed in agony. Both Liam and I were stumbling as our guides held us firmly by the ropes tying our hands behind our backs and led us around the bonfire. I took in the men by the other tents and couldn't miss the glares we were getting from Tribe Laith. None of them seemed to be mourning their now dead chief. If they shared the same view as Cairn, they likely saw Suin's death as a kind of justice for not having dealt with us as he should have.

Liam and I were soon shoved into the chief's tent, alone, no one to guard us. Animal skins lined the floor with a notable absence of furniture, although the perimeter of the tent was lined with weapons, and two solid wood chests sat side by side in front of a row of spears propped up against the tent wall. It looked as though the entire tent could be packed in a moment's notice and nothing would have to be left behind. We hadn't been given any clothes to wear, but at least we were clean.

"What's going to happen to us?" Liam asked.

Crying wasn't a good idea just now, but I couldn't help a stray tear. Our moment alone was brief. I didn't even have the chance to muster up a bit of bravery to tell Liam what awful things Ianthol was known for. He stood for a moment at the tent's entrance, then approached us.

"You'll find I can be quite affectionate. So long as neither of you balks at the state of my skin." Ianthol caressed my face, and I guessed that he was reminiscing about his lost youth and once uncorrupted body. "You're pale for a Cyndinari. Did they lock you up in that temple all summer? Forbidden from going outside until the walls pressed in on you too much that you had to sneak out? Yes, I recognize the fire in you, Jaerol. It reminds me of my own. Were you fantasizing about Cynethol's beaches? Thinking that a dip in a frigid river could replace your home? And that this lethien could replace your dead lover?" Ianthol quickly grabbed my shoulders to spin me around. His fingers ran down my body, exploring me.

"Get off of him," Liam yelled.

"There's fire in this one too, it seems. Yes, we will have fun together. You've found a fine replacement, Jaerol. Do all the kien wielders in the temple foster this fire? Perhaps they will serve a purpose."

What purpose could the lay votaries possibly play? It's not like they could simply walk out of the temple and join the Erynien Empire. Even if they wanted to, they were powerless in their positions—the temple knights would deal with them before they could get anywhere near the Chamber of Light and escape through the exit there. Thoughts of the temple faded when I saw Ianthol now staring hungrily at Liam.

"And what, tell me, is your story? Are lethiens common where you are from? I can't quite figure out which elven kin you belong to. Your appearance is muddled—no doubt from whatever filthy human also sired you. I wonder, which parent did the human genes come from?"

"Well, they're both dead, so let me know when you meet them," Liam said.

"Oh, I do like this one. I never thought I'd find myself attracted to a lethien."

Liam stood his ground. He wanted Ianthol touching me as much as I wanted the shadow elf touching him. Liam seemed ready to pounce on Ianthol and tackle him away from me even with his hands bound. And if the way he stood wasn't evidence enough, the fury lingering in his eyes was.

I looked at the walls of the tent, anywhere but at Ianthol

with his bulge pressing against me. His corrupted skin touching me was revolting. For the first time since we had been captured, I was grateful that it was the Dwonians who had abducted us. There were all those weapons stashed in the tent.

"Ah," breathed Ianthol. "You desire to kill me, don't you? You couldn't possibly know the life I've lived and suffered through. You think yourself brave for killing your young lover rather than taking his soul? Letting him flitter off to the myth that is Lumaeniel, to bask in Anaweh's light. Fool. You are nothing more than a coward—weak."

Ianthol easily threw me down on the piled animal hides, my sore and frail body in no shape to put up any resistance. I couldn't even brace myself because of the bindings.

"If you had been strong, your Kiron would still be with you. Just as my Didri is still with me. You think you were the only fool boy who had to face his lover in the Grand Tourney? Do you honestly believe that it was an accident?"

I cowered on the animal skin rugs while Liam stood by, uncertain whether he could come to my defense. I knew he felt as powerless as I did, too intimidated to act with Ianthol looming over us. We'd already seen how easily he had been angered by Suin's reluctance to immediately abide by Ianthol's wishes. Would he show any restraint if we too angered him? Or would he cut us down as he had to Suin?

Even lying down, I could barely support myself. I scuttled backward, as far from Ianthol as the tent's confines and my still-bound hands permitted. "What do you want from us?" I squeaked, whatever confidence I once had now dissipated and my raspy voice barely able to ask the question.

"I've already told you that I can be quite kind to my pets.

Don't make me repeat myself."

Whatever question I had hoped to follow up with vanished at the threat. Liam took a hesitant step closer to me, his loving expression telling me he wanted to console me, to try and tell me that everything would be okay. My heart ached. We wouldn't be in this situation if it hadn't been for me. We could still be safely in the temple, away from Ianthol and Tribe Laith.

"Go to him and give him whatever comfort he needs," Ianthol groaned. Liam moved to come to me. "Wait." Liam froze as commanded. Ianthol went to him and ran his fingers over his shoulders, along his biceps, and then down the rest of his arms before reaching his bound hands. Liam flinched as Ianthol went about untying the rope. Knowing Ianthol's reputation, I was sure he wasn't being modest as he went about his work. I couldn't tell if his eyes were focused on the rope or Liam's backside. Whatever he was looking at, he sneered as he spoke. "Yes, I believe we will have our fun together. Now go and untie him as well."

Liam hurried over to free my hands—he didn't take half as long as Ianthol had—then wrapped me in his arms. My ear was pressed against his chest and I heard his heartbeat racing. It sounded like a drum was beating inside his chest, with a quick and unrelenting rhythm. I shivered in his arms, my outer defenses gone now that he held me. I felt safe there. I didn't have to be the strong one just now. Liam didn't care, he was strong enough for the both of us. My back was to Ianthol and Liam's broad chest obscured much of my view.

"You are weak. I had thought you the stronger at the Grand Tourney, but now I can see that Kiron's death was more a loss than I had previously assumed. A shame that you lived and he died."

I buried my face against Liam's chest. He hugged me tighter, his arms squeezing the air out of me. I felt the familiar feeling of a panic attack take hold of me, and I knew I should practice the breathing exercise that Kiron had taught me. Liam just held me in my vulnerability.

"You're wrong," Liam said, I couldn't believe that he had decided to challenge Ianthol. Why couldn't he just let it be?

"And you are a fool." Ianthol turned away from us. "Sleep tonight. I won't disturb either of you, but you will serve me as my pets—in every way—starting tomorrow." Just before pushing the flap open, he turned to look back with a sneer before walking out the tent. "Pathetic."

Liam kept holding me, his hand rubbing my back comfortingly. My breath still came out in quick bits. "You're safe," he whispered into my ear, our heads touching.

Chapter Twenty-Two

I woke beside Liam, my burnt back tender and painful, making it difficult to move. Despite Ianthol's intimidating threat, I was surprised when I realized that it was the first night that I had slept all the way through since we had been captured. Two sets of clean linen shirts and trousers waited beside me, next to a bowl of fruit. I don't know when he had returned after I had fallen asleep in Liam's arms, but Ianthol had indeed come back and had been watching us sleep. He sat on a chest, one leg casually crossed over the other. I noticed a wash bowl on top of the other chest.

"You might have betrayed your kin, but you are still a Cyndinari. Even the lethien here deserves more respect than this band of barbarians gave him. However, Erynor would sooner see him and his ilk wiped off the face of Teraeniel. I could overlook what they had done to him, but not to one of my own. I had decided to kill Suin the moment I realized who you were and how he had treated you."

"You didn't take Suin's soul. I've seen it done often enough to know when it happens."

"Perceptive of you, especially considering the despicable state you were in last night. I'll pretend that it was lack of sleep and inadequate nourishment." He paused, as though he was considering whether to explain why he hadn't, and then went on. "Tribe Laith wanted Suin dead and the other tribes would have demanded the same once they discovered that he let the sun rise with you two still alive. But they are still our subjects. These Dwonians would not have reacted well had I taken their chief's soul. I could have easily killed them all if they had raised their weapons against me and claimed all of their souls for myself, but that would only lead to further unrest among the Dwonians and we still have need of their cooperation."

I didn't know what to say. He might have let me sleep peacefully last night, but his current demeanor was completely different than the previous night's. It was as though the rising sun had altered his disposition entirely, so that he was no longer lusting after Liam and me, but rather, wanting to correct an injustice.

"They forget their place. I'm sure they enjoyed pretending that they were better than a Cyndinari, but such grievances are inexcusable."

"What's to come of us?" I immediately regretted asking, but my drowsiness allowed the question to pass undeterred. "Forgive me, I didn't mean to ask again." I felt the shadow elf's eyes penetrating me. Perhaps his disposition hadn't completely changed. He had made it abundantly clear before leaving us alone last night that we would not be able to put him off a second time.

"Apologies go a long way but do not expect me to repeat myself after this. My attraction toward you will only go so far. You will become my pets. You did betray our people after all. Just because I will not stand for Dwonians to degrade you, does not mean you will be spared from my attentions. And don't think that Yloran will come to save you either. She'll never learn that you've become my pet."

"What happened to her?"

"She hasn't been seen since you competed in the Grand Tourney. But do not fret, little one, I can be kind to my pets. I reward the good ones." Ianthol's severely chapped lips cracked into a smile, bringing fresh blood to scab.

I grimaced; the bowl of fruit caught my attention again. My stomach groaned.

"Don't worry about eating. If I wanted you dead, I wouldn't use poison. Your death is more valuable to me in other ways. Besides, I thought it was clear that I want you alive."

Kiron blossomed in my mind. At least he was safe from this. Perhaps his early death was a mercy. Was it though? Would we have wound up in this position if our plan had been successful? Surely, he wouldn't have allowed anyone to find us in plain sight. And even if he had been the one to kill me at the Grand Tourney, he would never have ended up in this situation—he was too smart for that. He would have gone through with the original plan and allowed Yloran to get him away from the Erynien Empire to start a new life.

I again tried not to think about him, of what our lives could have been together. The heavy weight of depression had lifted slightly now that I was clean and had slept well. Having my physical needs tended to and being treated with decency went a long way in that regard. But it couldn't erase the past. It couldn't undo what I had done.

Ianthol grabbed the bowl and plucked several cherries from it before returning it to my side. The pear did look appetizing. I hadn't eaten since I'd shared that fish with Liam. The Dwonians had only provided the occasional drink of water. It was never enough, but I had cared little about food while the bonfire had roared against our exposed backs—cooking us alive.

Liam stirred, our conversation disturbing his sleep and he sat up in alarm once he saw how close Ianthol was sitting to us. Now that we were in a comfortable setting, he was clearly wishing it had all been a terrible dream.

"Ah, welcome to the waking world. I must admit, I'm more curious about you than about our dear Jaerol here. I know where he comes from. But you…" Ianthol stood and left my side to walk around where we lay and crouched beside Liam, his face only a handspan from Liam's. "There is mystery in you. I wonder how you came about."

Liam scooted away, coming even closer to me.

"Break your fast, wash your faces, and get dressed, or don't. The new chief's discomfort at your nakedness might be enjoyable to observe." Ianthol stood and walked to the tent flap. "I have to have a little discussion with Cairn. So please, tidy this place up before I return with him."

Liam and I were alone again, but for how long? I shifted to reach the pear and our thighs touched. Even in this state, captive, terrified, I felt an alluring jolt course through me. I handed the pear to Liam. He appraised it skeptically.

"Apparently, poison isn't something we have to worry

about," I said, repeating Ianthol. I stood to stretch then crossed the spacious tent to the wash bowl on the chest.

"Do we have any chance of escape?"

"Not while Ianthol still breathes. And moving against him now will result in him taking our souls before we can devise a better plan." I splashed the cold water against my face, sending chills immediately down my spine. I dried my face with the rag next to the washbowl and went to sit next to Liam again, taking the other pear from the fruit bowl.

"What about wielding? You can do that still, can't you?"

"I'm just as likely to harm us in the process. I can do small things without any significant consequences but I never learned to control the erendinth. And besides, even if I dared risk it, Ianthol is too powerful. He would snuff me out before my wield came anywhere near him. Our best option right now is to do as he says."

"You expect us to be his *pets*?" Liam asked, disgusted.

"I expect us to stay alive." Even as I said it, I heard my conditioned logic returning. It was a way of thinking that had only developed after I'd lost Kiron. Liam and I just had to stay alive. That was all that mattered, regardless of what it would cost us.

We finished our breakfast and dressed in the linen clothing, surprisingly more comfortable than I had given the fabric credit for. Even more shocking was how well the garments fitted us, as though someone had measured us before tailoring the clothing specifically for us. I squirmed at the thought of Ianthol being so near while we had slept, unaware.

Glancing around the tent, I couldn't see anything that needed to be tidied up. There weren't any discarded clothes to fold and other than the untouched weapons and chests at the perimeter of the tent, only the animal hides lined the ground as rugs. Were they supposed to be rolled up during the day? Were we expected to do something with the washbowl? A single collapsible table stood beside the entrance. I hadn't noticed it the night before, but a bowl of fruit, goblets, and a bottle had been placed on it. I had no idea where they had come from. Had someone brought that table and those refreshments in while we slept?

Ianthol returned with Cairn, his rage thinly masked. He groaned at seeing us dressed. Clearly he had looked forward to toying with Cairn.

"I don't approve of them staying in this tent," Cairn growled.

"There is much more that I don't approve of you, so if you want to end like your father, your ambitions extinguished in a flick of my wrist, you will be silent on the matter."

"Yes, my lord." Cairn kept his eyes on Liam and me, clearly regretting that he had not killed us the moment we were captured. "And which ambitions do you wish to accommodate?"

"Jaerol, pour the chief and me a glass of wine, the Cor'leran Blue, please." Ianthol instructed. It seemed that Cairn would have to wait until Ianthol had his wine before learning about which ambitions might be answered.

I hurried to do as told. Angering Ianthol was not advisable and neither was making him wait. I assumed that the only bottle I saw on the small table beside the entrance was the desired wine, and that Ianthol had already seen to the preparations for this meeting while Liam and I had slept. The blue ice wine splashed into the two glasses and I offered them to Ianthol and Cairn.

"One is already given, is it not?" Ianthol smiled at Cairn over his wine glass.

"I could have gone without my father's death in exchange for taking his place. I want what no other Dwonian chief has dreamt of attaining. And that, is yet to be given. Suin did not have to die for that."

"In time perhaps. That which you seek is not born overnight. And your father did not die solely for you to rise. His grievance against a Cyndinari was unforgivable."

"We kept them alive." Cairn grumbled.

"Covered in mud and urine. If you ever so mistreat a Cyndinari again, regardless of their crimes, I will steal your people's souls and erase Tribe Laith from Teraeniel. But not you; you, I will keep alive to watch what I do to your tribe. You will watch from a leash as your tribe burns, never to return to Dwonia and forgotten by history. Even when standing beside this traitor, you are still inferior."

"I won't repeat Suin's mistakes." Cairn stared daggers at me. He clearly thought the mistake was in letting us live.

"Good. As to the other proposition that you were promised, I believe I know of the perfect city for your ambitions to come to fruition."

"And? You don't intend on making me stay in Myrium after its people are slaughtered or cast into chains as slaves, do you? I'll happily take them as our slaves, but that city is too far from Dwonia."

"Do you believe you are in a position to bargain?"

"No, my lord. Forgive me." Cairn shied away from Ianthol, nearly spilling his yet untouched wine.

"Fortunate for you, we have other designs for the Jewel of the River, beginning with a siege which you will lead the Dwonians. And no, you will not be carting off her people as slaves. No. You will become the next King of Mindale. Binton is unstable at present. Its nobility is at each other's throats, and their king tries to appeal to them, but they all despise poor Lawrence Maroven. By removing him and pairing you with one of his numerous daughters, it should be easy to place you on the throne. Even after all his wives and mistresses, he has sired only one son. And the boy is young and sickly from what I hear. None of the nobles would question the prince's untimely death. And who would deny an unwed princess her exotic lover from the west? You can even choose whichever one you find most pleasing. As I said, he has countless daughters."

"I'll need more assurance than what-ifs."

"And you will have it. And if you excel at laying siege to Myrium, perhaps you'll even garner the support of the other tribes. That is what you want, is it not? To be king of all the Dwonian tribes? To reclaim Dwonia and force the remaining two tribes there to submit to your boot? We want this too. In their continued arrogance, they are spitting in Erynor's face from their concealment in Nynev's dunes and canyons."

Cairn smiled at the proposition. "How long will Myrium delay me?"

"The time it will take will only increase your support among the other tribes fighting beside you. You don't want to take Binton and become a Mindalean king before you have their support. Dwonians are stubborn and hold their traditions tightly. Patience is necessary for now. Especially if you want to break from your customs."

"Fine, but I want the other tribes and chiefs to know that I am first among them. That Erynor has placed me in that position."

"Fool! *I* am placing you in that position. Your allegiance is *mine*! As my allegiance is to Erynor, so is yours to me. The Tribes of Dwonia mean nothing to the emperor. You are a trifle to his imperial majesty. Now be gone from my sight, you desert rat." Ianthol thundered, making Cairn drop his glass of wine, having only taken a single sip from it.

Its contents spilled onto one of the animal hides, staining the tan fur blue.

"Do not stare at it. Liam, clean it up."

Liam hurriedly grabbed the rag by the wash bowl, and brought both to the darkening stain. He emptied some of the water from the wash bowl onto it, dousing the animal hide and dabbed at the spill, in hopes of cleaning the wine stain.

Cairn turned to leave the tent that now belonged to him as chief.

"Do not forget your place again, Cairn."

"My lord." Cairn bowed quickly and backed out the tent flap.

Chapter Twenty-Three

Ianthol, Liam, and I formed a triangle, seated at a low table laden with exotic dishes. We sat on pillows around it, tasting the various dishes. Most were recognizably Cyndinari inspired, especially the spiced fish. I had never seen the rest of the dishes before. They were probably Dwonian in origin, adapted to food common east of Dwota's Gap. However, Liam looked at every dish appraisingly. He clearly didn't recognize any of it. Even the peppered chicken was prepared in such a way that it no longer resembled chicken.

Serving men had brought the table and dishes into the chief's tent. None of them resembled Dwonians. Their blond hair and blue eyes identified them clearly as Sorenth refugees, now slaves. Still no women though. Ianthol had certainly indicated that he had received women as tribute. Had he already stolen all their souls to elongate his own life? How long would these men last before Ianthol claimed their souls as well? Would they live through the night? The more pressing question, though, was how long would he allow Liam and me to live? Did he intend to keep us as his pets until we were no longer pretty in his eyes?

"These Sorenth might not have been raised on Cyneth-ol, but their eel is nearly just as well prepared. I must find the chef, to make sure that that talent isn't lost." Ianthol swirled the eel in a bowl, offering more to Liam.

"I didn't realize that was eel…" His face lost its color at the revelation.

"Surely, there's no need for that. This is the least of the delicacies you'll enjoy when I take you to my villa."

"Your villa?" I asked.

"Naturally. I did consider keeping you at my residence in Broid, but I'm afraid you'd be too recognizable there. My residence *is* on the grounds of the Imperium after all. I might not have any desire to claim your soul for my own—at least not yet—but that is not the case for the rest of your past magisters at the Imperium. Dare I say, they might be just as excited to find you as I was. And as I'm sure you're aware, I do not like to share my pets." His hand clenched my thigh, his fingers dig-ging into me.

I shivered.

"Do not fret my pet, you are both safe with me. I believe you'll both enjoy my villa far more than staying in Broid. It's a two-day carriage ride from the imperial capital, and along the southwest coast. The gardens overlook the Blathn Channel. It's quite lovely and stunning when the sun sets. You can just see the hazy peaks of the Lintz Mountains in the distance. Truly, it's a magnificent landscape. I couldn't have painted a more picturesque backdrop."

I ate the offered eel. One of Ianthol's rules during this meal was that we could only eat what was offered to us and when it was offered to us.

"Although I will admit, if Yloran learns that you are in my care, I doubt even I could keep you safe from her. Which, naturally begs the question, how did you get involved with one of the Sha'ghol? Better yet, how'd you sway one of them to leave their Citadel and return to Cynethol?"

"*The* Citadel? The one on Cyndinare?"

"Are you aware of another one?" Ianthol returned.

I took the news with a deep swallow. "How?" I wanted to find Kiron, to tell him that we were right, that Yloran had been traveling to Cyndinare and more importantly that it was possible to travel to that Skyland. Maybe not for everyone but it was possible for the Sha'ghol.

"Interested in taking a holiday there? Don't expect the other Sha'ghol to treat you as Yloran did and they certainly won't be as good to you as I can be."

"No, but I thought it wasn't reachable anymore. That the Darkness prevents anyone from drawing near the Skylands."

"And for those who are responsible for that Darkness, do you think they too would be barred from it? That it would have the same effects on them as it has on others? How do you think Yloran and the other Sha'ghol are the way they are?"

"So, it is true," I breathed. "The Sha'ghol forced the ancient elves to abandon the Skylands."

"You give them too much credit. They are not gods. And whatever is said about them now, they certainly weren't divine back then either. Just like the rest of us, they were, and perhaps still are, instruments of Ramiel. Make no mistake, the Sha'ghol never wanted to leave the Skylands and would have every Cyndinari return to Cyndinare if they could orchestrate it."

"Then why bring the Darkness to Cyndinare in the first place?" I asked.

"All we can go on is speculation but no credible sources hold that they willingly or knowingly brought it to Cyndinare. An unhappy side effect of their pledge to Ramiel."

"What is the Darkness?" Liam asked.

"A manifestation of tenebrys is the easiest answer. But even that is not quite right. Some believe it is the negative of the Light that fills the Temple of Ceur, that in part, it is linked to Ramiel's essence—that a part of his power is imbued in it. It's more properly called the void, part of Ramiel's realm oozing into Teraeniel."

"So that would make the Shroud blanketing all of Krysenthiel…" I started.

"Child's play in comparison to the Darkness enshrouding the Skylands. Yet, Erynor thinks to attain godhood by it. He thinks to put himself on the same level as Ramiel. He is no different from the other Sha'ghol. All they have ever wanted was to attain divinity." Ianthol took another foreign morsel of food. "Now, stop avoiding my questions. How did you and Yloren meet?"

"She came to one of my uncle's soirées." I hesitated, pretending the display of food caught my attention. "Neither Kiron nor I wanted to become shadow elves, something we both decided too late. She had agreed to help us find a way to escape after the Grand Tourney, and said that no one would care if two recent graduates disappeared."

"Why not get you away before?" Liam asked.

"She said the Imperium's magisters would turn over every rock until they found us."

"I wonder if she knew that you two would be paired together?" Ianthol asked.

"Why would she do that? Just to toy with us?" I thought back on the precious little that I knew of Yloran. Would she have done that? I knew she hadn't seen us as equals, but she had never seemed cruel. She had seemed more interested in preventing us from becoming shadow elves than anything else.

"Truly, I'm doubtful that she did. Ever since the Shroud and our dependency on becoming shadow elves to overcome our mortality, she and the other Sha'ghol have looked down on us and withdrew from Cyndinari society. Except for Erynor, of course; he lusted for power and named himself emperor. She, in particular, despised what we had become. In fact, the years you were enrolled at the Imperium were her most visible years. As I said, she disappeared shortly after your graduation."

Liam grabbed my thigh. He didn't know the full extent of my past, but he did know enough that recalling it was painful for me. What if Yloran had known she couldn't save both of us? What if she knew that instructing us to wield umbrys was the best chance for one, not both of us, to survive? Did she still expect that either one of us would have been able to go through with the rest of our plan? My hands shook. I didn't care about anything after that—after Kiron. I didn't care about living freely of the Erynien Empire anymore. I didn't care about where I was sent or what was asked of me. Nothing mattered without Kiron.

"There's more to this story isn't there?" Ianthol's eyes flared as he looked hungrily at me. "Tell me about Kiron. How did you manage it?"

I choked on the eel which I had barely touched, leading to a coughing fit. My face reddened as I tried to clear my throat. I didn't want to talk about Kiron. Not to Ianthol—not to any shadow elf. Kiron would still be here if it wasn't for them.

"I've investigated some, and our records indicate that you are the only one to have managed to deceive the outcome of the Grand Tourney. There have been reports of contestants trying, but they never survived the event. There is no place for the weak in the Erynien Empire. You are not weak though, are you? You would not have survived if you were." Ianthol licked his lips.

My heart clenched. It felt as though Ianthol had driven his fist into my chest and grabbed hold of it. How did he know precisely which strings to pull and which emotions were still unresolved in me? I didn't want to think about Kiron—about what I had done to him. I felt myself lapsing into depression again.

"Please, he doesn't want to talk about Kiron." Liam said.

Ianthol caressed Liam's cheek with the back of his hand. "You will only speak when asked." The delicate tone oozed venom, the threat unmistakable. "Now Jaerol, tell me everything. I don't like to repeat myself and you'll like the consequences of maintaining a tight lip even less."

I felt myself tremble. It wasn't because of Ianthol's threat or proximity. Kiron's face flashed through my mind. His voice echoed somewhere inside of me, the voice that I was forgetting the sound of, the light and airy tone that always sounded like it had just stopped laughing or would soon start. Kiron's smile bloomed in my mind.

Liam's knee nudged my thigh, concern evident in his expression.

A powerful ping, the strongest I'd felt so far, rang through me. I hugged myself. If I had been standing, I would have collapsed from the sudden onset.

My first memory of Kiron flared. We had been very young, little boys, when we met. Neither of us was old enough for a formal education, and we had played together on the street we lived on the entire day. My heart raced and I could feel the blood rushing through my veins as other suppressed and once-cherished memories bloomed inside, memories which were easier to repress than relive.

I couldn't manage a deep breath, and panted shallowly instead. I knew I should try to steady my nerves. I remembered the exercises that Kiron had taught me when we were teenagers at the Imperium. Take a deep breath and hold it in, he would tell me, holding my hands as he said it. I loved him so much. The only way I was able to cope with his death was to stop thinking—to stop feeling. This Meridephaen had marked ten years since Kiron's death and I couldn't let go of him. I couldn't stop blaming myself.

"I'm waiting, Jaerol." Ianthol's tone was light, but menacing even so.

"I killed him. He was supposed to kill me. We had other plans at first, but that changed when we were paired against each other. *Everything* changed when we were paired against each other." I don't know how long I had stayed quiet. "He changed his mind in the end. We wielded umbrys together that day. Neither of us was strong enough to do it alone after we'd been paired together. I held him as he died, just after he kissed me goodbye. Our wield hid us from everyone else. We were alone in his final moment."

I started trembling again, my eyes wet from a rush of tears. I took a sip of the Cor'leran Blue ice wine, but my fingers couldn't hold the glass and it spilled from my hands. It splashed across the table, spilling onto the nearest dish.

"Liam, refill his chalice."

Liam took my cup and got up to get more wine from the table by the entrance while Ianthol cupped my face. "Only the strong survive, my pet."

I tried to slide away from his wrinkled and cracked touch. His skin should have turned to dust centuries ago. His decaying body held together only because of all the souls he had stolen over the years. He looked at me hungrily, his intentions and desires evident. He drew closer and started to kiss my neck. His hands pulled at me, and he began biting my neck as he groped me, clawing at my much younger and untainted body, lusting after what he had once had.

I felt Ianthol's hands between my thighs, and wanted to fight against the much stronger elf, that strength enlivened by the dozens, perhaps hundreds of souls he had stolen. I wanted to push him away and run from the tent. I shook all over, frozen where I sat, helpless against his focused attention.

Tears streaked freely down my face as I cried out, the sound covering Liam's hard thrust of a blade through the shadow elf's back, and through his chest. Liam pulled the sword out and drove it into Ianthol a second and third time.

Ianthol collapsed onto the low table, splattering the food and spilling his own wine.

Although stunned by the turn of events, I still shook, trembling uncontrollably as I gazed at Ianthol's corpse. A flurry of lights were flying out of the husk—too many to count. I crawled away from Ianthol, his body already turning to ash. Liam abandoned the sword in the quickly disintegrating corpse and rushed to me.

He grasped me by the shoulders, his gentle touch firmer than it had been before, almost commanding, and looked me in the eyes. "You're safe. It's me—it's Liam." He held on, waiting for recognition to return to me, my mind and body still in shock. "Jaerol, it's me. You're safe." He repeated, pleading.

I pulled away from the touch. Despite the words that I half heard and somewhat understood, I did not feel safe. I didn't feel like I'd ever be safe again.

Part Five

Acceptance

Chapter Twenty-Four

11 years earlier - 9057.3E

You know that I can't instruct you in the art of kien. So few still possess any degree of balance that it won't take a week until Erynor and the other Sha'ghol narrow their search to me. I'll be unmasked and then required to answer to them all. While none of us are necessarily honest with each other about our private schemes, it won't take the others long to uncover the truth." Yloran flicked a bug away, incinerating it in a puff of smoke. Ignys hung in the air.

"We won't tell anyone," Kiron proffered.

"You won't have to tell anyone, darling. What do you think people will think when a young kien wielder such as yourself manages to wield using his full strength without losing control?" Yloran cocked an eyebrow, clearly hoping that Kiron would find the flaw without her having to spell it out any further.

"Fine, but what about umbrys? You said you would help us with that, didn't you?" I said, coming to Kiron's defense.

"And that I did, but it's not something that you just learn, darling. You must recognize it within you—feel it inside you. I can't teach you something that is contrary to what you already know. Before Erynor started his childish war, we had spent centuries learning how to wield. And that was when the span during which we were considered youths was a millennium."

I felt the color drain from my face. "Is there no other way?"

"I might not have ever liked Kien and Kiara Lorenthien, but their names will ever be the answer you seek. *Giving to receive. Receiving to give.* Consider your special relationship. While it's not necessarily what those two pretentious elves meant, whether they meant it or not, it's not so different from sex. One partner giving and the other receiving. You two can quite literally swap roles whenever you wish. Granted, so can other partners, if they know how. Oh, how I miss being around immortals—experience is far from overrated."

Kiron and I were both blushing. That wasn't something either of us talked about around others. Quite the oddity for two Cyndinari lovers, since sex was all anyone talked about at the baths, and not so discreetly while walking around in public.

"You two are bashful, aren't you? A shame Erynor did what he did. I would have enjoyed having you around for another millennia or two. It's rare that I get excited around mortals. Even more rare that I involve myself with them. Fortunate that Teran hosts the best soirées on the entire island, otherwise, I would have never agreed to meeting either of you. How opportune for us all." Yloran chuckled, then plucked a grape and popped it into her mouth seductively. "Do be careful around Ianthol, though. You know him, yes?"

"The guest lecturer at the Imperium?" Kiron asked.

"That's him." She ate another grape.

"He disappears for months at a time. Why should we be cautious around him?" I asked. "Aside from being a shadow elf, he's always seemed pleasant."

"His appetites are unique. He's not choosy; he is a shadow elf after all. I doubt he can truly feel anything or enjoy any sort of company. But I do know he would never let you leave his villa if given the opportunity to have you." It was clear what she meant by *have*.

"We'll be sure to avoid him," Kiron replied.

"Happy to hear. I won't promise that I wouldn't become jealous if you two went to his bed instead of my own. If you hadn't been so foolish as to enroll in the Imperium, I would have secured you as my own attendants. Sadly, that's far too risky now—I can't appear to be favoring mortals. But don't think for a second that that very thought hasn't crossed my mind. I considered the favors I would have to pull for various magisters, to say nothing of what Erynor would require of me. It's simply too much to bear. I will not go into his debt for your sake." Yloran looked past the arcade, noting the lengthening shadows. "I believe we have spent quite enough time together for one day. Do be sure to practice." She stood to leave the terrace, even though Kiron and I were her guests.

We stood as well. We had been here for over an hour and while neither of us had pressed into kien, my mind whirled with possibilities. I didn't want to think about what Yloran had insinuated about kien and kiara while still in her presence though. The likelihood of becoming aroused was too high, especially when I was with Kiron. He often joked how I didn't need a second's notice before I was ready to make a move on him.

One of Yloran's attendants escorted us out of her sprawling mansion, nestled in the heart of Broid. Even in such a populated area, it still managed to have charming views over the city with the ocean as a backdrop. I shuddered at the thought of how many gorgeous young men were attending Yloran. This attendant wasn't the same young man who had been with her at my uncle's party, nor was he the one who had brought us to Yloran's terrace, but he was just as handsome and just as scantily dressed. As the warm climate rarely necessitated the need for a shirt, especially for Yloran's attendants, I was staring. Kiron elbowed me in the side.

"I can't help it," I whispered. "How does she have so many fine men *assisting* her?"

"You should ask." Kiron smirked. "A shame none of them are my type."

"You don't like well-toned, bronze-skinned men with red hair?" I asked.

"Oh, I have nothing against that. Clearly." Kiron winked at me, knowing full well what it would do to me. "There's just something lacking about them."

"Like what? I doubt Yloran would select any attendant deficient in anything."

Kiron stopped walking. Still holding my hand, he swung me around to face him, pulling me closer in the process. He smiled that smile—the one that appeared whenever he felt me pressed against him. "They're not you." He planted his lips on mine.

"Apparently, I'm not the only one who gets easily excited." I smiled as our lips touched.

"Apparently." We were only halfway across the grounds, but the entire property felt like a secret garden. We felt safe here. Safer than in any other public setting at the Imperium.

"When I said practice, I didn't mean immediately in my garden," Yloran called from a balcony. "I have plenty of rooms; all you had to do was ask."

Our illusion of privacy shattered. "Sorry," I hollered back, embarrassed, feeling its heat in my cheeks and ears, Kiron's just as red as my hair.

"More than mere kissing has been done in that garden and I'll apologize for none of it. Now, go on darlings, go and flourish as your best selves."

We hurried away after that, no longer caring to linger in the luscious garden. The blush on my face still hadn't faded and it would take even longer for it to recede from my ears. I wanted to run back to our apartment but forced myself into a leisurely walk, while Kiron and I both kept our hands in our pockets. Fortunately, Yloran's mansion was near the Imperium.

The sun was still high when we reached our apartment and we knew we should devote the rest of the daylight to our studies. However, the moment we made it back to our private apartment, a luxury given to fifth and sixth year students, we started peeling each other's clothes off. We had the presence of mind to close and bolt the door behind us, but that's where my thoughts had ended. We held each other, exploring each other, as though it was our first time and we knew nothing of the other's body.

His mouth again found mine and his breath poured into me. His arms held me firmly, strong yet gentle at once. I wanted him just as badly as he wanted me. "So, who's giving and who's receiving?" Kiron mocked Yloran, pushing me back to our bed in the process. I could see in his eyes what he wanted.

I smiled back as he nudged me backward, my legs bumping against the bedframe. Before I could fall onto the mattress, he lifted me, his forearms wrapped tightly around my bottom. He held me up for a moment, our eyes locking together, an exchange that lasted only a second, but felt like an eternity. I hoped that this moment would never end.

He lowered me gently, his arms careful not to slam me against the mattress. He moved from my lips to my neck, kissing my chest in a downward campaign. I clenched the covers as he held my thighs in place, his fingers pressing into the flesh. I could only see the back of his head, my eyes flashing between open and closed.

His arms crawled up my back, his face once again on the same level as my own. I almost pushed him back down. The temptation passed as I felt him swell between my legs. I didn't think it was possible for him to get harder. My breath caught as he eased into me.

Kiron lay in my arms after, his head leaning against my chest. I ran my fingers along his back where I could see a few of the freckles that he swore he didn't have. I knew we should get up, but neither of us moved a muscle, except for the occasional ripple across Kiron's back. He breathed heavily. Was he already asleep? Still in the thrall of our physical intimacy, I could sense the emotions underlying our actions. I felt all my being not only wanting that passion but embracing it. The emotions that had just whirled inside me had begun to subside. I focused on the emotion that came from embracing Kiron. Could it really be that simple? Kiron had pressed into me while I embraced him. Neither action was passive, but they were different, just as Yloran had described.

I debated whether I should wait to put my theory to the

test. I didn't want to wake Kiron so I couldn't really move with him still lying on top of me. Granted, I didn't have to move to wield. There was nothing physical about the erendinth and the elemental erendinth became physical only after the wielder interacted with the actual element. I looked again to Kiron. He hadn't moved and his arms were still wrapped around me.

I smiled at our entwined bodies. Everything about this moment was perfect. Keeping still, instinctually I pressed into the erendinth. I stopped myself. No, that wasn't right. I had to embrace them. I closed my eyes and took a deep breath, remembering the sensation, not the physicality of it, but what I had felt throughout me. I knew what I wanted to do—I had to learn to wield umbrys. It was the only way either of us would have a chance at deceiving the shadow elves at the Grand Tourney into thinking that we wielded tenebrys and consumed our opponent's soul, transforming us into shadow elves ourselves.

Eyes still closed, I envisioned shadows spilling across the room, darkening it to resemble night. I don't know how much time had passed or if I had fallen asleep, but Kiron stirred, repositioning himself. "Is it that late already?" he asked, pushing himself off my chest. He shook my shoulders in alarm.

"What's wrong?" I asked, opening my eyes to see him pointing fearfully out the window. The room was dark but the window showed a late afternoon sun just starting to set. Sunlight should be spilling through the window, practically blinding at this hour. I blinked at the sight trying not to lose my awareness of what I was doing. I had done it—I truly had done it! I had felt—still felt—that transcendental erendinth inside me. It was so different from the elemental erendinth I had come to know over the years. Yet, I held it inside me.

I began to manipulate it. I had no idea what umbrys was capable of, but I was equally aware that I could very easily lose control without warning. I was familiar enough with that sensation to know when to stop myself, but I did not want to get anywhere near reaching that point, especially when wielding umbrys for the first time. I swirled the shadows about the room, condensing them into a compact globe. I held it there for a moment, Kiron gawking wide-eyed at it.

"You did it," he breathed, afraid to speak any louder and break my concentration. "How?"

"Yloran was right. After what we had just done, I was still vividly feeling my emotions and I just embraced umbrys, pulled it inside of me." Worried about losing control by wielding for too long, I released my hold over umbrys. The shadowy sphere faded back to the corners and crevices of our room.

"Jaerol, we might actually have a chance to pull this off. We might actually get away from this place—all of this can be in our past next year."

We didn't leave our apartment after that. We didn't even bother getting dressed again. We chatted easily of our hopes and dreams, of where we wanted to go, living free of the Erynien Empire, a discussion we'd had before. Every time it came up, Kiron wanted to go to a different place. In the past year, he had mentioned every major city south of the Laudien Mountains. We didn't have any interest in traveling too far north.

We considered going back to Yloran tonight, neither of us thinking that she would mind. Hesitancy surfaced when we remembered that only I had wielded umbrys. I relayed my experience as best I could, but Kiron simply couldn't figure it out.

"We're just going to have to replicate what we did earlier, only in reverse this time." Kiron smirked, his eyes alight.

"Strictly for academic purposes, yes?"

"Naturally. Our studies are particularly important." Kiron couldn't keep a straight face as he forced out the bad joke, pulling me on top of him as we laughed and kissed.

Chapter Twenty-Five

Liam held on to me the rest of that night, through the following day and into the next, parting only to take care of basic needs. I knew that he held me, but I couldn't say when I realized it. I didn't even know when I had fallen asleep during that time either. Liam slept with me, his arms refusing to let go, trying to let me know that I was safe. At some point, my head had nestled into his chest.

I dreamt of Kiron. It was different this time though. He had never spoken to me in my dreams before. He had never accused me of anything, despite me wanting him to denounce me all these years. Instead, he now told me that he loved me and always would. He told me to let Liam love me too. He touched my cheek and brushed the tears away. He wouldn't let me say anything, not even that I was sorry and wanted him to come back to me.

Before I woke, he said he had never left me, and never would.

Just as I didn't know when I had fallen asleep or how long it took before I came out of my shock, neither could I say when I had begun to feel safe in Liam's arms. I considered waking him. We could not stay in the Dwonian chief's tent for much longer. The new chief and the other Dwonians were likely already suspicious. Ianthol had been quite explicit about not being interrupted, but those orders had been given nearly two days ago.

I watched as the light against the tent faded. Liam stirred beside me. I had no idea how he had managed to sleep in that position, but his arms still held me, sporadically squeezing even as he slept, as though to remind his sleeping self that he still held me.

"You're safe," he whispered.

"Forever?"

"Forever is too short."

I nuzzled against his chest and he held me tighter. "Thank you…"

"Don't," he said, enfolding me. "No one will ever force you to relive Kiron's death again."

I hugged Liam in return. "I miss him…"

"I know. He must have been special to make you fall in love with him."

"He was."

I stayed in his arms, unwilling to move as the tent grew dark. I didn't know how much time had passed, but Liam seemed content to give me all the time I needed as he rubbed my back. My skin prickled from his gentle touch, and not just because it was still tender from the bonfire.

"We need to get back to the temple. We can't stay here,"

he said at last, his voice low.

"I know...we're going to have to have a talk with Renaud and Stephen."

"I thought you said they already knew about us."

"If you think I'm sleeping without you right beside me after this, you are sorely mistaken. I honestly don't know when I'll be able to sleep alone again." I looked away, ashamed of my vulnerability.

"I'll sleep with you forever if you'll have me but one thing at a time." He chuckled, his chest making my head bounce slightly. "We still have to get away from Tribe Laith."

"How long should we wait?"

"It's dark out now. I doubt we'll get a better opportunity."

"There's something I have to do before we leave."

Liam turned away, knowing what I intended. "Is there no other way?

"It's not just about what they did to us—you heard them, they've been abducting Sorenth refugees and feeding them to shadow elves all this time. They've been here for eight months. How many innocent people did they hand over to Ianthol and others like him? To say nothing of what they did themselves to those people."

"Before that, we'll have to find something suitable to wear. Or do you think what we were wearing is fine?" Liam gestured to the white linen outfits crumpled in a ball. The bright fabric would surely make us easily noticed in the night. Liam looked toward the two chests.

"You'd have us dress as Dwonians while seeking re-entrance into Ceurenyl? Have you forgotten the guards still watching the gate?"

"The tunics we wore out of the city might still be where we left them, but our trousers were destroyed. I doubt any of the Dwonians gathered our belongings before they dragged us here."

"I hope you're right. Do Dwonians wash their pants? I was already planning on soaking in the temple bath halls for a week as it was."

Liam squeezed me instead of responding. Neither of us budged—each wanting to stay in the other's arms a moment longer. The noise from the Dwonians had long dissipated. They had not been raucous tonight, but neither were they a particularly quiet group of men. I thought I had overheard two fights outside the temporary safety of the chief's tent, in those moments when I had been in half sleep, safe in Liam's arms.

"Whatever you intend to do, we'd better see to it now while they're sleeping." Liam sat up, letting go of me for the first time since he'd killed Ianthol. My eyes had adjusted to the dark tent, and I could see Liam's back muscles narrow into a wedge shape before they rounded. Not even the statues in Broid were sculpted as masterfully.

Liam dug through a chest and tossed a pair of leather trousers at me, smacking my face. "I'm not sure if the length is right, but the waist felt about your size." Liam pulled another pair up his own legs.

"Have you been examining my waist?" I slid them on, a bit clumsily from my sitting position, tying them up the front. "Did the chief have any proper belts stashed in that trunk? My waist isn't as wide as you remembered."

"None that I could find. That was the smallest pair."

"I guess I'll manage. Should we wait until we find our

tunics? I'd rather not wear another garment belonging to these barbarians."

"The linen shirts should be fine. Even if we don't find our tunics, we'll never get past the city gate wearing Dwonian garments. Pants are one thing, but their vests are quite distinct."

I crept to the tent flap and pressed an ear against it. The crackling of the fire was all that I could hear. Before opening the flap, Liam handed over a sword, holding another in his dominant hand. I paused with the sword in my grip. Taking a final moment, I pulled Liam's head in for a kiss. I breathed him in. I never realized I had needed him so much.

Pulling away, I turned and opened the tent flap. The fire still roared in the center of the crescent of tents wrapped around it, stretching to either side of the chief's tent. A single Dwonian stood watch on the far side of the bonfire, his back illuminated by the flames. It would be so easy to end him here and now. I felt the erendinth around me—they breathed in and out, begging to interact with me. The Dwonian would likely alert the rest of the camp before he died though.

Light on my feet, I made my way to the nearest tent on the right and crept along the side to stay hidden. Two men spoke inside, laughing between pauses. I caught a whimper, not deep enough to be a man's. I hadn't seen a single woman the entire time we had been prisoners here. I looked to Liam, who had heard the woman as well. "Bastards." I kept my voice to a whisper.

I had intended to set every tent on fire—one so hot that not a single Dwonian would escape the blaze. But now, it wasn't just the Dwonians I had to worry about burning alive.

For a moment, I questioned whether I should do it anyway, then I felt ashamed of that thought. What hope did I have at saving the women kept secret in the various tents? Surely, the one in this tent wasn't the only one. Liam and I could potentially save one prisoner or two from a single tent but saving them all from the entire camp was unlikely.

"We could get the knights at the city gate and send for reinforcements," Liam whispered, his breath caressing my ear. I had been thinking the same.

"We would lose the element of surprise. No, whatever we're going to do, it has to be now." I leaned closer to the tent, the words clearer now, not muffled, forcing me to pause again.

"This one is with child, Cairn—you know what must be done. We cannot rejoin the others with her as she is."

"Yes, Bahnin, I know our laws," Cairn's voice was easily recognizable. I had to restrain myself from slashing through the tent's fabric and ending the new chief.

I wanted to be disgusted by what I heard, but I was numb to it. My upbringing in Broid had ensured that. What really caught my attention, though, were the others Bahnin had mentioned. Was there another camp the size of this one? Or was it a larger gathering?

"By right, you are Suin's heir. But the right to challenge will not be denied us. The tents must gather. We will either accept you as our chief or another man will take it from you. And if you do not dispose of this woman and the child, another will challenge you."

"We are at war, Bahnin. That can wait."

"This war which is not ours can wait." Both men were growing angry.

"Our fathers made this our war. Our laws hold only on our land—a desolate land where nothing grows and we are exiled from."

"You shame your fathers—the chiefs of Tribe Laith spit on you, Cairn. Son of none, I name you."

A grunt followed and the woman resumed her whimpering. "Take your condemnation to the grave, Bahnin. None are here to hear it. Laith will be a tribe no more. I'll carve a slice out of this continent for my own kingdom. This land that still has seeds will be mine. The other tribes will bow to Laith or die with you."

"You will die as the son of none—so you are cursed." Bahnin gasped.

I looked to Liam, unsure of what to make from what we overheard. From the sound of it, Cairn was likely to get himself assassinated by his own tribe. The little that I knew of the Dwonians allied with Erynor was that they had never sought a permanent settlement east of Dwota's Gap. That was treason to their people. But wasn't that what Ianthol had promised Cairn?

"Tribe Laith," Cairn shouted, no longer in his tent.

"We can't stay here," Liam whispered.

I sliced open the canvas in front of me and took in the tent's simple furnishings. Like the chief's tent, this one too was essentially bare, with furs lining the ground and a single chest. No weapons though. A young woman hurried to cover a corpse. She started when she saw me slip inside. "Come with me, hurry, before he returns."

Her eyes hardened. "I will not—not until I've planted a dagger in his heart." She spoke with a Sorenth accent in harsh contrast to the Dwonians.

"Are there others like you here? Others that are held against their will?"

"We are cycled through—only I have not been cycled out. Cairn thinks to enact a prophecy with my child. His tribe believes that only a child born of the east, south, west, and north will return the seeds to Dwonia. He intends to usher in a new age and claim all Dwonia for himself. He means to wed four women and have four sons, one from each direction the wind blows. Fool thinks they'll bring the seeds back to his desert."

"You aren't afraid to stay?"

"I'm terrified, but I will see his dreams destroyed, just as he destroyed mine. My child will never learn of his paternal bloodline. He will hate Tribe Laith as I do."

"Where are the others kept?"

"They are kept furthest from the chief's tent. The warriors use them as wanted; they return to their tent alone when done."

I recalled noticing that the warriors often visited a tent at the far end of the semicircle of tents. It had been in my periphery while we had knelt bound with our backs to the bonfire. I hadn't seen any women come out, only the warriors coming and going.

"Break camp—we've been summoned to Myrium, and after the city falls, we're taking Binton as our prize. Its weak king will crumble beneath our spears," Cairn yelled.

Liam yanked me out of the tent, leaving the woman behind. The warriors of Tribe Laith yelped and cheered, the light from the bonfire brightened, making the tents cast darker shadows. We crept along the outer perimeter of the camp, pausing behind each tent before exposing ourselves. Luckily, they were pitched closely together. Between the gaps of the tents, I glimpsed men dancing and stomping around the fire, chanting an odd tune. The sound echoed deeply, rising with the flames as they turned into smoke to waft into the sky.

Liam and I stopped at the edge of the camp. I wasn't positive, but I believed that the tent we now hid behind held the other captives. With any luck, there wouldn't be any warriors visiting just now, since their new chief demanded their attention.

Slicing the back of the tent open, I poked my head in. Over a dozen people, including two children, huddled together. Fortunately, there were no Dwonians present. I made a come with me motion with my hand as I pushed myself through the slit and said, "If you want to escape, you have come now, there's no time to waste."

The huddled mass began to break up, and a couple crept toward me, uncertain and silent.

"Others have tried to sneak out, and all have failed," a young man said.

"If you stay, you'll die to elongate a shadow elf's life and nothing more," I said.

"Where can we go?" a woman asked.

"Ceurenyl is not far. But we won't have another chance to get away," I said, as Liam poked his head into the tent.

"We have to go, now. The Dwonians are boasting of what their night will entail. It won't be long until they stumble in here."

"We can't delay; are you coming?"

The frightened Sorenth had no reason to trust us, but at least we weren't Dwonians. They shuffled forward, more concerned about getting away. I stepped out through the tear and into the shadow beyond. It hid our group well enough despite the fire growing brighter as the rowdy Dwonians celebrated.

Already at the edge of the camp, I looked down the path leading to Ceurenyl. The mountainous terrain hid the city walls rising somewhere in the east. I worried about how long it would take us to reach Ceurenyl's ruined gate. My sense of time had been dismal since we'd been abducted. How many days had it been since we had been dragged from our blissful night into the nightmare that followed?

Liam peered around the edge of the tent. "They'll see us if we don't have these tents to hide behind."

I scanned the area. There had to be some way to sneak past and get out of sight before our group was noticed. I brushed against the slaves' tent. "What did Suin say about his tent? Something about it being sacred?"

"What do you propose?"

"Giving a sign to Tribe Laith regarding their new chief."

"But that woman is still in his tent." Liam protested.

"That's not Cairn's tent anymore. The chief's tent belongs to him now." I pressed into ignys. The flames lapping up from the bonfire belonged to me. I didn't need an existing fire to wield ignys, but I did use that one. It had already reached a staggering temperature. I was shocked the warriors had drawn so near to the dancing flames especially as it grew hotter under my influence.

I no longer felt defeated. Something had changed over the past day while Liam held me, refusing to let go. I wasn't the same elf that had been bound naked before those flames, the flames I now wielded. The skin on my back was still tender from that same fire burning me.

The liberated Sorenth huddled together and couldn't see the bonfire from behind the tent, but Liam could. He realized what I was doing as the bonfire's size increased, growing outward from its node. The warriors also recognized something odd happening. The fire pulsed with my breath as though it too breathed in and out. I had no idea how to control the erendinth, only how to use them for destruction, and that was exactly what I intended to do. No one was going to stop me—the power thrumming inside begged, pleaded, for release. I felt the flames hungering for more. Entrenched in the erendinth, I too felt the need to expand and consume clawing at my insides.

I saw the worried look in Liam's eyes. I was scaring him. So much had happened between us. We had become something I never thought I would experience again. For a fleeting thought, I believed it was because I didn't deserve it. Not again. Second chances were nothing but a lie. Kiron had been my everything and I had killed him.

That thought did not linger. The look in Liam's eyes spoke to me. It begged me to be his everything in return. We both knew that if I lost control of ignys, we too would be consumed by the flames.

Instead of exploding the fire outward, I directed a single thread of ignys, only a spark, and ignited the chief's tent like a dried bale of hay. It took all my energy and willpower to only wield that small wisp of ignys—to abandon the full strength of that bonfire.

Liam stood frozen, looking at me as though he didn't

recognize me. I took a breath, a deep long breath. I knew I couldn't control the erendinth. I had been a step away from burning the entire camp, catching myself and Liam in the inferno.

The temptation did cross my mind though. I partly regretted that I hadn't. I could have stopped this entire gathering of Dwonians—Tribe Laith could have been cast into instability for years with the recent death of their chief and his heir. But even so, they would not stay here now, with Cairn urging them on to further destruction. The path before us would return to how it was before the Dwonians arrived and the scar they'd created would heal.

Taking Liam's hand in mine, I pulled us away from the camp, the Sorenth refugees stumbling along behind us.

Chapter Twenty-Six

Chaos had engulfed the Dwonians. I had never let myself hope that burning the chief's tent would prove so effective, but Liam and I could have skipped away from the Dwonian camp with the Sorenth refugees singing a merry tune and we would not have been noticed.

The trodden path created by Tribe Laith faded as we increased the distance between us and their camp. The orange glow of their bonfire and enflamed chief's tent had been swallowed in the night and only the waning moon and twinkling stars provided any light as we walked along the riverbank.

Our group of freed captives, Liam and myself included, quietly crept further away from Tribe Laith. We knew that as long as we remained outside the protection of Ceurenyl's walls, our lives were still in jeopardy. I tried to remember how far the Dwonians had dragged Liam and me away from our original place by the river. That night had blurred as I had fallen into a depression, blaming and pitying myself. I hadn't been able to look past myself, only seeing my likely death and Liam's suffering because of me.

Lost in my thoughts, I startled when someone sneezed. It sounded like it had come from one of the Sorenth, the sound resonating and telling anyone nearby that we were also nearby. Our entire group froze at the sound, too scared to take another step, worried that the pebbles under our feet would further attract a potential assailant. We knew that Tribe Laith had been occupied with dealing with the chief's tent catching on fire, but what if they had also discovered that all their captives were gone, slipped out of their camp in the confusion? Would they track us down before reaching safety? Would they care that we escaped, or would they move on without us, content to capture new prey on their march to Myrium?

Liam, the steadiest member of our group of runaways, assessed the situation. He gave me a quick glance, clearly giving more attention to listening at this moment. Those eleven years spent in Gneal's dungeons had sharpened his hearing. I remembered him telling Devlyn on the night of Erynor's attack that he could hear a mouse scrape across the floor. I had honestly thought he was bluffing, but after sharing a room with him over the past months, I found myself believing him. Even when I thought I was being as silent as possible when getting out of bed, he would reposition himself as though he had just woken because of me.

Liam looked from me to the group behind us to the river. "What's wrong?" I whispered, noting his concern.

"We're being watched."

"How do you know?"

"I can't tell if they followed us from the camp, or if a

scout already outside the camp picked up our trail after we left. But someone is nearby and they're getting closer. Before whoever sneezed, I thought it was just a nocturnal critter, but I had thought the same that night we were taken."

"What should we do?" I trusted Liam's instincts more than my own right now. I might have gotten past my state of shock, but that didn't mean I was in any state to devise a course of action. I trusted him and, more importantly, felt safe with him.

Liam glanced down at the sword I carried. "Depend on that instead of wielding. Let's not panic the Sorenth more than necessary." He lifted his own sword up a bit, preparing himself, then issued quick commands to the Sorenth. They huddled together as they moved off the pebbled beach and into the river, while Liam and I stayed on the beach with our swords now raised. I knew that water was freezing but it was safer for the Sorenth and made them harder to reach if anyone snuck up.

Our group shuffled in the direction of Ceurenyl, the great bridge spanning the river still hidden from sight, as were the city walls and any evidence that we were drawing near to Ceurenyl. What Liam had originally thought was a critter solidified into footsteps. I looked in the direction I thought they were coming from, not back toward Tribe Laith's campsite, but toward Ceurenyl. Hiding from whoever was coming near was not an option. Even if we had opted for that, our chances of keeping the Sorenth safe and unharmed would have severely dropped. They should be a more difficult target treading in the water.

My breath caught in my chest when I saw five silhouettes approach in the dark, visible only under the faint light of the stars and moon. Whoever this group was, they no longer tried to stay quiet, clearly not seeing our group of refugees as a threat.

"And what do we have here?" one of them called.

I gripped my sword tighter. That *was* a Dwonian accent.

"Looks like Cairn let the only good thing about this northern expedition escape," replied another man, and the rest of the group chuckled, striding toward us all the while. They all carried spears or swords.

"I was starting to think these nightly patrols wouldn't amount to anything. They haven't been fun since we took that first batch of refugees. Still, I'd prefer to find some new ones instead of this washed-up lot," the man at the center of the approaching group said, near enough now to make out his features.

In my peripheral vision, I saw Liam flinch. "What's wrong?" I whispered.

"That's the one who bound me that first night."

This man had applied the same abuse to Liam as Cairn had done to me. My heart ached at the realization. I tried not to think back on that night—not now. I couldn't afford to lose myself in that depression again. I had to stay focused on the task at hand. We weren't going back to the Dwonians. I'd sooner wield kien and lose control of the erendinth, risking all our lives, than return to that camp.

The group of five drew their weapons, daring us to challenge them. I looked back at the Sorenth, the water up to their knees. "Don't engage," I said, and I took my first step toward the Dwonians with Liam by my side.

Quieting my mind and inhaling deeply, I held it for a moment before exhaling, centering myself in the process. I wasn't the unstable elf that I had been for the past decade. I might not have complete control of myself, but thanks to Elayne, I was no longer as unbalanced as I had been. A sense of confidence poured through me. Two of the Dwonians came at me, the other three engaging Liam, noting his physique as the more threatening opponent. Liam might not be able to overcome three at once, but I was certainly capable of subduing two.

I fell into the jienzu forms, my sword flicking in the dark, diverting the first spear thrust, followed by a sword slash from the other Dwonian. Metal clashing against metal rang in my ears, the reverberations from the impacts running up my arms to my shoulders. I chanced a look at Liam, his sword flashing in the moonlight, commanding the situation as he held his three adversaries in check. He might be doing well and holding his own, but he was still at a significant disadvantage. Erynor hadn't recruited the Dwonian tribes all those years ago because they were inept warriors. They were some of the fiercest fighters on the continent.

I renewed my own efforts. The sooner I dispatched my two adversaries, the sooner I could even the odds for Liam. Swinging my sword low, it caught, digging into flesh, and the Dwonian I struck grunted in pain. He still managed to respond, his spear striking furiously at me. I barely managed to defend myself, his weapon flashing quickly, its next move difficult to anticipate while I also kept the other warrior at bay. Fortunately, the crazed and haphazard strikes gave my other assailant little space to draw near. He managed to swing at me between each flurry of blows from his comrade.

Forced backward, my feet now in the river, I glimpsed

an opening in the frenzied warrior's attacks. I parried a strike from the sword-wielding assailant, and the momentum from my swing took my sword past so that I managed to slice into the other's midsection just as he'd raised his spear to strike at me again. The spear slipped from his grip, clattering to the pebbled beach, and he fell on top of it as the other attacker slashed downward to end me.

I managed to parry, although it wasn't my smoothest move. With my back to the river and this Dwonian blocking my view, I could no longer see Liam. The sounds of metal clashing against metal still filled the air, but that did little to ease my nerves, especially when a series of grunts caught my attention. I couldn't tell who they came from and to make it worse, the sounds of the confrontation had ceased.

Terrified of what that might mean, especially after everything Liam and I had survived in the past days, I lashed out against my assailant. My instructors would have called my forms sloppy and my intended strikes obvious, but all that mattered just now was overcoming my enemy—the finesse I had previously exhibited no longer mattered. Raw strength was needed, and I struck another blow at the Dwonian. Our swords met in a powerful clash, my entire upper body thrumming from it.

Before I could ready myself for my next attack, I realized I had left myself exposed and so did the Dwonian. I caught his grim sneer as his weapon slashed downward. He wanted this. He knew who I was and why I had been taken a prisoner. Like the rest of his tribe, he wanted me dead because of my sexual orientation. I tried to bring my sword up to meet his own but I was too slow, and I braced myself for the impact that never came.

Confused, I looked from his sword seeming to hang in midair to his equally befuddled expression. And then I saw the steel protruding from his chest. The Dwonian fell to his knees before collapsing facedown into the riverbank. If he wasn't dead yet, his faceplant into the shallow water would certainly see the job done.

Liam stood behind the collapsed warrior, no longer hidden from my view. I looked in disbelief from him to the three fallen Dwonians he had left behind.

"You're okay," I exhaled, overcome.

"From the beating you gave me all those months ago, I had presumed you'd be the one coming to my assistance." He smiled, just as I noticed blood smeared on his arm. He lifted it to look at the mess. "It's nothing. One of them sliced it at the beginning of our fight. And honestly, the jolt likely gave me the strength and adrenaline to overcome all three of them. Even that rat who had dragged me to the Dwonian camp when we were first taken, spewing hateful slurs in my ear all the way. I still have the bruises from that night."

I dropped my sword and rushed to him, squeezing the air from his chest. The rush of emotions came without warning and I didn't care that the Sorenth stood behind me in the shallow part of the river, observing the entire exchange. Liam had saved me again. I had no doubt that this was becoming a trend, and part of me was glad for it. I was safe with him.

I released my hold, and tore a strip from my shirt and dipped it into the river. I washed Liam's bicep, cleaning the wound as best I could. Hopefully, it wouldn't be too long before he could visit Lillianna for a proper healing. Liam had enough invisible scars, he didn't need any physical ones. After the cut was as clean as I could get it, Liam tore off the bottom of his own shirt, and I used it to bandage his wound. I tried not chuckle at the sight of both our shirts now exposing our belly buttons. Despite my exhaustion and tumultuous emotions, my eyes lingered on his taut abdomen as he inhaled one deep breath after another.

"Later." Liam laughed, delighted that we were both alive. Given our current situation, I didn't believe for a second that he wasn't also thinking the same.

The Sorenth had all walked out of the frigid water at this point, even more uncertain about us, but with no other option. Without wasting any more time, we resumed our walk to Ceurenyl, and soon, we could hear the sound of the dual waterfalls on either side of the city gate.

As we'd hoped, our borrowed tunics still lay by the riverbank. The Sorenth had looked questioningly at us, wondering who we truly were. We quickly pulled the Septyl knight's tunics over our linen shirts and then led the Sorenth toward the winding path that led to the ruined city gate. Liam stayed at the back of the group to guard against any more Dwonians sneaking up on us. We passed under one of the waterfalls, the sound thundering in our ears.

The Sorenth had kept quiet during the entire journey, and none of them had said where or when they had been abducted, but it was clear that none had managed to make it to Ceurenyl. We finally reached the top of the path near the great bridge to Ceurenyl.

Every Sorenth, especially the two children, looked in dismay at the rubble that had been the city gate. They had come to Ceurenyl seeking a haven, leaving everything behind. They had been captured, beaten, raped, and promised to shadow elves, then rescued only to find the supposed haven compromised.

The nearest battlements glowed in the torchlight, but anyone looking out from them was too far from the gate to identify our small group. I couldn't see any guards at the bottom of the ramp, but they wouldn't be far. I brought us closer with caution. I had no intention of startling any of the guards in the middle of the night. I still gripped my sword, but held it pointing at the ground in a non-threatening manner.

Admittedly, without a torch of our own, our group did look like it was trying to sneak into the city. As we neared the temporary ramp that had been built over the rubble of the gate, I was surprised that the bottom had been left unattended. I didn't expect a heavy guard on this side of the ruined wall, but I had anticipated someone keeping a lookout. I looked for any sign of defense between the two torchlit battlements. Finding none, I assumed that whoever stood guard above must have chosen to forego torchlight. The possibility of the ruined gate being left unprotected seemed implausible. I led our group up the ramp, Liam now at the rear, and the Sorenth between us.

"I would not advise sneaking into Ceurenyl," a woman said from above us. A flash of light appeared at the apex of the ramp, lighting her face. The wielded globe of light made her easily visible and she was certainly not dressed as a soldier, but wore a simple dress and shawl.

"We weren't trying to sneak into the city, Ei'ana. But neither was there anyone to receive us." I didn't recognize this ei'ana, only the purple brooch she wore, identifying her as a

Vyoletryn.

"Typically, the gates are closed at night. And I am Indryl."

"Thank you, Indryl." I said, wondering how much I should tell here and now, out in the open.

"How is it that a Septyl knight ended up escorting a group of Sorenth refugees? Are these people under your protection? And is that another knight at the back of the group?"

"Is there some safe place where we can speak?" I asked, suddenly grateful for the tunic I was wearing. I had no idea what this ei'ana would have done to us if she hadn't recognized the Septyl knight's tunic, although she clearly had reservations about our right to wear that uniform. Hopefully, she wouldn't become angry once she realized we were imposters and had only worn the tunics so we could sneak out of the city.

"I can't just let you all into the city under these suspicious circumstances."

"I won't go back." A young woman pushed through the group to stand just behind me. "Please, I can't go back to the Dwonians."

Indryl eyed me, her question clear.

"It's why we need to speak somewhere safe," I offered.

"Very well, but you'll have to be satisfied with a guard house. This doesn't mean you have free rein of the city." Indryl's last comment seemed addressed to the Sorenth refugees behind me as she finished, just as five knights came up the city side of the ramp. They looked from Indryl to the people huddled just past her and I caught their eyes lingering on my tunic. Aside from the white trim and sigil, it matched their own.

"Sir Jon, do find proper accommodations for our guests

and something to eat. I must speak with these *knights* in private first. Don't take them far, I'll need to speak with our guests as well."

The Septyl knights saluted Indryl, then led the Sorenth away.

"Well, move on." She indicated that Liam and I should walk along the ramp toward the nearest battlement.

Like the gate, it too had been destroyed. I climbed over the rubble as instructed. This path had few deviations and I took the only manageable route my feet could find. Cracked and splintered debris had been pushed to the edge of a cleared path. I was soon looking at a ladder that led up a vertical drop. I looked back at Indryl for confirmation, but she only nodded, urging me forward.

I scrambled up the ladder, the topmost rung well over my head. As I pulled myself up and over the side, a partially ruined structure set into the wall greeted me. The entire thing tilted uncomfortably sideways.

"Did you expect our guardhouses to be in better shape?" Indryl asked, straightening up beside me after heaving herself over the ledge. "And don't bother pretending; it's too late for me to care that you aren't who you say you are. I can't believe we've come to putting ei'ana on guard duty, making us keep watch the entire night. Absolutely preposterous."

"I don't know what you mean," I said, suddenly very aware of my cinnamon hair and pointed ears. Indryl glanced at Liam as he too pulled himself over the ledge and stood beside me.

"It's late, so let's not play dumb. And while there are a few Cyndinari in the city including Mother Velaria, descendants of those who renounced Erynor because of Lucillia, we both know you are not one of them. Am I mistaken, Jaerol Solaris? And Liam Telvin, how did you get involved with this one?"

"How did you know?" I asked.

"Do you honestly think that the temple wouldn't have contacted Gwilnor after two kien wielders disappeared from their hallowed halls? You realize it's been over a week, yes? Do you need a refresher on the Councils of Telerius?"

I swallowed, suddenly very aware of the other knights on the ruined wall.

Indryl nodded at a broken archway. If there once had been a door, it was nowhere to be found, nor did it look like it would fit in the misshapen opening again. I shuffled through, careful not to lose my footing. Only one knight waited inside, and at a pointed glance from Indryl, he quickly left to join the other knights outside.

"Now, what is this business about Dwonians? Our scouts have reported no sightings outside the city."

"How is that possible? They've had a perpetual bonfire going every night we were held prisoner," Liam said.

"And where is this camp?"

"West, near the river. But they'll likely be gone by morning," I answered.

"Convenient."

"That's not all. They say they're heading toward Myrium to siege the city."

"We've heard rumors of an army gathering, but we haven't received any correspondence from Queen Karina Lariviere, nor from any of the ei'ana residing there. As far as we know, nothing of consequence is happening there, at least nothing that needs our attention. And aside from growing concerns about the refugees, none of the Sorenth nobility has raised any alarms."

"We heard it from the lips of a shadow elf, telling Chief Cairn of Tribe Laith that they're moving on Myrium. Can anything be done?" Liam asked.

"First, the both of you are going back to the temple. I don't know how you managed to get ahold of Septyl knight's tunics, but we will need them returned at once. Second, whoever oversees you will have to deal with you. Technically speaking, you are beyond the repercussion of Septyl. However, we do not take lightly two kien wielders outside the Temple of Ceur. Third, Suin is chief of that tribe; you were clearly deceived."

"He's dead. His son took his place several days ago."

"Truly? We'll have to verify that," Indryl said.

I dared a sideways glance at Liam. He looked just as nervous about the situation as I felt. "Those refugees we were with, the Dwonians were capturing them as gifts for the shadow elf. I have no idea how many had been handed over to him before we too were taken prisoner."

"Intriguing. That would explain why some of the refugees here have been asking about friends and family who never made it to Ceurenyl. What's the status of this shadow elf? Is he still with the Dwonians?"

"He's dead. Liam killed him. The souls he had stolen are free." Liam and I went on to tell Indryl everything we had overheard while among Tribe Laith. Despite knowing nothing of their presence camped outside Ceurenyl, she took the news impassively, asking pointed questions when details weren't clear. What was clear though, was that she found the information useful.

Chapter Twenty-Seven

When Indryl had finally let us go, and we had managed to get ourselves back into the temple without attracting any attention, Liam and I tried to sneak back into our room. The slightest turn of the doorknob had brought both Renaud and Stephen to their feet. I had thought sneaking back into the temple would be the tricky part. But it turned out that if you knew the proper phrase, the temple knights would let anyone in. I still couldn't believe that Indryl had simply let us go free after hearing our entire story. She hadn't even bothered to threaten us with possible repercussions if it was discovered that we didn't return directly to the temple. She did demand the return of the Septyl knight's tunics before we could go though, leaving us wearing only the torn linen shirts and much abused trousers we'd gotten from the Dwonians.

Our bunkmates sprang from their beds as Liam and I walked through the door, neither of us wearing the garments we had left in a week ago.

"Where in Ramiel's hell have you two been?" Stephen demanded. "Do you have any idea what we had to do to cover for the both of you? Bastien is ready to send you to the lower levels once he finds you."

Still frazzled, I teetered between fighting back and acting reasonably.

"It wasn't intentional," Liam supplied.

I crossed the room and collapsed onto my bed.

"Well, are you at least going to tell us? Bastien nearly suspended Stephen and me when he stormed out our room the second night you two were nowhere to be found."

"Maybe tomorrow." I hugged my pillow, turning on my side and toward the stone wall. The mattress dipped from the added pressure when Liam sat on the edge of the mattress beside me.

"Cover for us for one more day?" Liam asked as he moved to lie down as well. The Arenthylean bells indicated that dawn was only an hour off. I typically would not have heard them at this hour, too soft to wake anyone, but they seemed to grow louder with every bong.

"What should we tell Bastien?" Stephen asked, not commenting on Liam joining me in my bunk.

"The truth—we left the temple, enjoyed some time by the river, and were abducted and nearly killed by a Dwonian tribe and a shadow elf." Liam shifted so he could wrap his arms tenderly around me. Our backs faced our bunkmates.

For the first time since Kiron had changed our plans, I felt safe. Tears rolled unhindered down my face and I finally accepted Kiron's sacrifice. I loved him all the more for what he done for me.

My body shook. Kiron shouldn't have given me this gift. He was so much more deserving than me.

Liam held me tighter, his forearms against my chest and stomach. I didn't realize that I was already grasping his hands until I felt his fingers massaging mine. I didn't have to say what had so upset me—he knew. It wasn't Ianthol, the Dwonians, or our flight from their camp. It was Kiron. It was always Kiron.

"Liam?" I asked hours later. Neither of us had undressed for bed; we hadn't even kicked our trousers or shoes off to get more comfortable. Renaud and Stephen had left us alone while they went to morning drills, the same drills that we should have gone to. "Are you still awake?"

The returned squeeze was answer enough.

"I love you."

"It's about time you said it. I was worried that you'd never admit it."

The End

Appendix A

Glossary of Terms

Abbey School

The preferred system of education for children throughout Eklean. Those deemed capable are sent to higher studies, preferably at Gwilnor Academy.

Aelish

Native language of the elves. Largely forgotten, only used in academic circles.

Aerys

An elemental erendinth. The essence of air.

Albien

One of the seven Schools of Septyl. Albiens focus on truth and care for many of Eklean's libraries. Motto: Truth is discoverable. Emblem: A naked male and female elf holding unraveled scrolls with an owl perched behind, cast in gold on a white field. The chair of Albien is known as the Seeker.

Aldarch

Deific rulers of Aldinare who reigned from their sanctums.

Aldinare

Western Skyland of the Aldinari, one of the four elven kindreds. Lost to the Darkness. Only a hundred Aldinari escaped the Skyland with their lives.

Alicorn

A legendary beast native to the Skyland of Aldinare. A winged unicorn.

Anadel

Spiritual creatures that predate Teraeniel and Somnaeniel. Their native home is Lumaeniel. There are four known classifications of anadel: irythil, enthiel, lorendil, and naril.

Anacordel

Creatures of body, soul, and spirit.

Anaweh

The Creating Light.

Animys

A transcendental erendinth. The essence of spirit.

Aquaeys

An elemental erendinth. The essence of water.

Arantiulyn

One of the seven Schools of Septyl. Arantiulyns focus on strength and protection and oversee the Knights of Septyl. Motto: With fortitude, we will protect. Emblem: A naked male and female elf in a fighting stance with swords in hand with a lion prowling cast in gold on an orange field. The Chair of Arantiulyn is known as the General.

Arcane Gems

Sources of magic used by the Mages of the Kilnae Del.

Archsteward

Part of the Ei'ceuril hierarchy, they are elevated wise ones. Before kien wielders were restricted to the Temple of Ceur, archstewards lived in every major city of Eklean tending to those faithful to Anaweh, the Creating Light.

Arenthylean Bells

Twenty-four bells composed of four materials that ring every hour.

Aryl

The united head of an elven house composed of a king and queen or lord and lady.

Auburnis

One of the seven Schools of Septyl. Auburnises focus on inner peace. Motto: To love is our gift. Emblem: A naked male and female elf offering a garland with larks flying above, cast in gold on a brown field. The Chair of Auburnis is known as the Pilgrim.

Aurephaen

Feast day of the Luminari, commemorating Auriel and the dawning sun. Celebrated on the 15th of Aurenth, the spring equinox.

Azurelle

One of the seven Schools of Septyl. Azurelles focus on the advancement and training of the erendinth. Motto: The zealous soul must be temperate. Emblem: A naked male and female elf wielding the powers with a dragon behind, cast in gold on a blue field. The Chair of Azurelle is known as the Blue Dragon.

Belin's Watch

An Evellion city in the Vespien Mountains comprised of humans and dwarves. Named for Belin, the dwarf who sheltered Thellion refugees in their greatest hour of need.

Borephaen

Feast day of the Eldinari, commemorating Boriel and the sleeping sun. Celebrated on the 15th of Borenth, the winter solstice.

Bowl of Theniel

Sea set apart by the merpeople as sacred. The place where Theniel brought the waters to Teraeniel.

Centaur

Anacordel dedicated to protecting the forests of Eklean, particularly the Illumined Wood. The upper body is like an elf's but broader and more rugged while the lower body looks much like a four-legged horse.

Ceurendol

The Jewel of Life. Created by the Luminari by placing their life essence within seven jewels of incredible brilliance which allowed them to share their immortality with every race in 1.3a (7085.3E). Also known as the Light Diamond, the Lieben Stone, and the Heart of Hearts.

Ceurendol War, the

A cataclysmic war instigated by the Erynien Empire which began over a philosophical difference over the Jewel of Life and whether immortal life was proper for the 'lesser races.' The war divided Eklean in two factions, those faithful to the Luminari and those subjugated by the Erynien Empire. As the fate of the war grew clear, emissaries and merchants from other continents withdrew from Eklean, fearing the Erynien Empire. 322-500.3a (7407-7585.3E).

Ceurenyl

City founded by the ei'ceuril. Home of the Temple of Ceur and Gwilnor Academy. The only city not to fall into Erynor's control when Krysenthiel was lost to the Shroud.

Ceurtriarch

Leader of the ei'ceuril, known as High Archsteward and Arbiter of the Light.

Chancellor

The head of Gwilnor Academy under the authority of and appointed by the Seven Chairs.

Children

When capitalized, refers to the proto-race.

Cor'lera

A small village in eastern Parendior and in disputed territory claimed by both Lucillia and Perrien. The vineyards of Cor'lera produce the coveted ice wine, the Cor'leran Blue.

Crimsyn

One of the seven Schools of Septyl. Crimsyns focus on healing and run many hospitals and infirmaries throughout Eklean. Motto: Through healing, hope is given. Emblem: A naked male and female elf dancing with a dog, cast in gold on a red field. The chair of Crimsyn is known as the Physician.

Cyndinare

Southern Skyland of the Cyndinari, one of the four elven kindreds. Lost to the Darkness.

Cynethol

Home of the Cyndinari, situated among the Kinzdol Islands.

Daereneth

Continent south of Ogren and west of Ja'Horan. Tropical continent.

Deurghol

The Cyndinari directly responsible for the Shroud. They are neither living nor dead. Also known as the Deathless.

Draelyn

A half-bred ancordel of dragon and elven origins.

Dragon

Legendary creatures bound to the erendinth.

Druids of Kweil Aitch, the

Secluded faction of humans who learned to walk Somaeniel, the World-in-Between early on.

Dwarf

Anacordel who sought the deep roots of the mountains.

Ei'ana

An organized group of wielders. Since the Balance was lost during the Ceurendol War, there are only kiara wielders among the ei'ana. There has not been a kien wielder among the ei'ana for over a thousand years.

Ei'ana Counsels

A series of norms ei'ana are to follow in regards to wielding. The counsels prohibit men from becoming ei'ana due to their inability to wield safely after the Balance was lost. The counsels also require ei'ana to bring kien wielders to the Temple of Ceur for their own protection and the protection of their communities.

Ei'ceuril

A religious order, currently a majority of men, focused on serving Anaweh, the Creating Light. Because a kien wielder is not capable of wielding with control, every male ei'ceuril capable of wielding is confined to the Temple of Ceur.

Eklean

Continent where the anacordel first stirred as Children.

Eldin Wood, the

Home of the Eldinari.

Eldinare

Northern Skyland of the Eldinari, one of the four elven kindreds. Lost to the Darkness. The Eldinari were the first to evacuate their Skyland for the lands below.

Elemental Erendinth, the

Forces wielded to influence the elements. *See Erendinth.*

Elf

Anacordel who changed little when the different races were created. Because they wished to retain their original form, their immortality remained, and they were gifted the Skylands. There are four elven kindreds, the Luminari, Cyndinari, Aldinari, and Eldinari.

Elya

Powerful wielders born of any race who learn to wield instinctively and are not limited to the restrictions common to normal kien and kiara wielders.

Emradiel

One of the seven Schools of Septyl. Emradiels focus on beauty and life. Motto: Only the prudent thrive. Emblem: A naked male and female elf gesturing with open palms toward the beauty around them with a stag behind, cast in gold on a green field. The chair of Emradiel is known as the Tender.

Enthiel

Anadel dedicated to one of the seven irythil. The enthiel are very involved with the anacordel. A single enthiel guides an entire people.

Erendinth, the

The erendinth are the wielded powers believed to have created Teraeniel. Tradition says that there are seven powers, three transcendental: lumenys, animys, and umbrys; and four elemental: aquaeys, aerys, terys, and ignys. Much is forgotten or unknown about the full extent of the erendinth which are dependent on inner spiritual and emotional workings.

Erendinth Games, the

A game of wielding created at Gwilnor Academy, involving the wielding of all seven erendinth.

Faun

Short nocturnal anacordel with the hind legs of a goat from the navel down. Some fauns have horns.

Giant

Anacordel that were drawn to the frozen north. During the Great Blessing, their physical features became capable of withstanding the harsh tundra of Glacien.

Glacien

Northern frozen continent spanning the northern pole. Connects Eklean and Ogren.

Goblin

Anacordel native to the Kinzdol Islands. Known for their monetary shrewdness.

Goblin Guild

Infamous bank and guild of Eklean. Regulates the majority of Eklean's currency. The Goblin Guild is based in the Kinzdol Islands with branches in every city and most villages.

Great Blessing, the

Event recorded in the Theseryn where Anaweh blessed the growing differences among the anacordel and solidified their choices by making each their own distinct race.

Guardian Knights

Order of knights once based in Krysenthiel that served and protected all the land from injustice. The Guardian Knights were largely composed of Luminari and were defeated during the Ceurendol War.

Guardian Senate, the

An international body, crossing countries and continents to ensure the wellbeing of Teraeniel. Disbanded toward the end of the

Ceurendol War.

Gwilnor Academy

The foremost school dedicated to the education of wielders, located in Ceurenyl.

Holy Tomes

Volumes recorded by various ei'ceuril, some being prophets, and from which the ei'ceuril base their beliefs and practices.

Human

Anacordel that differ among themselves more than any other race. They traveled the furthest from the Valley of Saeryndol, migrating across the entirety of Teraeniel.

Ignys

An elemental erendinth. The essence of fire.

Illumined Wood, the

A vast forest with mysterious qualities and inhabitants.

Imperium

Selective school for Cyndinari youth. Its violent academic style educates the next generation of shadow elves.

Irythil

The seven anadel who, under Anaweh's guidance, introduced the erendinth, thereby creating Teraeniel.

Ja'horan

Continent south of Eklean. Inhabited largely by nomadic peoples.

Jahro Islands

Island chain in the Unarian Sea. Believed to be the home of pirates.

Jienzu

Forms used by the ancient elves to instruct in balance. Largely forgotten.

Judges of Yanil

An order that once ruled beside the Yanilean. The judges are now a secret organization that strives to uphold law and order with limited influence.

Keeper

Head of the time wardens and possessor of the time key.

Kiara Wielder

A female wielder. Kiara wielders learn to control the erendinth easily but require a kien wielder to reach their potential strength. Because the Balance was lost, kiara wielders are not able to reach their potential strength.

Kien Wielder

A male wielder. Kien wielders reach their potential strength easily but require a kiara wielder to learn control of the erendinth. Because the Balance was lost, kien wielders are not able to wield safely, and if any male begins to show an aptitude to wield, he is sent to the Temple of Ceur where wielding is impossible.

Kilnae Del

Order of mages native to Charren, headquartered in the Charrenese capital, Karithel.

Kinzdol Islands

An archipelago in southern Eklean, homeland to the goblins and Cyndinari.

Kweil Aitch

Island east of the Illumined Wood. The place where the veil is thin between Teraeniel and Somnaeniel.

Lay Votary

A non-clerical class of ei'ceuril.

Lethien

Half-elven and half-human anacordel. Largely extinguished by Erynor during and after the Ceurendol War.

Lorendil

Anadel that guard and protect individual anacordel. Some anacordel are known to communicate with their lorendil.

Lucillian Alliance, the

An alliance of the Eklean kingdoms established to return peace and order to Eklean following Emperor Erynor's disappearance.

Lumaeniel

The World-Beyond. Dwelling of Anaweh, the anadel, and those anacordel who have passed beyond.

Lumenys

A transcendental erendinth. The essence of light.

Luminare

Eastern Skyland of the Luminari, one of the four elven kindreds. Lost to the Darkness. The Luminari evacuated their Skyland for the lands below where they established Krysenthiel.

Mar'anathyl

City on the Skyland of Luminare. Governed by the Lorenthien aryls.

Masters, the (Seven Masters, the)

Vigyl Vyoletryn, Cyrelle Azurelle, Lanielle Emradiel, Lyon Arantiulyn, Mainor Auburnis, Caelyn Crimsyn, and Saeyrn Albien are the founders of the Seven Schools of Septyl and Gwilnor Academy.

Meridean Conclave

Governing council of the merpeople.

Meridephaen

Feast day of the Cyndinari, commemorating Meridiel and the noon sun. Celebrated on the 15th of Meridenth, the summer solstice.

Merpeople

Anacordel who longed for the depths of Teraeniel's oceans.

Miervae

Anacordel who longed to nurture Teraeniel's forests. Miervae are also referred to as Great Trees and begin their life as Settlings.

Minum

The least of Eklean's anacordel. A short half-bred creature of goblin and human origins. Before the elves migrated to Eklean, they were enslaved, sold by goblins to humans.

Naril

Anadel reminiscent of the seven erendinth. There are seven types of narils and they are commonly known as nymphs.

Nymphs

See Naril.

Observant

Non-wielders who have dedicated themselves to one of the Seven Schools of Septyl.

Ogre

Brutish anacordel covering the vast majority of Ogren. Half-bred creature of giant and human origins.

Ogren

Continent east of Eklean and west of Qien. Mountainous land with a mixture of forests and deserts. Inhabited by giants, humans, and ogres.

Phaedryn

Those bound with a phoenix.

Purged Desert of Dwonia, the

A vast wasteland in western Eklean that was rumored to have at one point been fertile. Home of the Twelve Tribes of Dwonia.

Return

The final stage of formation of an ei'ceuril toward becoming a steward. Often occurring in the Illumined Wood.

Sanctum

Expansive complexes housing the aldarchs and their courts on Aldinare.

Schtach

Language of the dwarves.

Schtam

(1) A dwarven people. (2) The dwellings of the dwarves.

Schtamite

The eight dwarven Schtams.

Seguian

A portal created to traverse space and time. Traversing time is restricted and only the keeper can use the time key to traverse time.

Septyl

(1) The order of Ei'ana composing the Seven Schools of Septyl. (2) The city of the ei'ana in Krysenthiel and now lost in the Shroud.

Septyl Knights

Order of knights dedicated to Septyl. The knights receive their training at Gwilnor Academy and vow to serve one of the Seven Schools of Septyl.

Servants of Shadow

Secret organization carrying out the orders of shadow elves and, in some instances, the orders of the Deurghol.

Settling

Tree-like creatures that wander about in their youth until finding an appropriate place to settle their roots and grow into a Miervae, also known as a Great Tree. Settlings have unique vitality qualities.

Seven Chairs of Septyl, the

The leaders of the Ei'ana. Each of the Seven Schools elects its own Chair who leads his or her particular School and participates in the leadership of Septyl. Responsible for admitting student wielders into Gwilnor Academy and selecting a chancellor.

Seven Schools of Septyl, the

The order of Ei'ana, composed of Albien, Arantiulyn, Auburnis, Azurelle, Crimsyn, Emradiel, and Vyoletryn Schools.

Shadow Elves

Cyndinari who consume the spirit of others to prolong their own life.

Sha'ghol

Past rulers of the Cyndinari. First to communicate with Ramiel and wield tenebrys.

Shroud, the

A diseased-looking fog placed by the Cyndinari over the entirety of Krysenthiel. It severed the Luminari from the Jewel of Life, cutting them off from their life essence and making them mortal, as well as any others who had benefited from it. An unanticipated result was that the Cyndinari also lost their immortality with that placement of the Shroud over the Jewel of Life. The Shroud's mysterious origin is one reason no one has been able to remove it.

Skylands, the

Four island countries, Aldinare, Cyndinare, Eldinare, and Luminare, floating in the clouds thousands of feet above the ground. The dwelling places of the elves before they were forced to evacuate to the land below.

Sojourners

The exiled of Dwonia who sought reentrance after forming an allegiance with the Erynien Empire.

Somnaeniel

The World-in-Between. A realm visited by dreamers. Gateway between Lumaeniel and Teraeniel.

Star Warden

An elven military unit, typically ensuring the protection of their lands.

Steward

A clerical class of ei'ceuril with the ability to wield.

Stewards of Shadow

Ei'ceuril stewards who forsook Anaweh to support Ramiel.

Temple of Ceur, the

Home to the ei'ceuril and pilgrimage site for the faithful. It is impossible to wield within the temple walls. All kien wielders are confined to the Temple of Ceur.

Temple Knights

Order of knights dedicated to protecting the Temple of Ceur and the city of Ceurenyl. Some of the temple knights are men who were brought to the temple when it was discovered that they could wield. These temple knights are prohibited from leaving the temple.

Tenebrae

An unrecognized School of Septyl intended to replace the other seven Schools. Its adherents focus on power and dominance. Motto: Might conquers. Emblem: A naked male and female elf standing triumphantly on seven broken emblems, cast in gold on a black field. The chair of Tenebrae is known as the Conqueror.

Tenebrys

A corrupted form of the erendinth, unrecognized by the Ei'ana of Septyl as one of the erendinth and absolutely forbidden to wield. The essence of Darkness.

Teraeniel

The World-Below. Composed of the continents Daereneth, Eklean, Glacien, Ja'Horan, Ogren, and Qien.

Terys

An elemental erendinth. The essence of stone.

Theseryn

Holy tome recording the creation of Teraeniel and the anacordel, written by the first Ceurtriarch of the Ei'ceuril. The Theseryn states that seven irythil, under Anaweh's guidance, introduced the erendinth thereby creating Teraeniel.

Time Key

An artifact created by the Luminari to restrict the ability to traverse space and time. It was entrusted to the minums, the least of Eklean's races.

Time Wardens

A select group of minums entrusted by the Luminari with the ability to create seguians, allowing them to travel to any place and any time.

Transcendental Erendinth, the

Wielded forces to influence the ethereal realities of lumenys, animys, and umbrys. The ability to wield the transcendental erendinth is forgotten.

Tree Spirits

Narils who agreed to bond with the trees under Sariel's guidance.

Umbrys

A transcendental erendinth. The essence of shadow.

Vaer

Fruit native to the Illumined Wood.

Valley of Saeryndol

Birthplace of the Children, the first anacordel.

Verakryl

A crystalline tree within Mount Verinien which brought life to the world and is connected to Anaweh. Also known as the Tree of Life.

Verathel

Sprouts of Verakryl, the Tree of Life.

Verathn

Weapons of power.

Vespephaen

Feast day of the Aldinari, commemorating Vespiel and the setting sun. Celebrated on the 15th of Vespenth, the autumn equinox.

Vyoletryn

One of the Seven Schools of Septyl. Vyoletryns focus on justice and diplomacy. Motto: With justice, peace. Emblem: A naked male and female elf holding a staff with an eagle soaring above, cast in gold on a violet field. The chair of Vyoletryn is known as the Watcher.

Wielders

Anacordel capable of wielding the erendinth.

Wise Ones

(1) Part of the Ei'ceuril hierarchy. There is no certainty how many are among the ei'ceuril. (2) Part of the Ei'ana hierarchy. There are seven wise ones for every School of Septyl.

Yanilean, the

The undisputed monarch of Yanil, always male. Used both as the monarch's title and as his name during his reign.

Days of the Week

(Based on the seven anadel involved in the creation of Teraeniel)
Gwynthaen–Thenaen–Uraen–Ramaen–Lerenaen–Saraen–Karaen

Months/Moons

(Based on the anadel attached to the elves)
Spring – Marenth, Aurenth, Delenth
Summer – Dynenth, Meridenth, Reventh
Autumn – Kyrenth, Vespenth, Orenth
Winter – Estlenth, Borenth, Lierenth

Currency

Goblin Guild currency – 16 iron angots for a copper lewt. 9 copper lewts for a silver jent. 13 silver jents for a gold crown. 3 golden crowns for a lumol.

Luminari currency – 8 kenols for a narol. 4 narols for a lumol.

Appendix B

Dramatis Personae

Agnelle Phanstienne

Luminari. Ei'ana and Chair of Auburnis.

Alesei

Queen of Tiel. Of the Royal House Ziera.

Alexander (Alex) Vaerin

Human from Perrien, whose family migrated to Cor'lera. Devlyn's cousin on his father's side.

Amry Thellion

King of Evellion. Married to Queen Lara.

Aren Lorenthien

Luminari. Led a rescue party to Aldinare and did not return. Now a Dark Phaedryn in service to Erynor.

Bastien

Human from Sorenthil. Temple Knight.

Cairn

Human of Tribe Laith. Son of Suin.

Daphnel

Human from Ceurenyl. Temple Knight.

Devlyn Telvin

Ward of Cor'lera's abbey school. Physical features indicate Lucillian ancestry.

Dolan Telvin

Father of Devlyn, Leilyn, and Liam. Husband of Evellyn. *Deceased.*

Dorien

Human from southern Eklean. Ei'ceuril Wise One.

Ealyndol Roendryn

Luminari. Ceurtriarch.

Elayne Thenrel

Luminari. Guardian Knight.

Ellendren Roendryn

Luminari. Princess of Lucillia. Student wielder at Gwilnor Academy.

Entiel Telvin

Human from Perrien. Ei'ceuril, steward, and abbot of the abbey school of Cor'lera. Devlyn's uncle on his father's side.

Erynor Meriden

Emperor of the Erynien Empire. Disappeared after Lucillia gave birth to the twins, Roendryn and Feolyn in 7857.3E. First Cyndinari born on Eklean.

Evellyn Telvin

Luminari from Cor'lera. Mother of Leilyn and Devlyn. Wife of Dolan.

Gordon Carvil

King of Torsil. Of the Royal House Carvil. Supporter of Erynor.

Harnyl Roendryn

Luminari. Aryl of Lucillia. Married to Queen Vernal. Father of Prince Aaron, Princess Kaela, and Princess Ellendren.

Ianthol

Cyndinari. Shadow Elf.

Indryl

Luminari. Vyoletryn ei'ana.

Jaerol Solaris

Cyndinari. Former Erynien emissary.

Josthiel

Human. Ei'ceuril Wise One.

Karina Lariviere

Queen of Sorenthil. Widow of the late King Dorian. Mother of Myranda.

Kiara

A mythical woman believed to be the first female wielder.

Kien

A mythical man believed to be the first male wielder.

Kiron

Cyndinari. Studied at the Imperium and defeated during the Grand Tourney. *Deceased.*

Lara Thellion

Queen of Evellion. Married to King Amry. Azurelle ei'ana.

Lawrence Maroven

King of Mindale. Of the Royal House Maroven. Supporter of Erynor.

Leilyn Telvin

Sister of Devlyn, believed to be living in the Illumined Wood. Daughter of Evellyn and Dolan.

Lenora Hanaryld

Human from Ceurenyl. Ei'ana and Chair of Arantiulyn. *Deceased.*

Lex Telvin

General from Perrien, key player in events surrounding Devlyn's family. Devlyn's uncle on his father's side.

Liam Telvin

Son of Dolan. Half-brother to Devlyn and Leilyn.

Lillianna

Human from Mindale. Ei'ceuril and formerly an Emradiel ei'ana.

Loretta Javie

Human of Sorenthil. Ei'ana and Chair of Crimsyn.

Lucillia

The woman who gave birth to the twins, Roendryn and Feolyn.

Melanie Birkwell

Human from Mindale. Ei'ana and Chair of Arantiulyn.

Myranda Lariviere

Princess of Sorenthil. Student wielder at Gwilnor Academy.

Oranna

Luminari. Azurelle ei'ana and chancellor of Gwilnor Academy.

Paurel Roendryn

Luminari. Ei'ana and Chair of Azurelle.

Razcul

Cyndinari. Shadow Elf.

Renaud Lariviere

Human from Sorenthil. Temple Knight recruit.

Selenya Waeyn

Luminari. Ei'ana and Chair of Albien.

Stephen

Human from Evellion. Temple Knight recruit.

Suin

Chief of Tribe Laith.

Teran

Cyndinari. Jaerol's uncle.

Therril

Ei'ceuril magister of theoreticals at Gwilnor Academy.

Velaria Treyven

Cyndinari born in Lucillia. Ei'ana and Chair of Azurelle.

Vernal Roendryn

Luminari. Aryl of Lucillia. Married to King Harnyl. Mother of Prince Aaron, Princess Kaela, and Princess Ellendren. Direct descendant of Lucillia.

Xanth

Cyndinari. Shadow Elf.

Yelaris

A free dragon of the Blue Flight bound to Velaria.

Yloran Eth Gnashar

Cyndinari. One of the Sha'ghol.

The Seven Irythil and their Associated Enthiel

Uriel – Lord of the Stars, whose name means Anaweh is my Light. Irythil who brought Anaweh's Light to Teraeniel.

Auriel – The Dawn Star. Guardian of the elves of Luminare.

Meridiel – The Noon Star. Guardian of the elves of Cyndinare.

Vespiel – The Evening Star. Guardian of the elves of Aldinare.

Boriel – The Night Star. Guardian of the elves of Eldinare.

Gwynthiel – Lady of the Lorendil, whose name means Strength of Anaweh. Irythil who brought Anaweh's spirit to Teraeniel.

Ramiel – Lord of Death, whose name means Arrogant toward Anaweh. Betrayed Anaweh and all creation. Irythil who brought shadow to Teraeniel.

Theniel – Lady of the Seas, whose name means Anaweh Heals. Irythil who brought water to Teraeniel.

Nauto – Guardian of all humans living along the coasts.

Aquae – Guardian of the merpeople.

Sariel – Lord of the Land, whose name means Command of Anaweh. Irythil who brought substance to Teraeniel.

Tera – Patroness of harvest and nourishment. Often referred to as Mother Tera.

Mundi – Guardian of the dwarves.

Lereniel – Lady of the Winds, whose name means Friend of Anaweh. Irythil who brought air to Teraeniel.

Kariel – Lord of Peace, whose name means Who is Like Anaweh. Irythil who brought fire to Teraeniel.

About the Author

Ryan D Gebhart first started writing the Jewel of Life series in 2012 in Philadelphia, PA, shortly after concluding his undergraduate studies in philosophy. This unexpected passion evolved over the years and has remained a constant companion through his career changes, from a Franciscan Friar, to a Claims Processor, receiving a Graduate Degree in Architecture, and now working at an Architecture Firm in Washington, DC. Ryan D Gebhart is originally from Wilmington, DE.

Keep up with Ryan D Gebhart at www.RyanDGebhart.com

www.ingramcontent.com/pod-product-compliance
Lightning Source LLC
Chambersburg PA
CBHW030526310726
48979CB00010B/1814/J

* 9 7 8 1 7 3 2 6 3 5 5 7 9 *

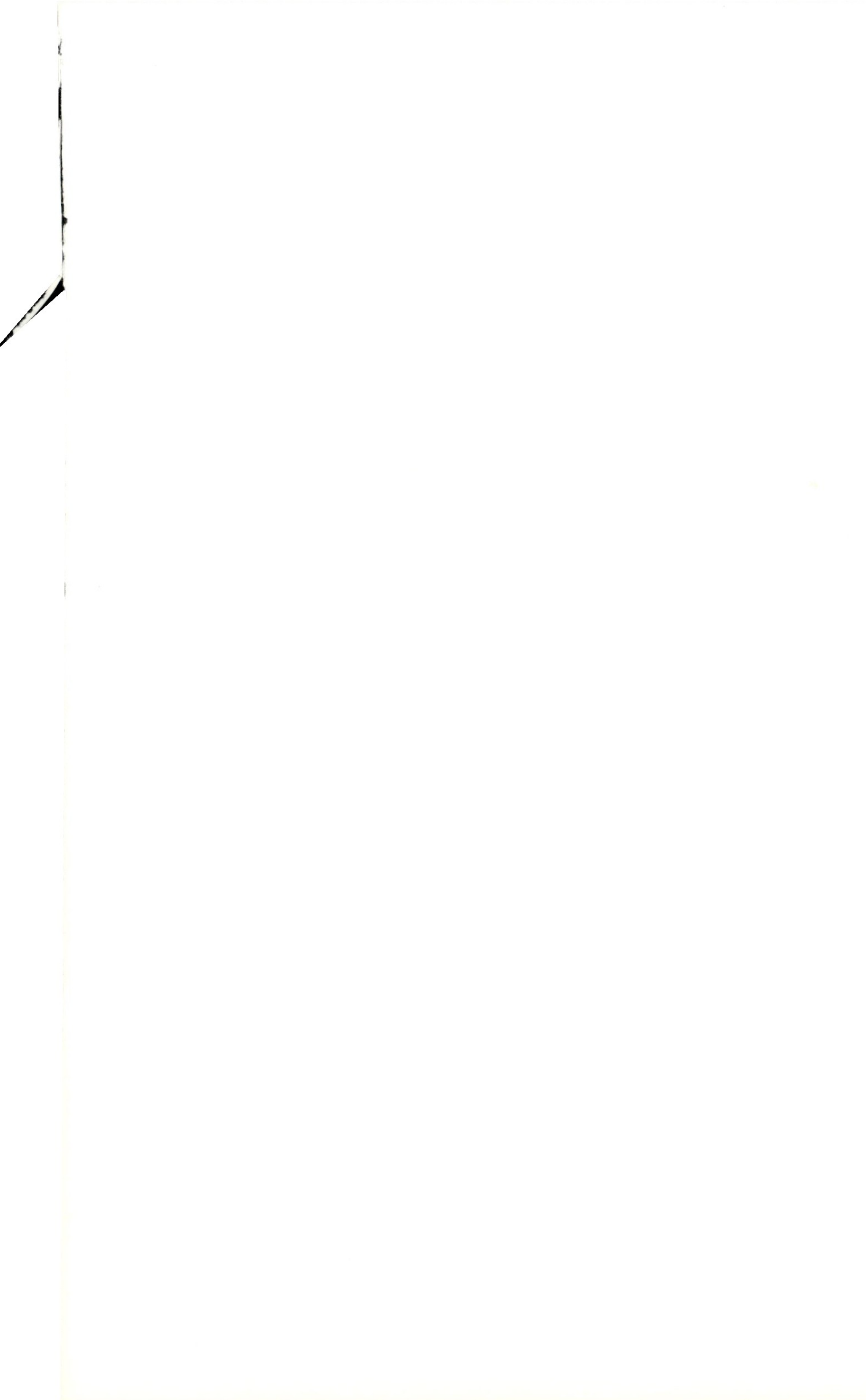